Contents

When the blast of war blows in our ears,
Then imitate the action of the tiger.

William Shakespeare

Part One
The Mountains

The game's afoot

William
Shakespeare

Recent Titles by Alan Savage from Severn House

THE COMMANDO SERIES
COMMANDO
THE CAUSE
THE TIGER

THE SWORD SERIES
THE SWORD AND THE SCALPEL
THE SWORD AND THE JUNGLE
THE SWORD AND THE PRISON
STOP ROMMEL!
THE AFRIKA KORPS

THE TIGER

Alan Savage

severn
House

This first world edition published in Great Britain 2000 by
SEVERN HOUSE PUBLISHERS LTD of
9–15 High Street, Sutton, Surrey SM1 1DF.
This first world edition published in the USA 2001 by
SEVERN HOUSE PUBLISHERS INC of
595 Madison Avenue, New York, N.Y. 10022.

British Library Cataloguing in Publication Data

Savage,   Alan
    The tiger. - (The Commando series ; bk. 3)
    1.   Great Britain. Army. Commandos - Fiction
    2.   World War, 1939-1945 - Fiction
    3.   War stories
    I.   Title
    823.9'14 [F]

    ISBN 0-7278-5645-6

This is a novel. Except where they can be historically
identified, the characters are invented and are not intended
to portray actual persons, living or dead.

Typeset by Hewer Text Ltd.,
Edinburgh, Scotland.
Printed and bound in Great Britain by
MPG Books Ltd., Bodmin, Cornwall.

The Mission

B ehind a blaring horn the jeep slowly made its way along the pothole-littered road. Although the sky was presently clear, it had rained recently, and the wheels scattered mud and water; the windscreen wipers whirred ceaselessly. But it was not the poor surface that made progress so slow. The jeep was going against the human tide that proceeded in the other direction, heading east. The soldiers tramped along, steel helmets at jaunty angles, rifles slung, boots splashing in and out of the puddles, chins unshaven and khaki uniforms filthy – but in the best of humours, laughing and joking. Interspersed between them were their vehicles, trucks and even tanks, all following the retreating German Army.

Apart from the jeep, the only people heading west were groups of despondent, grey-clad German prisoners, guarded by the occasional Tommy.

Overhead, darting in and out of the clouds, myriad aircraft roamed to and fro. But these were all British or American. It was August 1944, and from an Allied point of view, everything was looking good.

Major Harry Curtis, seated in the back of the jeep, thought it had been a long time coming. Still only twenty-three, powerfully built, fair-haired and boyishly good-looking, his true qualities were only occasionally revealed in the sudden hardness of his blue eyes, the way his mouth could close like a steel trap. Harry Curtis's active war had begun on the beach at Dunkirk . . . could that possibly have been only four years ago? Since then, as one of the first of the Commandos, he had seen action the length and breadth of Europe as well as in North Africa – wherever it could be accessed by sea or by parachute. His achievements were illustrated by his medal ribbons, which included the Military Cross, the Distinguished Service Order, and in front of them both, the crimson ribbon of the Victoria Cross. Yet through all the triumphs and tragedies of the past three years, the catastrophes of St Nazaire and Dieppe – he had missed the second after just surviving the first – the loss of so many good friends and comrades, the two severe wounds and several additional superficial injuries that had from time to time overtaken him, he still remained able to smile, and to look forward to the victory that now seemed certain.

What would happen then, on a personal level, he had no idea – beyond marriage to Belinda, which was the most certain thing in his life at the moment.

But victory! There was clearly a lot of fighting still to be done; the Germans had not been able to prevent the Allies from landing in Normandy, and thus they were withdrawing, but the Reichswehr remained a most powerful fighting force and there did not seem to be any doubt that they would resist to the end. On the other hand . . .

The jeep reached the top of a slight rise, and Harry looked down on the city of Caen and beyond to the waters of the Bay of the Seine – calm waters now, where a month ago they had been so turbulent that the invasion had nearly been postponed. But that narrow stretch of water was every bit as actively crowded as it had been on the sixth of June. Ships came and went, the surviving Mulberry Harbour was crowded, and the beaches were thronged with men and *matériel*, disembarking and being martialled for their journey to the front line.

Harry reflected that if the Germans still possessed an active air force they would never have a better target. But the great days of the Luftwaffe were history.

Caen was a wreck. Here the Germans had held out with determined gallantry for several weeks, while the British had slowly pounded the ancient city into rubble. Now progress was even slower, as the jeep had to negotiate shell craters and collapsed masonry as well as human beings, and these now included civilians, picking their way amidst the wreckage in their search for relatives and belongings, food and shelter. But at last the vehicle drew to a halt before one of the less battered buildings, outside of which there flew the Union Jack as well as the Brigade standard.

"Am I to wait, Major?" asked the driver.

"You'd better, until I find out just what I'm doing here," Harry said, and went up the steps of the building.

At the top an MP stood to attention. "Sir?"

"Major Curtis, First Commandos," Harry said. "I am required to report to Brigade."

"Inside, sir." The MP opened the door and Harry stepped into a corridor, a place of dislodged plaster and hurrying khaki-clad orderlies, both male and female.

"Major Curtis?" asked one young woman, clearly taken aback by the conjunction of Harry's youth and rank. "Brigadier Martin will see you right away."

She led the way up the stairs, while Harry reflected on the stocking-clad legs which emerged primly from beneath the knee-length skirt. He had always had a weakness for a trim pair of female legs, and he had not seen any at all for the past eight weeks.

On the gallery there were several doors, one of which the ATS sergeant knocked on before opening. "Major Curtis is here, sir."

Harry stepped inside, stood to attention, and saluted. The sergeant closed the door, remaining on the gallery.

"At ease, Major." The brigadier returned Harry's salute, then came round the desk to shake his hand; he was a short, generally small man, but very trim. "We haven't met."

"No, sir."

"Rough trip?"

"Slow, sir."

"I can imagine. Sit." The brigadier returned to his seat behind the desk. "Smoke?" He indicated the silver-plated box.

Harry sat on the straight chair before the desk. "I don't, sir."

"Must always be fit, eh? How are things going up front?"

"At the moment, quietly – for us. We're enjoying some R and R."

Brigadier Martin would know this as well as himself. He opened a file. "Colonel Bannon speaks highly of you."

"Thank you, sir."

"Well, he should. Unfortunately, he's been taken ill, so he can't be here today." Martin turned a page. "Your battle honours sound like the Brigade of Guards. You began in the Guards, didn't you?"

"Yes, sir."

"And served with them up to Dunkirk, where you were badly wounded, and briefly afterwards, before being seconded to the Commandos. Which means, I assume, that you are fully recovered from that wound?"

"Yes, sir."

"Since then . . . Lofoten, Ardres – wounded again – St Nazaire, Algiers, Spetsos, and then here in France before D-Day. And then, on D-Day itself, holding the bridge over the Orne until we could get up to you."

"I was not in command of that operation, sir."

"But you were there, Major. Colonel Bannon says that when it comes to a special operation, there is no man like yourself."

"That is very kind of the colonel, sir. I had hoped to remain with my unit until this business is finished."

"Because of what happened outside Lisieux in May? You completed your objective. You blew the railway line and the munitions dump. Had the weather permitted us to launch the invasion at that time, what you accomplished would have been of vital importance to our success."

"Only the weather did not permit it, sir. And by the time it did, the Germans had repaired the line, and possibly even the dump. And I lost my entire squad, either killed outright or taken prisoner. And then, presumably, shot – considering Hitler's orders regarding captured Commandos."

"And you are bitter about this."

"I'm human. And perhaps unlucky. You know what Napoleon said."

"That he'd rather have a lucky general than a good one? But your record suggests that you have been fairly lucky on more than one occasion. And equally, that you have never let personal feelings interfere with the job."

"I hope not, sir."

"Still, a little bit of personal antagonism does no harm. We need you, Major, for a job of the greatest possible importance – and one of the greatest imaginable danger. In fact, it may almost be called a suicide mission. I wish you to be quite clear about this. However, it is the opinion of Colonel Bannon, and some others, that if any man can pull it off, you are that man. Are you interested?"

"Certainly, sir." Harry grinned. "Interested."

"Very good. What I am about to tell you is obviously top secret. It therefore follows that should you, having heard the proposal, decline to carry it out, while that will involve no blemish on your record or your future prospects, you will have to be placed in detention until a suitable replacement is found and the job has been completed. Understood?"

"Yes, sir."

"Very good. Let me begin by putting you in the picture. We have our toehold in Europe, and Jerry is presently in disarray. But we are a long way from Germany, and an even longer way from victory. The Wehrmacht still has several million men under arms, and they have each and every one of them taken a personal oath of fealty to the Führer, so that if he commands them to fight to the death, as he probably already has done, they will do just that, and may well hope to take one of us for each of them. That kind of casualty figure is totally unacceptable. Would you agree?"

"I would agree, sir."

"Thus the key to our success, at an acceptable cost, is Hitler. Were he not there, the Germans would willingly call it a day."

"You mean they would accept the unconditional surrender we are demanding?" Harry was doubtful.

"Our information suggests that they would. All except Hitler's close circle of associates, of course. But the generals know they're licked; their interest now is to save what they can from the military mess and preserve as far as possible the infrastructure of the country. We have recently learned that there has actually been an attempt on Hitler's life, at his East Prussian head-quarters, in which several leading generals were involved. The attempt failed. The bomb which was to do the trick exploded all

7

right, but in some miraculous fashion he didn't go up with it – although we understand that he was pretty shaken up. Meanwhile, all hell has broken loose in Germany, with some very distinguished people being tried before kangaroo courts and hanged. Now, I'm sure you'll agree that the very existence of such a plot, at such a level, indicates that the German generals are getting desperate. Unfortunately, as this attempt has failed so disastrously, and Hitler appears to be in total command of the situation, we cannot anticipate any more plots in the immediate future – the surviving generals are simply too afraid of the consequences of failure. However, were Hitler to be removed by an outside agency, we estimate the whole house of cards would collapse."

"I hope you are not thinking of mounting a Commando raid on Rastenburg," Harry commented.

"It did come under discussion," Martin admitted. "But the logistics involved are simply impossible. However, we have been presented with a very viable alternative. As I say, Hitler was quite badly hurt, and certainly shocked, by the explosion. He has been advised by his doctors to take a complete rest for at least a month, and we have been informed that he is doing this at his favourite retreat, Berchtesgaden in the German Alps. It is pretty mountainous country, and there can be no question of putting an aircraft, or even a glider, down. It will have to be a drop. On the other hand, you are not required to take the Führer, or anyone, prisoner. You simply shoot everyone in sight, including Hitler. Then you will make your way across Austria into Italy; the distance is about fifty miles, which is a lot closer than attempting to reach Switzerland. Getting to Italy will also mean there will be no question of internment. We are in touch with the various partisan groups in the north of the country, and once we confirm that you are on your way, which will be immediately after you have completed the job, they will expect you and take care of you. I'm afraid they're mostly Communists, but we're all on the same side at the moment. Anyway, we will get you out, p.d.q. But even if we don't, with Hitler gone we estimate the War will be over by Christmas, and you will be out then. Will you do it?"

"Is there anyone on the ground?"

"I'm afraid not. We do have agents in Austria, but it would be too risky for them to become involved."

"I take it we have detailed maps of the area, and a house plan of wherever it is he is staying?"

"We do. He has his own house there. Captain Forester will give you everything you need."

Harry's head jerked. "Did you say Captain Forester?"

"Yes. Colonel Bannon's secretary. Do you know her? Well, I suppose you must, as you have worked under him for so long. She's a real go-getter."

"Yes, sir," Harry said.

Belinda, here in France? It seemed too good to be true. They had not seen each other for nearly two months, and then her divorce had just been coming through. They had agreed that they would not get married until after the shooting stopped – they had both seen too many of their friends killed – but now with the shooting about to stop . . .

"Major?" Martin inquired.

"Sorry, sir. I drifted off."

Martin frowned. That was not what he expected from one of his more important officers at such a vital briefing.

"Does this mean that Captain Forester knows of this plan, sir?"

"Yes, she does. She is absolutely trustworthy."

"Oh, indeed, sir. I don't doubt that for a moment. But does she know I am to command?"

"No, she does not. It was only decided yesterday. Now tell me what you will need. How many men, to begin with."

"What would be the German establishment at Berchtesgaden?"

"If Hitler is in residence, we must assume something like battalion strength. Most of these would be quartered in the town itself – Hitler's house is situated on the hillside above it – but obviously they could be summoned. When you carried out that raid on Darlan's headquarters in Algiers, what was the strength of the opposition?"

"Virtually the entire French garrison. But there was an important difference. We knew the Americans were landing the next day, so we didn't have to get back out – just sit tight and wait to be rescued. There was also the point that not all the French were our committed enemies. I assume Hitler's body-guard will be SS people?"

"I'm afraid we have to assume that, yes. We understand, as I have said, that this is a very high-risk mission. That's why we are inviting you to lead it. Again, as I have said, the feeling is that if any man can bring it off, you are that man." Martin paused, expectantly.

"And something simpler, like a bombing raid, is out."

"It doesn't offer much chance of achieving our objective. Our information is that there are deep air-raid shelters built into the mountainside, into which Hitler and his people will simply disappear until the raid is over."

"And equally, providing me with a battalion of Commandos isn't on."

"Well, no. The number of aircraft required would be spotted long before you reached your objective. This can only succeed by complete surprise."

"Point taken. Well, if it is to be done by stealth rather than force, the smallest possible number of men must be taken. I'll have to study the plans, but I would say four, certainly not more than six."

"That few?"

"The fewer the better, from the point of view of evading detection, both before the assault and – presuming we come through that – getting across Austria afterwards. I'll pick the squad myself."

"You understand they have to be volunteers."

Harry nodded. "However, I do also require the assistance of the RAF."

"To do what? Apart from dropping you, I mean."

"To launch a raid on Berchtesgaden at the appropriate time. I will give them the time. This is to cause sufficient confusion to enable us to make our escape."

"And suppose they hit you and your men?"

Harry grinned. "I imagine that is less of a risk than being shot by the SS."

"When? Time is important. We know Hitler went to Berchtesgaden a week ago, and that he is still there. We don't know how long he means to stay."

"Three days."

"Excellent." Martin stood up to shake hands. "Keep me informed. And if there is anything you require that cannot be obtained by normal means, you have but to say."

"I will, sir. Where can I find Captain Forester?"

As if it mattered, in these circumstances – save for one final embrace.

How casual it had been, as it always had been. There is something we would like you to do, old man. Of course we understand that the odds are you will not come back, but this is war and it has to be done. Besides, you have always come back in the past, have you not?

Leaving a trail of corpses behind him. Sometimes he could not escape the feeling that the Army, while happy to use his talents whenever necessary, were actually hoping they could one day set him a task from which he would *not* return. He was, after all, a killing machine – for whom it might well be difficult to find an adequate niche when the guns finally fell silent.

In many ways he supposed that was a compliment. Not that he had ever considered himself as a killing machine, or any kind of machine. He merely had the ability to concentrate his mind – perhaps to a greater extent than his comrades – to which was added a total belief in his own survival. Thus when it had become clear on that last disastrous mission to France that he and his men would only escape the burning village in which they were sheltering – and which was entirely surrounded by German troops – by shooting their way out in one wild death-or-glory charge, he had done just that, and was alive to tell the tale. His squad had been perhaps less determined, less certain that they could do it, thus he had been the only survivor.

Now he had been commanded to create a new squad . . . and lead them to death too. Yet he would do it, because having gone straight from school to Sandhurst and thence into the Army only a month before war had been declared in September 1939, he knew no other way of life.

So . . . what could he possibly say to Belinda, in such circumstances? But she would know the circumstances, even if she did not yet know he was involved.

Her office was just along the gallery. Harry hesitated before knocking. He felt oddly nervous. His career, brief as it was to date, had been littered with women; he had a weakness for them – and quite a few of them, it appeared, had a weakness for him. Several had let him down, and he supposed he had let several down. One he had had to execute, but another had actually laid down her life for him. They were a sex he could not resist, but with each new experience he had become increasingly wary of dangerously close relationships.

However, throughout the past three years, beginning when he had first joined the Commando training camp in Wales, Belinda Forrester had been constant. She remained as she had been when they had first met, secretary to the CO. It had once been somewhat amusing to reflect that if, as seemed likely in the course of time – if he survived that long – he became a battalion commander, she could be *his* secretary. That was now a remote possibility, as she had moved up to being the brigadier's secretary. And long before he could hope to attain such an exalted rank . . .

He had been attracted to her from the moment of their first meeting, at least partly because she had been so obviously unattainable. They had been acquainted for more than a year before she had suddenly become very attainable indeed. He had never been sure what had turned her in his direction; he had known he was far from being the only man in her life, and that amongst the others was their then commanding officer, David Lightman. But slowly, following that first weekend together, she had replaced all the other women in his life. That is, until Deirdre Hale had so unexpectedly drifted across his consciousness. She had been the girlfriend of his lieutenant in the raid on Spetsos. Poor Simmons had been killed, and Harry, as he always did, had visited both the parents and the girl personally to break the news.

Never before had he been so instantly attracted to anyone, and he had a strong suspicion his feelings had been reciprocated. But he had just asked Belinda to marry him!

So . . . ships that pass in the night.

He summoned his courage and knocked on the door. "Come," called a voice from inside.

He opened the door, and they stared at each other. Belinda was always worth looking at; she was short and slim-hipped, but with a very full bust – perfectly made to wear a uniform. Her straight black hair was cut just below her ears, her clipped features were always anticipatory. And now, totally astonished.

"Harry?!"

He closed the door behind him, and waited. She hesitated for a moment, then came round the desk for a long, slow kiss.

Her obvious consternation at the sight of him was disconcerting. "Where did you spring from?" Harry asked.

"I came across with Bannon. The day after D-Day."

"You have been in France for damn near two months, and I never knew?"

"I understand you've been fairly busy."

"Fairly," he said thoughtfully. "But as I'm not busy now . . ."

"How long have you got?" she asked, suddenly breathless, as if they hadn't been lovers for the past three years.

"Tonight, anyway."

"Oh, gosh. I'm sharing a billet."

"And I haven't even got one yet. Maybe you can sort that out. We need a private room and a double bed. There must be one spare somewhere in this dump."

"I'll see what I can do."

She disengaged herself and returned to her desk.

"You also have some info for me," Harry said. "Maps and things. I'm to pay a visit to Berchtesgaden."

Her head jerked. "You? I thought you were serving with the Commandos."

"I am. Which is why I've been seconded for this mission."

"But . . . Harry . . ." Her hand, which had been hovering over the telephone, dropped to the desk. "That's a suicide job."

"Now, where have I heard that before?"

"And you're still here," she remarked. "So you always say. But there will come a time . . ."

"If this comes off, it'll be the last. You said you wouldn't marry me until Adolf was dead and gone."

"And you said you'd have to hurry him on his way. I thought you were joking."

"So did I, at the time. But now I've been given the opportunity . . . and to end the War maybe at a stroke."

"I think you're crazy. But then, I always did." She unlocked one of the drawers in the desk, and took out a manila envelope.

Harry sat down, opened the envelope, and studied the various papers inside, while Belinda began telephoning. Berchtesgaden was certainly difficult for even normal access. It lay in the shadow of an 8,000-foot-high mountain called the Watzmann, behind which there was a lake called the Königssee; the town had apparently been a royal spa as far back as the last century, and was situated about fifteen miles south-west of Salzburg. A few years ago it would have lain even closer than that to the Austrian border, but of course that no longer existed. As Martin had said, to get out he and his men would have to go south across the Alps and then for some fifty miles to gain the Italian border and the hopeful assistance of the Italian partisans. With the Germans close behind!

At least in August they should not encounter any massive snow. But it really was a suicide mission. Then again, he had supposed that about Algiers, before he had settled down to thinking about it – and worked out how it could be done.

There appeared to be a single main road in to the town, as well as a railway line. Both of these were obviously out. It would have to be approached by way of the foothills of the Watzmann, but this was to their advantage: the Hitler House, along with several no doubt other delectable residences, was situated on a ridge above the town, some distance from the mountain itself. There was a road leading up to this ridge, but there was also a funicular railway, which presumably was used by the high and mighty. And by the SS when they relieved their comrades at the house?

The house itself appeared to be unremarkable as regards layout, the normal reception rooms opening on to a large terrace overlooking the view, and the first floor comprising various bedrooms. Hitler's was marked, and beside it another, belonging to Eva Braun. Harry sighed. Kill everyone you see, Martin had said, so presumably she would have to go too. Once upon a time it had been his private boast that he had never killed a woman. But even that had gone by the board in North Africa.

He stroked his chin. He almost felt this job needed doing by a single assassin. But he would need *some* back-up, if only for the additional firepower, in case something happened to him before the mission could be completed. He would also need a rearguard to keep the SS busy. But not more than four altogether, he reckoned.

"How does it look?" Having been chatting vigorously and also apparently having tried several numbers, Belinda replaced the phone.

"Nasty. But I never expected anything better. What have you accomplished?"

"I have a room for the night."

"Did anyone ever tell you that you're brilliant? I suppose lots have. When do you get out of here?"

She looked at her watch. "I could manage four."

"That seems a hell of a long way away. Have you lunched?"

"I snacked."

"I haven't even snacked. I suppose there's a canteen around here?"

"In the basement."

"Join me."

"I simply can't, Harry. I've so much to do. Come back at four."

He frowned at her. This was not the totally positive young woman he remembered, and with whom he had fallen in love, at least partly, for that same positivity, the feeling that nothing would ever faze her. But his appearance certainly had, although she had known he was in France and would surely turn up sometime.

Nor would the woman he remembered have spent more than a month only just behind the lines and not let him know she was there. And however distressed she had appeared to be on learning that he was going on another highly dangerous mission, he couldn't escape the feeling that the operative word was "appeared". Perhaps, for all Martin's denial, she had known all along that he had been selected for the Hitler raid. That was the most reasonable explanation. So she had merely been acting. He wasn't prepared, at this moment, to look further than that.

"Four o'clock," he said, and replaced the maps in the envelope. "May I keep these?"

"They're yours."

"Thank you." He stood up. "See you later."

"I'll require a list of everything you may need."

He nodded. "When I can think straight."

Harry went down to the front of the building. "You can have the rest of the day and tonight off," he told the driver. "Do you have a billet?"

"That's not a problem, sir. I'll get a bed at the motor pool."

"What about food? There's a canteen here."

"I'll go along to the pool, sir. They'll feed me."

Harry guessed the corporal would be happier with his mates. "Fine. Be here at zero eight hundred. I shall be returning to Battalion."

The driver saluted.

Harry went to the canteen. The kitchen was closed, so he had a beer and a sandwich. He tried to concentrate on the mission, which meant he had to stop thinking about Belinda and the coming night. Four men, he thought, including himself. And massive firepower. That would be the key. But there was also the weight factor, even if they wouldn't be bringing any of the gear out.

The question was, where was he going to find three men as willing to risk their lives for him as in the old squad?

"Major Curtis, sir?"

Harry looked up and frowned at the man in uniform standing beside his chair, lost for the name for a moment "Good Lord! Corporal Green." Then he saw the insignia on the sleeves. "I beg your pardon. Sergeant-Major Green. Well done, Sergeant-Major. Sit down, man, sit down. My God, I haven't seen you since . . ."

16

"Calais, sir, during the escape from Ardres." Sergeant-Major Green took off his cap and sat on the far side of the table.

"That's right. I'm not sure you didn't save my life."

"You'd have managed, sir. I was merely your crutch. But you're all right again now, I would say."

"Just a scar. I've one on each leg now. But you . . . you've left the Commandos?" Harry signalled the waitress to bring two more beers.

"Well, yes and no," Green said. "I'm still in the Medical Corps. I was only seconded to your outfit for that one raid. I tried to sign up permanently when I got back to England, but they reckoned I was more useful as a medic. So I get stuck behind the lines organising the wounded. Would you believe that after the first couple of days I haven't heard a shot fired in anger?" He raised his glass. "Your health, sir. It is very good to see you again, and looking so well, if I may say so."

"Thank you, and the same to you, Sergeant-Major. You're looking pretty fit yourself."

"Well, sir, I keep in training. I reckon I might get called on again, one day. To operate with you, I mean."

Harry studied his old comrade. Green was about thirty, a big, solid man who had proved unflappable in the most extreme circumstances as they had fought their way out of Ardres and through a burning Calais. Harry could not think of anyone he would rather have standing at his shoulder in a shoot-out. And Green appeared desperate to see action. But had he the right to ask him to go to his death?

"Tell me something, Sergeant-Major," he said. "Are you married?"

"Me, sir? Good Lord, no. My old man always said why buy a cow when you can get milk by the pint?" He grinned. "Time enough for that sort of thing when this show is over."

"But you have a family?"

"Oh, yes. My mother and father are still about. And my two brothers."

"Ah," Harry said. That was a relief.

"I suppose you were in on the first drop, sir," Green suggested.

"Yes, I was."

"And been in the line ever since, I reckon." He eyed the crimson ribbon above Harry's left breast pocket. "And picked up the big one."

"Oh, that was way back at St Nazaire. One of those reflex actions which happen to get noticed."

"So, now it's on to Berlin. You leading, and me bringing up the rear." Green finished his beer and stood up. "I've taken up enough of your time."

"I have some, right this minute. Sit down," Harry said.

Green obeyed, frowning.

"Would you really like to see some more action?" Harry asked.

"Would I!"

"I should tell you that it will be a very dangerous assignment. The odds on survival are just about non-existent."

Green grinned. "That's what they said about going in to Ardres. But you got us out, Major."

"Some of you," Harry agreed. "These odds are even worse."

"And you'd like to take me along?"

"I can't think of anyone I'd rather have. If you wish to volunteer."

"Oh, I volunteer, sir."

"I want you to be very clear about this, Sergeant-Major. We are going in behind enemy lines. Well behind them, so there is going to be no substantial back-up. When we have done what we have to do, we are going to have to get out on our own, if we can. As you probably know, the German General Staff, acting on orders from Hitler himself, have instructed all their people to shoot any Commandos on sight, whether they have surrendered or not."

"So we don't surrender," Green said. "But you believe we'll get out."

Harry shrugged. "If I wasn't an optimist, I wouldn't be in this job in the first place."

"That's good enough for me, sir."

"Right-ho. Your CO will receive a letter tomorrow morning, seconding you immediately for special duties. You will tell no one what these duties are."

"With respect, sir, I don't *know* what these duties are."

Harry nodded. "But you won't even let on that it's a mission behind enemy lines. Very good, Sergeant-Major. I'm delighted to have you on board. As soon as you are informed of your secondment, report here."

"Sir!" Green stood up again, replaced his cap, and saluted.

Harry reflected that he had at least made a good start.

By the time Harry had finished his lunch, it was past four. He went up to Belinda's office, where she was just packing up.

"What have you got for me?" she asked.

"Nothing, regarding the job. I'll give you a list tomorrow. Right now I have a lot for you, and I'm not going to be able to think straight until you have it."

She put on her tunic and then her cap, surveyed herself in the mirror, and tucked away a wayward strand of hair. "You sound desperate."

"Do you realise it is nearly two months since we last got together?"

"War is hell," she agreed, and led him down the stairs.

It was a brilliant summer afternoon, disturbed only by the constant rumble from the east and the incessant stream of aircraft overhead, coming and going.

"They're taking the devil of a pounding," Belinda remarked.

"Well, they dished out the devil of a pounding whenever possible, over the past few years," he reminded her.

"True. We'll go to my billet first to get some gear."

He walked beside her along the rubbled street, both of them returning salutes to various servicemen, being watched with abstract curiosity by the occasional civilian.

"I wonder if they regard us as destroyers or saviours," Belinda commented.

"Bit of both," Harry suggested.

They stopped before what might once have been a convent. "You'd better wait here," she said. "This place is full of women."

"I have no objection to that."

"But they might. Or they might not let you out again in one piece. Won't be a minute."

Harry let her go and began walking up and down the pavement. Two ATS privates approached and saluted smartly, then went inside, heads together as they exchanged whispers; the officer was obviously waiting for someone.

Belinda was as good as her word, emerging five minutes later with a small bag. "Now," she said. "It's just a couple of blocks."

It actually was a hotel, which had been damaged but was still apparently operating. "Captain Forester," observed the clerk in reception, in surprisingly good English. "We have a room for you, for one night."

Belinda nodded.

The clerk looked at Harry, without excessive curiosity. "It is on the first floor," he said. "I am sorry, but there is no porter, and the elevator is out of action."

Harry observed that there was also a hole in the roof above the desk.

"We'll walk up," Belinda said, taking the key.

"Please mind how you go," the clerk recommended.

Harry followed Belinda up the stairs, which definitely creaked beneath their weight. "One can't escape the feeling that this whole caboodle could come down at any moment," he remarked.

"Can you think of a better way to go?"

"Providing it doesn't happen for say half an hour."

"We should be able to make that."

There was no light in the corridor, and they had to peer closely at each door to find their room. "This looks like it," Belinda announced.

"Tell me something," Harry said. "Shouldn't that chap have asked for a passport or something?"

"Do you have a passport?"

"Well, no. But some sort of identification . . ."

"We are very obviously soldiers – and officers, too – in the great British Army," she pointed out. "No Frenchman worth his salt is going to quibble about that right this minute."

"Even if we are obviously . . ."

"Even if," she said, and unlocked the door. "The French approve of this sort of thing." The blinds were drawn, and the room smelt musty, but at least that indicated there were no holes in the walls or ceiling. However, the blinds were superfluous, as there was no glass in the large window, just a sheet of plywood.

Belinda tried the light switch, without success. "Fumble, fumble."

"I've been looking forward to that." Harry took her in his arms and did a little fumbling of his own. Eventually she freed herself and tried the bed.

"At least it's made up, and the sheets are dry. I wouldn't like to swear how clean they are."

"What about bugs?"

"Ah. I have a remedy for that." She handed him her cap, opened her bag and took out a small spray gun. Then she raised the sheets, got her head underneath and pumped the gun several times; the smell of the disinfectant filled the room. "That should discourage the little beasts."

"What about us?"

"Well, you don't want to get any on your willie, that's for sure. It'll be dry in a few minutes. Fancy a bath?"

"Might be an idea."

She went into the bathroom and turned on the taps. "Just a trickle. And there is no way it is going to be hot. But it's a warm evening."

He undressed, joined her, watched her release her suspenders and roll down her stockings, then took her in his arms. "You are the sort of woman a man dreams of."

"That's because you've been bereft for too long. I think I'm overweight."

Harry squeezed her bottom. "In all the right places." He watched as the bath slowly filled. "Soap," he suggested.

"I have some." She returned to the bedroom and again delved into her bag. "Here we go. I'm afraid it's heavily scented."

"Don't tell me you were a girl guide in your youth. Always prepared and that sort of thing. Spray gun, soap . . ."

"I just happen to have a nodding acquaintance with French hotels. Even in peace time they seldom supply soap."

For some reason the vague sense of unease he had had that morning returned.

Belinda was bending over the tub, and he simply couldn't resist holding her again, which went a long way to reassuring him. "That looks like enough, and we mustn't run them dry. We're going to need some more later."

She sank into the water and he sat opposite. As it was still broad daylight outside, the sun's rays were seeping in through the various boards on the windows, so there was sufficient light for them to see each other.

"Now tell me," he said. "What's the problem?"

"Problem?"

"You have something on your mind."

"It'll keep."

He couldn't determine whether that was a reassuring reply or not. Could she somehow have found out about Deirdre? But that was impossible, and, in any event, what was there to find out? The girl had been desperate for comfort, and he had provided that, once. He had no idea whether or not she had fallen for him as he had fallen for her; she had given no indication of it beyond saying that she would like to see him again. But he had never been back to her shared flat since that day; he had been committed to Belinda.

"We'll catch pneumonia," she said, and climbed out of the bath, drying herself before handing him the one towel and getting into bed. Once he was there beside her, his doubts again disappeared. Belinda had, at times, a single-mindedness to match his own; when having sex she seemed to surge, almost silently, although occasionally there were little grunts of pleasure. Nor did she ever fake, in his experience; when she had climaxed she lay on her back, breasts rising and falling in great gasps.

"I think you needed that as much as I," he suggested, leaning on his elbow to kiss her mouth.

"If you look in my bag, you'll find a bottle of gin," she said. "Well, half a bottle."

He got out of bed and found the liquor. "Neat?"

"It'll have to be tap water."

"You reckon?"

"The gin should kill the bugs. Throw me the fags."

He obeyed, poured a liberal measure of gin into the one glass he found in the bathroom, topped it up and allowed her the first sip. She sat up in bed to smoke. "How come you haven't taken this up yet?"

"Never felt the urge."

"In your stressful profession? You amaze me."

He sat beside her and they passed the glass to and fro.

"Have you anything on Yasmin Le Blanc?" Harry asked.

"That Algerian woman who wanted to kill you?"

"I imagine she still does. I did execute her sister."

"I thought her husband did that?"

"On my orders."

"Well, as far as I know, as she did for her brother-in-law in rather a macabre fashion, she's going to spend the rest of her life in Holloway. So you don't have to worry."

"That's nice to know." He looked at his watch. It was still daylight outside, although it was past seven. "You reckon this place rises to a restaurant?"

"I think it does. I'm not guaranteeing the food."

"You're going to have me supposing you've been here before. I almost felt that reception clerk knew you."

"If I had been here before, would you be madly jealous, and beat me up?"

"Not my scene. I'd be disappointed, though. I thought we'd agreed no more sleeping around."

"Are you going to tell me you haven't had a go at any French bit?"

"I have not had a go at any French bit," Harry said, carefully stating the absolute truth. "I'd have been arrested. So tell me about your recent love life."

Belinda got out of bed and walked round the room. However attractive to watch, this was again unusual behaviour for her. She came back to the bedside, took the now empty glass, and refilled it with an even more generous proportion of gin.

"I didn't really mean to say this until tomorrow morning. Actually, I didn't mean to say it at all. I had intended to write you a letter."

"Dear Harry?"

"And then you just turned up . . . I was so surprised. And

when you told me you were being sent on this crazy assignment
. . . I suppose I lost my cool."

"You, Belinda Forester, lost your cool?"

"It does happen. More often than you think."

"So what were you going to put in the letter?"

She took a deep drink, made another perambulation.

Harry sat up in bed and leaned back on the pillows. "You're
making me think you've found somebody else."

Oddly enough, he almost felt a sense of relief.

"No," she said. "It's not someone else."

"Then I'm totally mystified."

She sat at the other end of the bed. "You'll never guess who
turned up a couple of weeks ago, right out of the blue. Just as you
did, today."

"Sorry. You have me."

"Jonathan."

He frowned. The name certainly rang a bell. "Who's Jonathan?"

"My husband, idiot. He's a lieutenant colonel. In the Buffs."

"My God!" She had told him her estranged husband's name,
and he'd forgotten it. "But he's no longer your husband. You're
divorced."

"The nisi hasn't come through yet."

"You told me—"

"That it would take another couple of months."

"And you slept with him and put it back another six months."

"Well, not quite like that." She sighed. "I do love him, Harry. I
always did. We split—"

"Because he had been unfaithful to you. That's what you
said."

"Yes, I did. And it's true. But since then, I've been unfaithful
to him. And not only with you. You know that."

"Indeed I do."

"So . . . well . . . he wants to let bygones be bygones. And . . . I
agreed. I do love him," she repeated.

"And obviously you never did love me."

"Oh, I did. I do. It's just that . . ." She gazed at him.

"But you reckoned I was worth a last fuck."

24

"Well, knowing what you were going to do . . ."

"And from which I would probably not come back."

"I know," she said.

"The condemned man has a hearty final meal," he said.

"Would you like me to leave?"

"I think you had better," Harry said. "You have a billet, and I don't."

The Squad

H arry did not suppose any bed had ever felt so lonely. If his initial feeling had been one of relief, that very soon dissipated into bitterness. Perhaps he had always known that marriage to Belinda would be a disaster. She was too used to command, to doing as she thought best: authority could be her middle name. When they had first got together, in the summer of 1941, he had still been young enough, junior enough, innocent enough, and confused enough about the various women who had already bedevilled his emotional life, to welcome her assumption of superiority, her calm certainty that she knew what needed to be done, for both of them. He had surrendered his personality to hers both as his mistress and as the officer who, on behalf of their superiors, gave him his orders and supplied him with the know-how and the *matériel* to carry them out.

But three years was a long time in a war, and he felt that in his experiences he had grown past her, and not only in rank. She was unchanged, still totally confident, still passing on the orders and the background information, still in charge of her own destiny and, at least, the immediate destiny of whichever man happened to be sharing her life. As far as he knew, she had never seen a man or a woman – and more especially a comrade and friend – killed, had never known the mixture of exhilaration and apprehension of going into battle, or the fearsome responsibility of taking a life – however good or urgent the reason for doing so.

Thus they had been steadily growing apart over the past three years, something of which she had seemed to be unaware. But why should she have been aware? At home, whether in her flat or with his parents at their home in the village of Frenthorpe outside Worcester he had always appeared the same slightly bewildered youth who did not know how he had got into his present situation. They accepted that the medals he had earned, as he told it, had been the result of reflex actions rather than considered gallantry. And if Belinda had known there was more to it than that, even she had no idea of the change that could come over him when in action – that his medals were a result of neither accident nor gallantry, but of the ruthless determination to destroy the enemy, no matter at what cost to himself.

There was no way he could convey that to those who had not fought. He wondered if that meant that he would never be able to marry, and share true mental intimacy with any woman?

But he was still human enough to feel resentment, even anger; for all the physical desire Belinda had demonstrated, he had apparently never been a total commitment to her – her love had always been directed elsewhere. Leaving him . . . with a job to do.

His duty had always been the only part of his life that truly mattered. He wondered what they would say of him when he was dead?

Harry was up early, relieved that Belinda's spray had seemed to work and he was free of bug bites. He shaved, dressed, had an attenuated breakfast in an otherwise empty restaurant, and reported to Brigade Headquarters.

Belinda was already at her desk. Harry had the impression that she hadn't slept very well.

"I need to requisition the services of Sergeant-Major John Green of the RAMC," he said. "He's stationed in Caen, or close by. Will you see to it? He should report here tomorrow morning."

She made a note.

"I am now going to return to Battalion to do some recruiting. I shall be back here tomorrow. At that time I will let you have the list of what extra *matériel* I shall require. I shall need it to be available in twenty-four hours, so have someone standing by."

"Yes, sir."

"I will also require billets for four men – myself and three others – for tomorrow night. Not that hotel. I don't mind sharing."

"Yes, sir."

"And I wish a meeting with the air officer commanding, for tomorrow afternoon."

"With respect, sir," she said, "he is an air vice-marshal."

"That should do."

"You are a major, sir."

Harry grinned at her. "Refer the matter to the brigadier. Carry on, Captain."

She gazed at him, looking as if she wanted to say something, then stood up, put on her cap, and saluted.

The driver was already waiting outside. Harry refrained from asking what sort of a night *he* had had with his friends in the motor pool; he looked cheerful enough anyway. The drive back to Battalion was just as slow as the drive in, and it was midday before they arrived.

"I'll need you again tomorrow morning, Corporal."

"Yes, sir."

Harry reported to Colonel Lord Lovat.

"What's on their minds?" Lovat asked.

"Special mission." Harry laid the seconding order on the desk.

Lovat glanced at it. "Which is no doubt top secret."

"I'm afraid it is, sir. I need to recruit."

"How many?"

"I think two, sir. With two in reserve. They will have to be volunteers."

Lovat nodded. "For how long?"

"I'm afraid it may be for some time, sir."

They gazed at each other.

"Damn," Lovat commented. "What will you tell your volunteers?"

"That we are going on a highly dangerous mission which could end the War sooner rather than later and therefore save a great number of lives, including those of their comrades."

"I assume you have the men you want in mind."

"A couple. But as I said, they will have to volunteer."

"Give me the names and I'll have them in, together with some others. When?"

"This evening if possible. The mission is urgent."

"You're a glutton for punishment. Aren't you engaged to be married? What would your fiancée think of all this?"

"What fiancée?" Harry asked.

As he had been quite sure would be the case, there was no shortage of volunteers. These included the two men he most wanted, and who he knew were available; several of the others had to be disregarded because they were either married or only sons. However, as was necessary, he narrowed the applicants down to four.

"I do not wish anyone to be under the slightest misapprehension about what you will be taking on," he said. "This is a highly dangerous mission. We will be operating behind enemy lines. Well behind them. Our objective is heavily guarded, and while I believe that we can get in, I cannot promise that we will be able to get back out again. You are all well aware of the German orders regarding captured Commandos. And even if we do manage to withdraw from our objective, there is no prospect at all of extraction, and only very little of us being able to rejoin this command for some considerable time. We have been given an escape route, but it will be long and difficult. I can only say that if we are successful, the end of the War, and thus our ability to rejoin our comrades, will be considerably shortened. Any man who wishes to leave this room, may now do so with no reflection on either his courage or character."

Predictably, no one moved.

"Very good," Harry said. "Now, only two of you will join the squad; the other two will be reserves. I would very much like to take you all, but any more than four men would become a liability. I already have one member of the team waiting in Caen. We will be operating in highly mountainous territory, therefore abseiling ability and training will be necessary. I know you have all completed abseiling courses as part of your Commando training. Were any of you top of your class?" Of course, Harry already knew how they had ranked in training, but for the sake of morale they had to pick themselves, as it were.

Lieutenant Manning stepped forward. "I was top of my section, sir."

He was a tall, lanky man, who wore a little moustache; he was a wartime soldier who was actually a couple of years older than Harry – but Harry had become used to this inverted situation. "Very good," he said. "No dependent relatives, girlfriend, that sort of thing?"

Again he knew the answer, but again Manning had to pick himself.

"Not at the moment, sir."

"Right. You're on. Anyone else?"

Private Lawton stepped forward. "I was third in my section, sir."

This was hard to accept, although Harry knew it was true. Lawton was a short, chunky man. But there was obviously enormous strength in his heavy shoulders.

"Dependent relatives?" The private was older than the average Commando, in his early thirties.

"No, sir. I'm divorced. If I don't come back, she'll lose her alimony. Then her current boyfriend will have to support her."

"No children?"

"She never had the time, sir."

"Very good. Tell me something, do you still smoke?"

"Ah . . . I'm afraid so, sir."

"Let's see your hands." The private held them out, and Harry gazed at the stained fingers. "You'll have to do without on this trip."

"Yes, sir. I understand that."

"Very good. You're accepted." He turned to the other two men, a sergeant and a private, who were both looking distinctly disappointed. "I know you both have the highest qualifications, but as I have said, I'm limited to four men. You are, however, members of this squad and you will accompany us into Caen tomorrow morning. You will remain there, as reserves in case of accidents, until after the mission has been completed, then you will return to Battalion. Now check all of your normal gear, and report here at zero five zero zero tomorrow morning. Do not discuss this with anyone. Any questions?"

"Clothing, sir?" Manning asked.

"You may each bring a couple of changes of underwear and socks."

"I was thinking of civilian clothing, sir, for when we withdraw."

"We shall not wear civilian clothing. It wouldn't do us any good if we are captured. We shall wear battledress throughout."

"Won't that make us easier to spot, sir?" Lawton asked. "When withdrawing?"

"If we are spottable," Harry said. "We will be moving only at night, and lying up during the day. There will be an issue of special equipment at Caen. Dismissed."

They saluted and withdrew.

Harry turned to Lovat, who had remained seated behind his desk, a silent witness of the interviews.

"Permission to second Lieutenant Manning, Sergeant Thomson and Privates Lawton and Roberts for special duties, sir."

"Permission granted. When will Thomson and Roberts be returned?"

"Hopefully the day after tomorrow, sir."

"Realistically," Lovat said. "What are your chances?"

"That you'll see us again at the end of the War? I would say virtually nil."

"But you do hope to come back. That means you either anticipate being taken prisoner, which isn't on, or you have someplace to go to ground. I'm not prying. I really would like you to come back, no matter how long it takes."

"So would I," Harry said.

They reached Caen in time for lunch, and found Green waiting for them at Brigade. He had never met Manning, Lawton and the two reserves; Harry left them to get to know each other while he went up to Belinda's office.

"Your billets are arranged," she said. "And the brigadier is waiting to see you. Do you have that list of equipment?"

He had written it out the previous night, and gave it to her.

"Looks like you mean to blow up the entire mountain," she commented, scanning the list.

31

"That could be an idea," Harry agreed, and went to the brigadier's office, where he found Air Vice-Marshal Hartman waiting for him.

"Just tell me what you wish," Hartman said.

"Well, sir, in the first instance, a drop."

Hartman nodded. "I gather we're talking about a twelve-hundred-mile round trip. That's a long way for a Lysander, but we can do it. There'll just be the four of you?"

"That's correct, sir. But we will have some fairly heavy equipment."

"Weight?"

"Say one and a half more men, sir."

"Very good. When do you wish to go?"

"It's a matter of careful timing, sir. We need to be dropped as soon as it is dark."

"We'll call that twenty-two hundred. Then you'll leave here at eighteen hundred."

"Yes, sir."

"And you wish to be dropped on a mountainside, in the dark?"

"No, sir. That is not practical. There is open farmland . . ." Harry leaned over the map that had been spread on Martin's desk. "Here, by the railway line."

"That is five miles from the town and the mountain."

"Yes, sir. It will take us a couple of hours to get into position. We shall open hostilities at zero zero one five, immediately after the guard will have been changed – hopefully."

"Why do you say, hopefully?"

"Because I don't know precisely when the guard is changed. I am relying on German method and efficiency. What I would like from you is a bombing raid to be carried out at zero one hundred."

"You estimate the mission will take you forty-five minutes to complete? Suppose you finish early?"

"We must take our chances on that. We intend to use the mountain as an escape route. We must presume that the enemy will be in hot pursuit. In that case, the raid will be our best chance of getting out while they are distracted."

"Very good. So we are to bomb Berchtesgaden and the lower slopes of the mountain. With you, presumably, still on it."

"We'll take our chances on that too, sir."

Hartman looked at Martin.

"He's done this sort of thing before," the brigadier explained.

"Very good." The air vice-marshal was still sceptical. "When is this to happen?"

"Tomorrow night, sir."

"That quickly?"

"We do not know how much longer Hitler will be in residence, sir. And tomorrow is ideal, because moonrise is not until zero two hundred."

"Very good. Radio contact?"

"We will carry radios, sir. But we will not use them, either for sending or receiving, until after we have linked up with the Italian partisans, which will be after we have made our way across Austria. If the schedule is adhered to, it should not be necessary before then, and would only alert the enemy."

"Very good. You will take off at eighteen hundred tomorrow evening. The bombing squadron will take off at twenty-two hundred, being somewhat faster than the Lysander, and will deliver its attack on Berchtesgaden at zero one zero zero."

"Thank you, sir."

Both senior officers shook Harry's hand. "We'll wish you good luck."

Harry saluted.

Harry returned to Belinda's office, where he found a quarter-master-sergeant waiting.

"Is that stuff ready?" he asked.

"It will be tomorrow morning, sir."

"Have it delivered here."

"Yes, sir. May I ask, sir, are you going to jump?"

"Is that any business of yours, Sergeant?"

"It isn't, sir, except that jumping with gelly is a hazardous business."

"So is fighting a war, Sergeant. But if it will reassure you, I have done it before."

"Yes, sir. And the bazooka, well, it's quite a weight. As are its shells. Have you ever fired one, sir?"

"Yes," Harry said. "And my people have been trained to do so."

"Very good, sir. The equipment will be here at ten."

"Don't forget the black overalls, and the boot black."

"With respect, sir, why don't you try one of these new woollen headgear. They cover not only the head but the entire face, with just openings for the eyes and mouth. Very effective. I have one with me, if you'd care to look at it."

Harry took the woollen cap and tested it for strength. He reckoned it would be quite warm to wear, especially in mid-summer, but it was certainly all-concealing and would do away with the necessity of blacking their faces.

"All right, Sergeant. We'll give these a whirl."

The sergeant saluted and withdrew.

"When is the off?" Belinda asked.

"I really don't think that is any business of yours."

"Meaning you don't trust me any more."

"Is there any reason why I should?"

"I can easily find out, you know. I'm the brigadier's right-hand woman."

"Then I suggest you ask him. Where is my billet?"

"I can offer you a choice of three."

"I told you, I am perfectly happy to share . . . with a brother officer."

"By which I assume you mean, male."

"That is what I mean, yes."

She sighed. "There's a room available at Headquarters Reserve. I've put your Lieutenant Manning in there. Is that all right?"

"I think that's excellent."

Harry actually didn't know Manning very well. They had both been dropped behind the German lines on the night before D-Day, but that had been part of a pretty big operation, and once they had been relieved by the main Commando force they had gone their own ways – Manning continuing with his company and Harry joining Battalion Headquarters. But he did know that the lieutenant had been mentioned in despatches and was in line for a Military Cross for having shown conspicuous gallantry and ability under fire; that, plus Manning's known ability as a mountaineer, had made Harry pick him in the first place. Not to mention his obvious enthusiasm.

"Gosh, sir, am I glad to be sharing with you. I was afraid I might talk in my sleep."

"What would you talk about?" Harry asked.

"That's true. Are you the only one who knows where we're going, and why?"

"Apart from a couple of senior officers, yes." And a two-faced female adjutant, he thought, still bitter.

"And we find out when we get there?"

"No. You'll find out when I tell you, which will be tomorrow."

"I was wondering . . . well, you know, when we got the green light back on the fifth of June, I wrote to my folks. Just to say goodbye. They actually got the letter about three weeks later. I've had a reply."

"And now you'd like to write to them again," Harry suggested.

"Well . . . am I saying goodbye?"

"It might be an idea, at least for a while. Let's go and find somewhere to eat."

In an amazingly French fashion, little restaurants were already re-opening all over the city. The food was somewhat limited and the wine distinctly *du pays*, but the ambience was as evocative as ever.

"I suppose this special mission stuff is old hat to you," Manning remarked.

"Nothing like this is ever old hat," Harry told him.

"Oh, quite. But you have done it, over and over again."

"Let's say, more than once."

"And you're still here."

"People keep reminding me of that," Harry said. "What they forget, or don't know, is that of the fifty-seven months this war has been fought, I have spent something like nine in hospital. That's a fairly high proportion."

"Gosh. How many times were you hit?"

"Seriously, twice. Once on the beach at Dunkirk . . ."

"Good Lord! Were you at Dunkirk? I was still a civvy. But . . . the Commandos hadn't yet been formed."

"I was a Guards officer at that time."

"Good Lord!" Manning said again. "And the second?"

"During the raid on Ardres. Sergeant-Major Green got me out, which is why he's coming with us on this one."

"But you were at Dieppe."

"No. If I had been, I probably wouldn't be with you now. I had actually only just got back to England from Portugal, where I wound up after the St Nazaire mess – courtesy of the French resistance and our agents."

"And that time you weren't hit."

"Amazingly, no. They missed me, although they hit just about everyone else." Harry found himself beginning to brood about all the very good men – some of them close friends – who had bought it on that occasion, and hastily got his thoughts under control: now was no time for memories.

"Good Lord!" Manning remarked a third time. "The drop last month was the first time I'd seen action."

"I've an idea it won't be the last," Harry said.

Next morning the weapons and explosives were waiting for them, as promised, together with the special outer gear. As Commandos, they were in any event equipped with tommy-guns and pistols, knives and hand grenades, knuckledusters and lengths of steel wire for when the killing had to be silent. Commandos also carried, in their backpacks, emergency rations for three days, water purification tablets, a first aid kit, a compass, and of course spare magazines for their firearms. The rations for this mission were increased to seven days for each man; the main ingredient was bars of chocolate, which, while not providing a balanced diet, would keep a man going for a considerable period.

To this personal equipment were added a haversack with twelve sticks of gelignite and their fuses, two further haversacks containing the small but weighty shells for the rocket launcher, and the bazooka itself.

"This is your baby, Sergeant-Major," Harry said. "Until we get down."

Green was the biggest and undoubtedly the strongest.

"Lieutenant, you and Lawton will be in charge of one haversack of rockets each. I will handle the gelignite. And as we will be operating at night, we will wear this black gear over our uniforms, together with these special caps. Try them on."

Harry spent the rest of the morning with the squad, making sure they were all familiar with handling the bazooka, and after lunch, when they had assembled in a private room at Headquarters, was the time to tell them what they were going to do.

"We are going to take out Herr Hitler," he said when they were all seated in a semicircle facing him.

There were several gulps, but no one moved.

"We know that he is at present at his country house, in the village of Berchtesgaden in south-east Bavaria. Berchtesgaden is very close to the old Austrian frontier, but of course that border no longer exists, so we cannot regard that as an asset. Now, unfortunately, the only information that we possess is that Hitler is in residence. We may presume that he is accompanied by several close aids, and possibly also by his mistress, Eva Braun. We also know there is a garrison of SS men in the village, possibly as much as battalion strength, but we do not know what are the actual guarding arrangements, how many there are and when the personnel are changed – we must assume the guard on duty will be of some strength. However, Hitler's house is situated on the high ground above the village, virtually on the lower slopes of the mountain, here; you'll see there are several houses, and we do not know how many are presently occupied." He indicated the map. "There is a road down to the village, but the funicular railway, here, is the normal way of going up and down. We will have to blow that railway, and thus at least partially isolate the houses.

"Now, when we go in, in view of the fact that once our presence is known we shall be facing enormous odds in manpower, our objective is total destruction. This plan indicates the layout of the house, and as it will be just after midnight when we attack, we may presume that most of the inmates, but possibly not Hitler, will be in bed. In any event, we are going to blow that room apart. The same goes for the rooms on either side. One of these, you will notice, is marked as belonging to Miss Braun. That goes too. I am sorry about this, but we will not have the time to discriminate.

"Now, as to getting out again. I will lead the attack on the house, with Sergeant-Major Green. Lieutenant Manning, you and Lawton will destroy the funicular railway at the top end, and then you will hold the road, long enough for Green and I to complete the job. Once we start, all hell will break loose. That is when you will detonate the railway, and, using the bazooka, you will retreat on the house. We will join forces and go to the mountain. Of course the SS people will very rapidly work out where we have gone and come after us, but they won't know our strength and will have to bear in mind the possibility of a counter-attack. At zero one hundred the RAF will carry out a bombing raid on the town and the lower slopes. This is designed to throw the entire area into some confusion, long enough for us to circle the mountain on the far side of the town, and make our escape into the lower Alps and thence across Austria. As I have already explained, it will be a matter of concealing ourselves by day and moving at night. I estimate it will take us about a week, for which we have rations. Once we reach Italy, we will contact the Italian partisans, who by then will know we are coming. They will conceal us, and hopefully be able to make arrangements for us to be extracted. If this cannot be accomplished, well, we shall finish the War fighting beside them. Questions?"

"How do we get in, sir?" Lawton asked. "By drop?"

"Yes, but not directly on either the villa or the town. That would be a dead give-away. We shall be dropped here . . ." He indicated the position on the map. "That is open farmland. It is also five miles from the village. We shall make our way up the lower slopes of the mountain, high enough to be able to circle to a position immediately above the houses, and descend from there. I'm afraid both going in and coming out will require a good deal of mountaineering in the dark." He grinned at them. "That will probably be the most dangerous part of the operation.

However, as I explained at camp, this whole operation is extremely hazardous. It is being undertaken because our superiors consider that if Hitler could be got rid of, the War will end that much sooner. And if it can be done at the cost of just four of our lives everyone will be ahead." Another grin. "Except us. But I believe it can be done, and I believe that at least some of us will get away again. But it will only be done – and we will only escape – if we are totally committed, both before and after. There can be no question of anyone surrendering. Anyone seriously wounded will have to be abandoned, with a grenade. He must not be taken alive. The whole essence of the operation is that Jerry must not know who and how many he has been hit by, and thus, how many he is looking for. Understood?"

He looked from face to face, and certainly saw apprehension, but their eyes were steady.

"Right," he said. "Now, I am going to ask for the last time: if anyone has had any second thoughts and wishes to drop out, this is your final opportunity to do so. As I have said, this will carry no slur upon either your personal courage or your record. However optimistic I may be, any sane person would regard this as a suicide mission."

Green, Manning and Lawton looked at each other, while the two reserves waited; it was impossible to tell whether they were holding their breath for the chance of being a replacement, or sharing mental relief that they would not have to go.

"Very good," Harry said, "and I am proud to have you aboard. Thomson and Roberts, thank you again for volunteering. You will have your opportunity. I'm afraid I can't release you right now."

"We would like to see you off, sir," Thomson said.

"And so you shall. You'll be returned to camp first thing in the morning. Well, gentlemen, shall we go?"

A command car drove them and their gear to the airfield, where to Harry's surprise, both Martin and Hartman were waiting for them . . . together with Belinda.

It was a fine evening, still broad daylight and hardly a cloud to be seen.

"Flight-Lieutenant Carpenter, Flight-Sergeant Morris," Hartman introduced. "We need two for a long flight like this."

The Commandos shook hands.

"I've told them you're very precious," Hartman said. "At least until you're dropped."

"We'll get you there, Major," Carpenter said.

"And get yourselves back?" Harry asked.

"We think so. The aircraft has been specially adapted with an extra fuel tank. This lops off a bit of speed, but we should still be able to do one-fifty."

"And over there," Hartman said, "is your back-up."

The six Lancasters waited silently; their crews were not yet in evidence, but ground personnel were loading the bombs.

"Then it's all systems go." Harry looked at his watch: ten minutes to six.

"I'll wish you good luck," Hartman said, and shook hands with each of the four in turn.

Thomson and Roberts waited to one side.

"My turn." Martin also shook hands.

"You'll see that Sergeant Thomson and Private Roberts are sent back to Battalion, sir," Harry reminded him.

"You'll attend to that, Forester," the brigadier said.

"Yes, sir. First thing in the morning."

"Very good."

"May I bid you Godspeed as well, Major Curtis?" Belinda asked.

"Thank you, Captain."

They shook hands, her mouth twisting.

"Time to go," Carpenter said.

The Commandos loaded their equipment, put on their black suits and strapped on their parachutes – they were all experienced jumpers – and climbed into the aircraft. The watchers on the ground saluted, the engine started, and the aircraft taxied past the waiting bombers to the end of the runway.

"Quite a send-off," Manning commented. "Makes one feel like royalty."

"This is nothing to the welcome we'll get," Harry pointed out. "When we come back."

He was, as always, surprised at his calmness. Gone – as if with a snap of the fingers – was all the uncertainty, the apprehension, of the past few days. Even the bitterness towards Belinda. Only the mission now mattered. He had no doubt that he would succeed, at least in reaching Hitler's villa and destroying it and everyone inside it. What would happen after that was in the lap of the gods – but he had been in that position before, and was willing to trust in the deity.

The watchers waited until the aircraft was lost to view. It would have to cross the battlefield, but would be too high to be identified. In any event, the Germans had all they could do attempting to shoot at the Allied bombers and fighters who constantly strafed their positions; they would have no time to fire at a lone observer high in the sky.

"I feel like a drink," Martin said. "Several drinks."

Hartman nodded. "I know just the place. Has a neat little restaurant, as well." He glanced at Belinda. "Would you care to join us, Captain?"

"I'd be delighted, sir."

Thomson and Roberts were driven back to their barracks; they were given the evening off, but enjoined not to discuss the mission with anyone, and to report to Brigade Headquarters first thing in the morning. Then the three officers went on to the restaurant.

"Do you have champagne?" Hartman asked the proprietor in excellent French.

"Champagne, no. I have white wine."

"Then send over a bottle and the menu."

"Don't you think champagne would be more appropriate when they come back, sir?" Belinda asked.

"We should drink to the success of the mission," Hartman said. "I understand Major Curtis is very highly thought of."

"He is the best we have at this sort of thing," Martin said. "Would you agree with that opinion, Forester?"

"Absolutely, sir. The very best."

"You've known him a long time, haven't you?"

"I met Major Curtis – he was Lieutenant Curtis, then – on the day he joined the Commandos, in 1940, sir."

41

"And since then you've directed him at the enemy on God knows how many occasions, and he's always carried out his mission, and come back."

"Not always in one piece, sir. But he has always come back, yes."

"So what makes him tick so successfully?" Hartman asked.

If you only knew, she thought. If *I* only knew. Oh, Harry, Harry. But hadn't she known all along that they would never be able to share the rest of their lives without a war, without a constant involvement in so many things greater than themselves? Compared with Harry, Jonathan was a rest cure. But that was what she needed now, and wanted most of all.

Yet the man had to be answered. "A combination of several things, I would say, sir. The will to succeed, to conquer, certainly. Then there is the sex drive."

"Eh?"

"Have you never noticed, sir, that many very successful men have a pronounced sex drive? You could say that men with such a drive are more forceful, more determined, more macho, if you like, than others."

"Interesting point," Martin commented, studying the menu. "Oysters. Oh, indeed, we'll have oysters. Now they do wonders for the sex drive, so I'm told."

"Tell me, Captain Forester," Hartman said. "Have you any first-hand knowledge of Major Curtis at work?"

"Only the results, sir," Belinda replied, but there were pink spots in her cheeks – as the air vice-marshal noticed.

"You do understand that he may not come back from this mission?"

"That has gone for all of his missions, sir, since he became a Commando. But I should say that another of his assets, perhaps his greatest, is that when he goes into action he does not care whether he lives or dies; he is only concerned with the destruction of the enemy."

"And he's always turned up," Martin observed. "Let's hope his luck holds. I shouldn't think he's ever been on a mission quite this important before."

The meal was a convivial one, and it was just going on ten

when they returned to the airfield to watch the bomber squadron taking off.

"Good show," Hartman said. "And Curtis and his people will be dropping about now. Well, there's damn all we can do now. We'd better get you back to your billet, Forester."

"Thank you, sir," Belinda said, and watched a telegrapher hurrying across the tarmac towards them. Lead balloons gathered in her stomach. Although she was relieved that she would not have to spend the rest of her life sharing the intensity of Harry's personality, she still felt like a heel. And she certainly did not want anything to happen to him.

"Sir!" The telegrapher saluted.

"Yes?" Hartman's voice was suddenly strained.

"We've just had a report, sir, that Herr Hitler has addressed a rally at the Sports Palace in Berlin."

"When?" Martin snapped.

"Tonight, sir."

"But he's in Berchtesgaden, recuperating from the bomb blast!"

"He left Berchtesgaden this morning, sir."

"Oh, shit," Martin commented.

"We must abort the mission," Hartman said.

"They're on the ground. And specifically not using their radios."

"Four of our best men," Belinda lamented.

"Shit!" Martin said again.

"At least we can recall the bombers," Hartman said.

"No," Martin said. "The raid is the only hope of Curtis and his people getting out."

Hartman looked at Belinda. "What a cock-up," he said. "What *are* we to do?"

"Pray," she suggested.

The Fiasco

" Five minutes." Flight-Sergeant Morris came back to act as
despatcher.

Harry nodded, and looked at his men. They seemed alert
enough, and there was no sign of nerves. "Hoods on," he said.

They had removed them for coolness during the flight.

"Equipment," he reminded them, himself adding the haversack of gelignite to his load.

"Only a light breeze," Morris said. "You shouldn't scatter,
Stand by."

Harry took his place at the door, waited for the light, and a
moment later was floating through space. A brief recollection of
the other times he had been dropped into enemy territory drifted
through his mind. But previously he had either been part of a big
operation or had been sure of a welcome on the ground from
resistance groups. This time he and his band were entirely on
their own.

The drone of the aircraft faded, and in its place he heard
the rumble of a train engine followed by the blast of a whistle.
That would be the last train from Berchtesgaden to Munich,
he estimated. Neither engine nor carriages were blacked out,
and he reckoned the railway line was only about a mile to his
left.

A moment later he was on the ground, staggering to his feet
while he gathered up his parachute. As Morris had indicated, the
breeze was so light as to be almost non-existent at ground level,
so he had no difficulty. Neither did his men, who were now
landing around him.

"Do we bury these?" Manning asked.

Harry looked at his watch: ten past ten. "Bundle them up and stow them in those bushes," he said. "By the time they're found they'll be meaningless. You all right, Sergeant-Major?"

Loaded with the bazooka strapped to his back, Green had gone down, but now he was on his feet again. "I'm all right, sir."

The Commandos stowed the parachutes, while Harry surveyed their position. They had landed, as intended, in open fields about a mile from the railway line and the road. The fields were fenced, but he didn't reckon that was going to be a handicap. To the south-east was a gleam of light, which was undoubtedly Berchtesgaden itself; the Germans obviously did not apprehend an air raid this far from the front and where there was no industrial target. Just to the right of the glow the dark shape of a mountain deepened the night.

"Check your weapons," Harry said, and himself made sure the gelignite was stable; until they were fused the sticks were perfectly safe, as long as they were dry. Then he spread his map on the ground and checked their position by flashlight, while the squad stood round to conceal the glow, just in case there was someone near enough to see it. "Check watches. Ten seventeen. Check compasses. Direction is one-seven-eight degrees. All correct? Let's go. Stay close."

They made their way across the fields, cutting barbed wire fences where necessary, and even where it wasn't, in keeping with Harry's idea of leaving the impression that a large body of men had been put down. Several of the fields contained cows, but these regarded the intruders with only mild curiosity.

It was slow going, but by eleven thirty they were on rising ground and some half mile from the town itself. There were certainly lights in the lower houses, but only a glimmer on the ridge. It occurred to Harry that this was not Hitler's usual routine, which was to work quite late at night and sleep late in the morning. But of course Hitler was recuperating rather than working, and if he was already in bed it was probably on doctor's orders.

"Now for the tricky bit," he told his squad.

They began climbing. On the lower slopes it was actually quite easy, even in the darkness; the difficult climbing would be after they had completed the mission and would be trying to get up and round the mountain, presumably both in haste and under fire. But even now there was the odd stone that got dislodged and went rattling down the slope into the valley. At each such mishap they paused, pressed to the ground, waiting and listening. There was no general alarm, however, and they had climbed above the upper houses and were beginning to traverse round the hillside when they heard voices.

Harry flapped his hand, and the squad went to ground while he listened; he spoke fluent German.

"Nothing to report," a man said.

"A nice night," said the other man.

They were not in sight, but Harry estimated the two men were somewhat below the Commandos. He mentally cursed. It simply had not occurred to him that there might be a guard above the house. But at least his timings were being proved right: there would not be another change for at least two and probably four hours, as it was summer.

The Commandos continued to wait while the two men exchanged some more conversation, then they bade each other good night, and the clump of boots receded. Harry realised that they might actually have gained an advantage; he had anticipated having to abseil down the last slope, but there was obviously a way down.

His men looked at him questioningly, but he shook his head and continued to wait, checking his watch. Ten past midnight. He gave it another ten minutes, enough time for the replaced guard to have reached the bottom and hopefully to be making for his barracks. Then he touched Green on the arm. With great care the Sergeant-Major laid the bazooka on the hillside, wedged it against an outcrop of rock, and followed his commander.

Harry crawled round the corner, and discovered that there was a rough path cut into the mountainside to provide a platform for the guard, who was at this minute marching up and down. Obviously he did not do that all the time, but he was more accessible while moving. Harry reached into his haversack for one of the lengths of steel wire he carried.

The sentry reached the far end of his platform, turned, and marched back towards them. He was armed with a tommy-gun rather than a rifle, and this was slung from his shoulder under his right arm, but his hand was resting on the trigger guard and it was reasonable to suppose it would close even if he were taken by surprise: Harry was not afraid of being shot, but he couldn't risk the noise that might alert any of the men on the ridge below.

Again the guard halted, stamping his feet as he faced about. Harry stood up, virtually beside him, swinging his hand down to land on the right arm and knock it away from the gun. Green moved to the sentry's other side, seized the weapon and whipped it from his shoulder, while in virtually the same movement Harry turned his victim and got the wire round his neck, twisting it into a tightening loop.

The soldier had only time to utter a startled gulp before his windpipe was constricted and he sagged in Harry's arms.

"Keep still," Harry whispered, and the three men waited while he carefully laid the dead man on the ground. Then they listened, but there was no sound from below. Harry checked his watch again: twelve twenty.

He waved the squad forward and they followed the path, moving slowly and carefully; now was no time to dislodge any more stones. Within five minutes they were above the houses, of which there were several. But Harry had marked the position of the Hitler House in his mind, and knew just where it was. They reached the position immediately above it, and gazed down the slope.

There was a gleam of light emanating from the house itself, but no sound apart from the tramp of feet as the guards moved up and down in the yard; all the other houses were in darkness, and the terrace of the Hitler House was deserted. Harry listened very carefully, and deduced that there were only two guards on patrol – which meant that there were probably at least two more on duty. He studied the other houses, but there was no sign of life from any of them. He knew that both Goebbels and Goering also maintained residences here, and wondered if they were actually here at the moment, perhaps with Hitler. What a coup that would be! That there were no flags flying from any of the poles – each house had one, Hitler's being situated on the terrace – was no indication of residence, as the flags would all have been lowered at sunset.

Harry studied the road leading from the houses and down to the town below. This looked deserted, as did the funicular railway that ran close by. That guard too would just have been changed, and would be settling down for the usual uneventful night – but they were certainly far fewer in number than he had anticipated, and far more lax than he would have supposed possible when guarding the most important man in the country. But it was not his business to look a gift horse in the mouth.

He cast about and saw, immediately to his left, a series of steps cut into the hillside leading down. They were situated two houses away from the target. He crawled along until he reached them, looked down, and saw two more guards standing together at the foot; it was impossible to tell whether they were passing their time of duty in a chat or saying goodnight before going to bed. In any event he couldn't afford to wait any longer – it was twelve thirty.

"Slight change of plan," Harry whispered to Manning. "Green and I will go down by rope. You and Lawton wait here. Only go down if those chaps move; there's no hope of taking them out without giving the alarm. Either way, stay here or at the foot of the steps until Green and I open up. Then you, Lawton, will have to take out every guard you can see. Manning, you'll get the bazooka and the explosives to the head of the railway and the road, and the moment anyone starts to come up, blow it and anyone *you* can see." He gave the lieutenant six of the sticks of gelignite, and together they fitted the fuses to all twelve sticks. He then turned to face Green. "Sergeant-Major."

Green divested himself of the bazooka and the bag of shells, and Manning added them to his already extensive equipment. "If I get hit carrying this lot . . ." Manning ventured.

"You won't know a thing," Harry assured him. "Now, when you have destroyed the railway and discouraged anyone trying to get up, come back to Lawton and both of you get back up to this ridge and move out, going south and then up. If you feel in the mood to go on using the bazooka you're welcome – just remember you'll be exposing your position."

"And you?" Manning asked.

"We'll be doing the same thing just the moment we've got our man."

"Well . . ." Manning held out his hand. "Good luck."

Harry squeezed his fingers. "And to you. Let's go, Sergeant-Major."

Harry and Green made their way back along the platform until they were again immediately above the Hitler House. Here they unslung their ropes and after making several tests found a sufficiently solid outcrop of rock to which an end could be made fast. This was done, and the two ropes were carefully lowered into the darkness, behind the house. The two men went down, letting the rope slide through their thickly gloved fingers, and landed lightly. The house rose above them, and now they could hear, faintly, the sound of a gramophone.

There was a short flight of steps up to the back door. Harry went up and tried this; incredibly, it was unlocked. Little alarm bells began to tingle in the back of his mind. But he told himself that the Germans had every reason to be relaxed in this remote spot.

Carefully he turned the handle and stepped into a lighted kitchen, where a uniformed maidservant, flaxen-haired and buxom, was putting away some cutlery. She turned at the sound of the door opening, and gazed in total consternation at the black-clad and hooded figure emerging from the night. She opened her mouth to scream, but Harry swiftly stepped against her – his knife already drawn from its sheath – and closed his left hand on her throat.

Green joined him, waiting, his breathing heavy. Their orders were to destroy everyone in the house. But that meant anyone either important or able to resist. This girl was neither, and they were only going to be in the house for fifteen minutes at the most. He nodded to Green, who understood, drew and reversed his pistol, pushed the girl's cap to one side while she stared at them with wide eyes, and used the butt to strike her across the head. She gave a groan and collapsed in Harry's arms. He laid her on the floor, sheathed his knife, stepped over her and listened at the inner door.

Now the gramophone was quite loud. He simply could not

believe that Hitler was sitting up listening to a gramophone after midnight. But there could be no turning back now. He nodded to Green, drew a deep breath, and opened the door.

In front of him – as he remembered from the house plan – there was a corridor leading to a hallway which backed the terrace, and thence on one hand to the dining room and the stairs to the first floor, and on the other to the lounge. The gramophone came from the right hand, the lounge. Harry cautiously looked round the corner; the hallway was empty, but the door to the lounge was open, and he could see several people in there, mostly legs. Disconcertingly, at least two pairs of them belonged to women.

Yet again, what he was looking at did not conform to the mental picture he had formed of Hitler or his habits – but of course the man had to have a lighter side too.

He signalled Green, patting his tommy-gun. Green nodded, and stood beside him. Harry drew one of the sticks of gelignite, lit the fuse, waited to let it burn down, and then heard someone say, "There is something burning."

Harry threw the stick into the room. There was a chorus of screams, and a man – with more courage than sense – picked up the burning explosive and ran at the door. Green fired a burst from his tommy-gun and the man fell backwards, the gelignite flying from his hands. It was still in mid-air when it exploded.

Harry and Green had flattened themselves against the wall of the corridor, but even so they were shaken by the blast and some plaster fell from the ceiling.

"Finish the job," Harry said, and ran into the hall, turning left for the stairs. Green followed him, turning right, and advanced on the smoking drawing room, tommy-gun chattering. As they did so there was a rumble of sound from outside and down the hill, more tommy-guns firing, people shouting, sirens wailing.

Harry was up the steps in seconds, looking down another corridor between the bedrooms. One of these doors now opened, and a couple staggered out. They were both naked and extremely tousled, but the man carried a revolver. Harry gave them a burst from his tommy-gun, and they both went down in a scatter of blood. He jumped over them and reached the door. This time, as the room would be much smaller, he used a grenade, throwing the door wide at a count of two and slamming it shut just before the door blew open again. Tommy-gun thrust forward, he stepped inside. The grenade had landed on the bed, which had disintegrated. But there was no evidence that anyone had been in it.

Beginning to feel vaguely sick, Harry returned to the corridor and threw open the door of Eva Braun's room. This was also empty.

Now he heard the rumble of an explosion from outside: Manning had blown the railway. The operation was going like clockwork . . . with the vital ingredient missing.

He ran along the corridor, throwing doors wide, but all the other rooms were empty, and now he smelt, and heard, flames from below. Some smoke drifted up the stairwell, together with the clump of boots.

"Major!" Green called.

Harry went to the stairhead and looked down.

"They're all dead, sir."

"Hitler?"

"Not so far as I could see, sir. I thought . . ."

"So did I," Harry said. "There's been a cock-up. Let's get out."

They went down the stairs. The drawing room was well alight; the glass doors had shattered and the flames were leaping into the air. No one in Berchtesgaden could have any doubt that the Hitler House was being destroyed. From outside there continued the sound of firing, but there was no point in exposing Manning and Lawton any longer.

Harry ran to the end of the terrace and shouted, "Withdraw!" Then he rejoined Green, and the two Commandos ran through the corridor and back to the kitchen. The maid was just stirring, moaning and holding her head, which was bleeding. Harry grasped her under the armpits, dragged her to the door and down the back steps, laid her on the ground. At least she would not burn to death.

The firing from behind them was now growing louder, presumably as Manning and Lawton withdrew and the SS men from the town began to make their way up the slope; there did not appear to be anyone apart from the Commandos and the maid left alive on the ridge. Harry and Green went up their ropes as quickly as they had gone down, reeled them in and untied them. There was still no sign of Manning and Lawton, so they moved back along the platform to the top of the steps, where they looked down and saw Lawton starting up, half carrying the lieutenant.

"Shit!" Harry growled. "You'd better give him a hand, Sergeant-Major."

Green went down the steps, while Harry unslung his tommy-gun and surveyed the ridge below him. There was a good deal of shooting, and bullets were flying all over the place, but none of the Germans, who were now slowly coming up the road, were exactly sure where their enemy was.

"What happened?" he asked, as the three men reached the platform.

Manning was still carrying the bazooka. "Some blighter we never saw at all," he gasped. "Must have been asleep. Woke up when we started firing and took a pot-shot at me."

"Keep their heads down," Harry told Green and Lawton, who both opened fire with their tommy-guns. "Let's have a look." He bent over Manning, already suspecting the worst, for blood was seeping through the black overalls. He tore open the rent to see inside, using his flashlight regardless of the risk. Inside, the battledress trousers were also torn, and when he opened this as well he saw the splintered bone.

"Shit," he muttered. "How do you feel?"

"It's just starting," Manning said. "Oh, Jesus!"

Hitherto he had been spared the pain by the shock, but this was now wearing off. The important thing was that he couldn't walk, much less climb, and they had several hours of that ahead of them together with several days hard walking after that.

"I'll give you a painkiller," Harry said.

"No," Manning said, gritting his teeth. "I need to stay awake. Just leave me here." He forced a grin. "That was the deal, right? And I still have the bazooka; you won't need that again."

That had indeed been the deal, but it still went against the grain. Harry looked over the houses to the end of the road, and saw a cluster of dark figures. Several were on the ground, but there were far too many standing – and advancing. They would be here in minutes.

"Blow those steps," he commanded.

Both Green and Lawton tossed grenades down the slope, and the steps disintegrated.

"Now clear off while you can," Manning said.

Harry hesitated a last moment, then clasped the lieutenant's hand.

"Just one thing before you go," Manning said. "Did you get the bastard?"

Harry looked past him at Green, then looked down again. "Sure we did," he said. "The mission has been a success."

The Fugitives

T he three men hurried along the platform. None of them spoke; there was nothing to say. Harry looked at his watch: ten to one.

Behind them the bazooka exploded, and again, followed by a burst of tommy-gun fire and the deeper crack of a revolver; the Germans had determined Manning's position. The platform ended. "It's up from here," Harry said, looking up at the immense dark mound above them. As he did so, the night – already loud with noise as Berchtesgaden came to life – was seared by the wail of an air-raid siren. "Hallelujah!" he said, and hurled his rope upwards. It came back down with a rush, but on his second throw the grapple lodged and held; he swung himself up.

The night rocked to the sound of the first explosion, drowning the noise of the still-firing bazooka. Now a searchlight beam rose; it was not directed at the mountain but rather at the aircraft, and was joined by the sharp cracks of an anti-aircraft gun.

Harry reached his lodgement, where there was a spur of rock on which he could sit; he gave a jerk on the rope. Lawton came next, followed by Green. Harry estimated they were about forty feet above the burning villa. They looked down at the ledge, but could see nothing. There was no more sound from the bazooka, but they could hear men shouting. However, these shouts were lost in the explosions as bombs began dropping in earnest. Berchtesgaden and its environs became a mass of flames, turning the night as bright as day.

"Round," Harry said. "They won't be far behind."

The men climbed a little higher, then made their way round the hill towards the mountain at a height of perhaps eighty feet, taking turns to be the lead, passing their ropes back one after the other. Inevitably there were slips in the darkness; on one occasion Lawton at the lead, fell some twenty feet down an unseen crevasse, and had to be dragged up hand over hand. Fortunately he was only bruised, but by the time he had been recovered the raid was over, and the bombers disappeared into the night.

So far as Harry could ascertain, none of the planes had been hit, and they had done their job; behind them fire-engine bells clanged and the clamour was enormous; much would depend on how distracted the Germans soldiers had been. The Commandos had a fair start in terms of time, but very little in actual distance – they were still only in the foothills of the Watzmann. Now, to their left, they could see the broad sweep of the Königssee.

Harry checked his watch and his compass. It was one thirty, which meant that the moon would be rising in half an hour; already he could see the gleam beyond the hills. On the other hand, there was still no immediate sound of pursuit.

"We keep going until daybreak," he said. "That's just over two hours, then we'll hole up."

"Reckon they'll be after us tomorrow, sir?" Lawton asked.

"I reckon," Harry said.

There was no point in attempting to climb up into the mountain itself, Harry decided. They wanted to get as far south as they could before first light. He had memorised the map, and between them and the Italian border – which he reckoned was now some seventy miles away due south instead of the originally estimated fifty – there was only the occasional scattered hamlet and isolated farm. The land itself was often more than six thousand feet above sea level, and seldom less than three. It was also totally unsuited to tracker dogs, most of it being bare rock and close to precipitous. Providing they could find concealment during the day, he thought they had a reasonable chance of making it.

But what a waste, Harry reflected, as they crawled their way across the slopes, now well illuminated by the bright moonlight, the sounds of chaos gradually fading behind them. Neither Hitler nor any of his more important underlings had been in residence, and a very good man had died needlessly, however gallantly. That could not be forgotten – supposing any one of them survived.

By dawn they had covered some eight miles, so far as he could estimate. With hopefully a full night ahead of them he reckoned they should be able to double that every night from then on; they were all in superb condition and, even as heavily laden as they were with their weapons and survival packs, found traversing the mountainside hardly more difficult or exhausting than negotiating a road.

Now it was necessary to find some place to conceal themselves. They all surveyed the land before them through their binoculars. Green pointed at a hopeful position perhaps a mile away to their right, while Lawton spotted a rushing mountain stream immediately beneath them. They drank the last of their canteens, then Harry and Green handed them to Lawton to refill and went across to the tumbled rocks which made a shelter.

"What do you reckon, sir?" Green asked.

"Pretty good," Harry agreed. "So long as no one comes within fifty feet or so. It's our best option." He waved at Lawton, and at the same moment heard the distant drone of an engine. "Down!" he shouted at Lawton. "Inside, Sergeant-Major."

Green ducked into the rocks, and Harry followed. Lawton threw himself full length on the ground and lay still. He was still wearing his black overalls, but the rocky slopes were, fortunately, dark from shadow. The important thing was that he lie still.

Harry and Green watched the plane – a single-engined monoplane – swing round the mountain, as low as it dared in the midst of so many hills. Now it flew directly towards them, at about four hundred feet.

"If I had a rifle, I could bring him down," Green muttered.

"Not a good idea," Harry said. "He will have radio, and a rifle shot would echo for miles in these hills."

The plane flew right over their little cairn, and disappeared again. "Think he noticed anything, sir?" Green asked.

"We'll soon know," Harry said.

Lawton was starting to get up, and Harry waved him down

56

again. They waited while the plane, and the sound of its engine, slowly faded.

"Okay," Harry said.

Lawton ran to them, the three canteens strung round his neck. "Do you think he saw me?" He was very agitated.

"If he identified you as a human being and not a shadow, he'd have come back for another look," Harry said. "Now let's get some sleep. We have fourteen hours to play with."

They took off their dark overalls and balaclavas, ate some chocolate, drank some water, and tried to relax. They kept their weapons beside them, but they all understood that if they were discovered they were going to die, no matter how many of the enemy they might take with them.

It was actually one of the more restful days in Harry's experience. There was absolutely nothing to do save wait for darkness. He didn't even dare switch on his radio, in case the Germans had the use of some sophisticated tracking device. Instead he thought about Italy. He had never been there, and he didn't suppose he was going to see it at its best. But he knew it was still going to look like heaven.

Green was equally relaxed, and spent most of the time with his eyes shut, even when he was awake. Lawton was more of a problem. His nerves were obviously frayed by having been caught in the open by the spotter plane and he was clearly dying for a cigarette. To Harry's consternation, he suddenly produced a packet of Craven A from his haversack and regarded it lovingly.

"What the devil is that?" Harry demanded. "You agreed not to bring any of those."

"With respect, sir, I agreed not to smoke."

"Well, having a packet of fags is just too tempting. Get rid of it."

"Couldn't I have just one drag, sir? I don't reckon there's anyone for a hundred miles."

"I suspect they're a lot closer than that," Harry told him. "And if they do come this way after we've left, and find a cigarette stub, they'll know they're on the right track. If you had some German cigarettes, now . . ."

"Muck," Lawton growled. But he remained fingering his own pack for several seconds before putting it away. Harry didn't much like the look of that, and wondered if he should confiscate it, but their survival depended on their total commitment to each other, and he was reluctant to risk the slightest discord until and unless it became absolutely necessary.

Throughout the day there was no sign of any pursuit, and although another plane flew over in the afternoon, this was much higher than the first, and again showed no evidence of knowing where they were.

"Think we've got away with it, sir?" Green asked.

"I wouldn't count on it, Sergeant-Major. I would say they know that looking for us on foot in these mountains would be like looking for a needle in a haystack, especially as they don't know how many of us there are or what arrangements we may have made for extraction. But they'll be reckoning we've got to show up somewhere, and are waiting for that."

"And when we don't show up anywhere?" Lawton asked.

"They'll get agitated. But I would say we've a day or two."

They ate some chocolate, and as soon as it was dark resumed their black clothes, refilled their canteens at the stream and set off again, making steadily south. Entering one valley about midnight they saw a gleam of light about a mile to their right, but they were too far away from the village to cause even a dog to bark.

They made good progress that night, and, checking his map against the various mountain peaks which surrounded them, Harry reckoned they had covered something like twenty miles, which, added to the eight of the previous night, meant they were very nearly halfway. On the downside, they could find neither water nor really adequate shelter at daybreak, and had to huddle in a copse of trees while several planes flew overhead.

"Like you said, Major," Green remarked. "They're starting to get agitated."

"By now they'll have eliminated all possibility of us having gone north, or west, or east. Therefore it has to be south. It's still a lot of country to cover."

"On bars of chocolate," Lawton said disgustedly, folding up the wrapping paper to put it into his haversack. "What would I give for a big plate of steak and chips."

"Three more days, and you should be sitting down to at least a plate of spaghetti," Harry told him.

"Think he's going to make it?" Green asked, when the private had left the trees for a movement.

"He's a Commando," Harry said.

"They're not all heroes," Green pointed out.

"We'll just have to keep an eye on the situation, Sergeant-Major."

"I will do that, sir," Green agreed, and looked up as Lawton returned rather more quickly than he had left.

"People!" he gasped, dropping to his hands and knees.

"Soldiers?" Harry asked.

"I don't think so. Just people. But heading this way."

Harry peered through the trees, and made out three men. They wore civilian clothes but carried shotguns, and were obviously hunting. And, as Lawton had said, they were steadily approaching.

"We may have to take them out," Green said.

"Only if we have to," Harry told him. "For three locals to disappear or be found dead will tell the Germans where we are as quickly as if we sent up a smoke signal. Let's just keep our heads down."

They lay on the ground, waiting and watching. Soon they heard voices, but the men were walking past the copse rather than into it. Harry was just breathing a sigh of relief when the Austrians stopped, peering at the ground.

"Shit," Lawton muttered.

"That's exactly it," Harry agreed.

The men were looking right and left. From the freshness of the movement they would be able to tell that whoever had relieved himself had to be close. There was nothing for it.

"Single shots," he said, adjusting his tommy-gun. "Lawton, left. Green, right. Me, centre."

They levelled their guns, and the three shots were simultaneous. The hunters went down together, while the noise reverberated to and fro from the slopes around them.

"What a fucking racket," Green commented.

"They came here to shoot," Harry said. "Anyone close by will have expected to hear shots. Cover me."

He got up and walked towards the three men, tommy-gun thrust forward. It had been an act of cold-blooded murder. But then, what was war but murder? These three men, out for a pleasant day's shooting, had endangered Harry and his comrades just as much as if they had been armed members of the SS.

But more and more, with every assignment, he found himself wondering how many more men he would have to kill before the end came. Even more, how would he cope – supposing he survived the last shot – when killing suddenly became illegal? He had known no other way of life as an adult.

He got right up to the scattered bodies, and saw movement. His reaction was instantaneous, leaping to one side while firing another single shot. But the dying man had already squeezed the trigger, and Harry went down. For the moment he felt nothing, was not even sure where he had been hit, but he knew the shock would soon wear off.

Boots pounded, and Green and Lawton arrived.

"The bastard," Green said.

"He was only doing what came naturally," Harry said.

"Well, he's dead now," Lawton pointed out.

"Anybody about?" Harry asked, gritting his teeth as the first sharp slivers of pain ran up his leg and into his back.

"Not that I can see, sir," Lawton said.

"Right," Harry said and tried to rise, only to go down again.

"Easy, sir," Green said. "You've got some pellets in that leg, and maybe higher up. We'll get them out."

"First things first," Harry said. "Get me back to the copse, then bring the bodies."

Actually, he found he could walk while leaning on Green's shoulder, but progress was very slow. Green laid him on the grass under the trees and went back to help Lawton bring the bodies, humping them over their shoulders to prevent any tell-tale drag marks on the ground. Then they collected the men's haversacks, the shotguns, and the spent cartridge cases. There was little they could do about the blood, save kick some earth over it.

"When do you reckon they'll be missed, sir?" Lawton asked.

"What's in those haversacks?" Harry bit his lip as Green divested him of the black overalls.

The private opened the first. "Christmas Day! Ham and bread and a bottle of beer."

"That means they were out for the day. They won't be missed until this evening at the earliest. How is it, Sergeant-Major?"

Green had pulled down his pants and was kneeling by the exposed and bleeding leg. "Half a dozen pellets. Mainly in the thigh, but one or two in the buttocks. I'll have them out in a jiffy. It may hurt a bit." He pushed Harry's battledress blouse higher. "Shit!"

"Bad?"

"There are some in your back as well. Could be pretty deep."

"Just do what you can," Harry said, lying on his face and gritting his teeth again as Green opened his first-aid box and got to work with a pair of tweezers.

"OK to eat some of this stuff, sir?" Lawton asked.

"Why not. And I wouldn't say no to some beer."

"Here we go." Lawton opened a bottle and gave it to him. Harry drank deeply; nothing had ever tasted so good.

Green was busily cleaning up the wounds and applying antiseptic.

"How does it look?" Harry asked.

"Messy," the sergeant-major said. "But when I have it bound up it'll be better. There's one in the back I can't get out. Too deep. I'd have to cut, and we don't have that kind of gear, or anaesthetic."

"Then it'll have to stay put."

"There's a chance of septicaemia."

"I'll have to take that chance. What about walking?"

"Strictly speaking you shouldn't," Green said. "But as in our circumstances you have to, I'm afraid you'll have to grin and bear it."

"What you mean is, I'm going to be a liability."

"I wouldn't say that, sir. We'll manage."

"Sergeant-Major," Harry said. "As of this moment you're in command."

"Very good, sir."

"Therefore, you'll carry out your instructions. Any wounded man will be abandoned with a grenade. Leave me my tommy-gun as well, and a canteen of water. I should be able to hold them up for a while." He grinned. "That makes septicaemia irrelevant."

"Your mean to stay here, sir?"

"That was what we decided."

Green looked at Lawton, who shrugged and drank some beer.

"If I am in command, sir," Green said, "then from here on, I make the decisions, and I give the orders. Am I right?"

"You are right."

"Then, sir, with respect, it is my decision, and my command, that you will accompany us."

"Now, Sergeant-Major . . ."

"I have made my decision on strictly practical and military lines, sir. Firstly, you may be wounded, but you can still move – and fight; three of us have got to be better than two. So you may slow us down a bit, but that may turn out well for us. When the Germans find these bodies they will determine, both by logistical and forensic evidence, that they must have been killed early this morning. They must already have worked out that we are travelling only by night. Thus, working on where we were this morning, they will also be able to calculate that in one and a half nights we have covered twenty-eight miles. Now, sir, as they cannot know that you have been wounded, they will have to assume that we will move some twenty miles a night. Thus they will expect us to be farther ahead than we are, which may well turn out to our advantage. The other important point is that you are the only one of us who speaks German with any fluency, and this may be very important before we reach Italy. Do you agree with that reasoning, Private Lawton?"

"Whatever you say, Sergeant-Major," Lawton said.

"Right. Then we sit tight, eat the grub these fellows have so kindly provided for us, and move out at dusk. With respect, sir."

Harry clasped his hand.

Obviously this was not as pleasant a day as the previous one. Quite apart from the presence of the three bodies, Harry's leg now began to hurt quite seriously. Green offered him a pain-killer, but as the sergeant-major acknowledged that it would certainly make him drowsy, he had to decline – at least until they had reached shelter for the next day. On the credit side, the change of diet, not to mention the beer, was most acceptable.

"All right if I have a smoke, Sergeant-Major?" Lawton asked. "I mean to say, when they find these stiffs they're going to know we've been here, so a cigarette butt isn't going to tell them anything new."

Green looked at Harry, who gave a brief nod; a moment later Lawton was puffing happily.

At dusk they moved out, Harry using one of the shotguns as a crutch, and Green and Lawton dividing his gear between them. Thus both handicapped and overladen they made slow progress, but at least it was progress. At midnight they came on a stream, so that they were able both to slake their thirst and refill their water bottles.

"Once they have a point to start from, Sergeant-Major," Harry said, "they can use dogs."

"Good thinking, sir. You up to wading a while?"

They entered the water and went upstream for about two hundred yards, before emerging on to the south bank to resume their march. As it happened, they needn't have bothered, because before dawn it started to rain quite heavily.

"Now they'll have footprints to follow," Lawton grumbled.

"Not that easily," Green argued. "The ground is only soft in patches. If we stick to as much rock as we can we should be all right."

This involved a certain amount of zig-zagging, which slowed them even more. By now Harry was in considerable pain, and, although he refused to complain, he was very relieved when it began to lighten. Green inspected their situation through his glasses. They were now well into a large valley, although in front of them were mountains they would have to cross.

"How far to those humps, Major?" Green asked.

"Ten, fifteen miles," Harry said.

"And on the far side?"

"Italy."

"Hallelujah!" Lawton said. "You mean we're going to make it?"

"If we get to the hills, yes," Green said. "But we won't reach them today." He made another sweep with his glasses. "There's a small wood over there. Another mile, maybe. That's our best bet." He looked behind them and up at the sky; it was still drizzling and the cloud cover was both low and complete. "At least we're protected from the air. How close do you reckon they are, sir?"

"Let's be logical," Harry said. "The hunters were supposed to be back, presumably, by dusk. Dusk, their families would have started asking questions. Say eight o'clock they'd have started getting a search party together, but I don't reckon they'd have found the bodies, in the dark, much before midnight at the earliest. What happens next would depend on how clued-up they are, but let's suppose the worst, that they have heard all about what happened at Berchtesgaden on their radios, and know there are some British soldiers loose in the area. So they contact the local military. These would need both organising and taking to the start point. They'd want to get hold of some dogs. I very much doubt they'll be starting to look sooner than an hour ago. But we can expect some air activity fairly soon."

"We've time to make that copse," Green decided. "Let's go."

They hurried forward, Harry limping as fast as he could, Lawton out in front. But the private suddenly stopped, waving his arm. When they reached him he pointed. "A bleeding road."

They had crossed several mountain tracks over the preceding two days, but this was an actual road, stretching across their path.

"It needn't be important," Green decided. "Keep going."

They moved forward, climbed the slight parapet, and reached the metalled surface. Lawton was just helping Harry down the far side when they heard the roar of an engine, and almost in the same instant saw a motorcycle with a sidecar come over the slight rise about a quarter of a mile away.

"Take cover!" Green shouted, and unslung his tommy-gun. Lawton gave Harry a push to send him rolling down the second parapet into the ditch beyond. He landed on his back, and listened to the sound of shots from above them. Then, sitting up, he saw the bike itself leaving the road to plunge down the parapet. It was unoccupied.

Harry turned on his knees, unslinging his tommy-gun as he did so, and went up the embankment on his belly. Lawton seemed paralysed, uncertain what to do. Harry pushed his head over the edge. The rider had apparently been killed outright and lay on his back, arms flung wide. But his pillion passenger seemed unhurt and was on his feet, pistol drawn and aiming at Green, who was on his face.

"Stop there," Harry shouted.

The soldier turned, firing as he did so. His bullet went wide, and Harry cut him down with a burst from his tommy-gun. Then he crawled forward to reach Green.

The sergeant-major was dead; he had been hit in the chest and Harry reckoned had gone instantly.

"Shit," he remarked. "Shit, shit, shit!"

"With bags on," Lawton commented. "We're done."

"Not necessarily," Harry said. He had seen the aerial rising from behind the motorbike's pillion, and the radio was crackling, apparently undamaged. Harry slid down the parapet and found the mike.

"Heinrich," a voice was saying. "Where are you, Heinrich."

"I am here," Harry said.

"Where? I have been calling for the past five minutes. What has happened?"

"I am on the road, as ordered," Harry said. "But I have a flat tyre."

"Have you seen the Englanders?"

"I have seen nobody," Harry said. "They have not come this way."

"Well, go on into Fusch, and see if they have anything to report. Then return here."

"As soon as I have mended my tyre," Harry said.

"Make haste. You will be required further south."

"Over and out," Harry said.

"That was brilliant, sir," Lawton said. "Do you think that will put them off?"

"For a few hours, anyway."

"But if they call back and get no reply . . ."

"They still won't react immediately."

"We can't bury the bike," the private pointed out.

Harry nodded. "It won't be easy to spot, down the parapet. But we're going to have to move in daylight, for at least a few hours."

"With respect, sir, now that poor Green has bought it, do I get the command?"

"No, Lawton, you do not," Harry told him.

"Yes, sir. What do we do with these bodies?"

"Drag them down the parapet beside the bike. That way they should be spotted from the air, at least until the weather clears."

Harry took Green's haversack, with its spare magazine for the tommy-gun and his extra chocolate bars and canteen. He knelt beside the sergeant-major for a brief moment, then stood up to allow the impatiently waiting Lawton to drag the sergeant-major's body to the edge of the road and roll it down the slope beside the two Germans.

It was not the end he would have wished for his old friend and comrade, but he had now to think of the living.

They made due south, for the mountains. Progress was again slow, partly because of Harry's wounds, and partly because they had to keep taking cover as planes appeared. But, aided as they were by the constantly changing pattern of the ground – which was sometimes dark and at other times quite light – as well as by the tree cover which was plentiful, they avoided detection. Harry supposed they were being very lucky, apart from the fact that they were dropping dead with some regularity. On the other hand, that half of the original party should have reached this far was a plus. The minus was that there could be no doubt that the net was closing, or that the Germans had now worked out where they were heading.

By mid-afternoon they came in sight of a farm. They had passed quite close to several of these during the preceding night, but always in darkness. Now Lawton spent some time studying the buildings and outhouses through his binoculars. The drizzle had stopped and the skies were beginning to clear, making it imperative that they find shelter very rapidly. Additionally, they were both soaked through and were feeling chilled; Harry indeed found that he was constantly shivering, and deduced that he was running a fever.

"Cows," Lawton said. "And people. One, anyway." He looked again. "A woman. And is she a looker."

"Well, you can dream about her tonight," Harry told him. "What else do you see?"

"Another of those little copses, sir. What do you reckon?"

"That'll do. Let's get over there."

"We'll have to keep our heads down, sir, in case that popsie looks over here."

"Very good, Lawton. Let's go."

They crawled until Lawton reckoned they were out of sight of the farm. Then they got up and hurried into the wood, which was thicker than Harry had either expected or hoped. By the time they were in shelter he was exhausted, his aching leg now accompanied by a gonging headache.

"You look pretty done up, sir," Lawton remarked. "Hurting much?"

"Yes," Harry said.

"Well, sir, may I suggest that you have a bite to eat and then take a couple of these painkillers of Sergeant-Major Green's. It won't matter if they lay you out for a couple of hours; we won't be moving on until about ten, anyway. Will we?"

Harry looked at his watch; it was just four o'clock. And he desperately felt like a few hours sleep – painless, if possible.

"I'll keep an eye on things, sir," Lawton said. "I mean, if they find us here, there's not a lot we can do, is there?"

"Not a lot," Harry agreed. "All right, Lawton, I'll take a nap. But if we are approached by Jerry soldiers, I wish to be awakened immediately."

"Yes, sir."

"And remember, no smoking. In a couple of days' time you'll be able to puff all day long."

"Yes, sir."

Harry took the pills, made himself a bed in some soft

undergrowth, and was asleep in seconds. When he awoke, it was dark in the wood and the night was quiet, save for the buzz of one or two insects.

He sat up. His brain felt quite clear, and if his leg immediately started paining again, he felt fresh enough to cope with it. He looked at his watch: nine fifteen.

"Let's eat, Lawton," he said. "And then we can move out."

There was no reply.

"Lawton?" he asked, and then realised that he was alone. "Shit!" he muttered. What could the crazy fool be up to? He knew it was an unworthy thought, but he couldn't avoid the reflection of how much better it would have been if Lawton had stopped the motorcyclist's bullet and Green had survived.

He used his shotgun crutch to reach his feet, and moved towards the edge of the copse. It was not quite dark in the open air, but there was no sign of the private. He frowned, and returned to where they had made their bivouac. Lawton's tommy-gun was not there, but his haversack and night overalls were; he had certainly not decided to abandon his wounded officer and go off on his own, which was a relief.

Then where the devil was he?

Harry picked up his own tommy-gun and returned to the edge of the wood. They needed all the hours of darkness they could get if they were going to reach the mountains before tomorrow morning. He peered into the gloom, and to his consternation saw two figures approaching him, one in front of the other. As they came closer, he identified the one behind as Lawton, carrying his tommy-gun and a bag of some sort, which was slung over his shoulder. The one in front . . . Harry swallowed as he made out the flutter of hair.

Oh, the fool! The crazy fool!

"Major!" Lawton called, as he came up to the trees. "Are we in luck."

Harry kept his voice even with an effort; he could now make out that the woman's wrists were bound behind her back, and that the bonds had a tail, which was held by Lawton. "Just what sort of luck?"

"Well, sir, you won't believe this, but this baby is alone in that

68

farmhouse. Seems her husband is in the militia, and he had to report to the village to join his pals in looking for us."

"Leaving his wife alone, knowing that we may be in the neighbourhood."

"Well, sir . . ." Lawton grinned. "Seems the locals have this idea that all the English are gentlemen."

"A ridiculous concept of which you have no doubt dissuaded her."

"Well, sir, a caper like this sure does make the heart pound."

Harry gazed at the young woman; he estimated she was in her middle twenties, tall and well built, with wavy auburn hair and good, strong features that remained composed no matter what might have recently happened to her. The rest of her was concealed beneath a somewhat shapeless dress which ended in mud-stained boots.

"What is your name?" he asked in German.

Her head jerked in surprise. "Jutta."

"And has this man raped you, Jutta?"

She hesitated before replying. "He assaulted me. It was not rape."

Lawton had been listening to the exchange. If he had only a little German, he could have no doubt as to what Harry was asking.

"She didn't put up no fight, sir," he said. "All I did was search her to make sure she wasn't carrying a weapon."

"I'm sure. You do realise you have done us?"

"I don't accept that, sir. Her husband won't be back until tomorrow morning. By then we should be in those mountains, with Italy just a march away."

"And you don't suppose her husband may telephone tonight to see how his wife is, and get alarmed when there is no reply?"

"There's no telephone, sir. I made sure of that. The man was called this morning by someone on a motorbike." Lawton grinned. "Could have been the same blokes we ran into."

"Only if they were able to be in two places at the same time."

"And there's all this food, sir," Lawton went on, eagerly. "Went through their larder, I did."

"Brilliant," Harry said, sarcastically. "I suppose things could be worse. But from here on, Lawton, you are forbidden to leave the squad – which means me – except on a direct order."

"Yes, sir."

"So tell me, what are your plans for the woman? Cut her throat and leave her here?"

Jutta was looking anxiously from face to face. Harry didn't know whether or not she understood English, but she could certainly deduce that her fate was being decided.

"Well, sir, we could do that, of course," Lawton agreed. "But why shouldn't we take her with us, at least for tonight? She can't do us any harm, and she'll be a bit of company, eh? She can carry some of the gear, take a load off that leg of yours."

Harry didn't doubt he had an ulterior motive, but as long as he was in command it wouldn't happen. And he didn't really want to add this innocent young woman to the list of those he had killed. Still, even if they left her bound and gagged, she might well work herself loose and raise the alarm before they could reach the mountains.

"All right," he said. "Untie her."

"You reckon that's all right, sir?"

"Lawton, how can she possibly carry anything with her hands tied behind her back?"

"Good thinking, sir. I never thought of that."

"Leave the rope tied round her left wrist, and give me the tail," Harry instructed. "That way I can bring her up short if she tries anything."

"Yes, sir."

Lawton untied Jutta's wrists.

"Are you going to kill me?" she asked.

"I don't want to," Harry said. "And I won't, unless I have to. But I can't leave you here. So you will have to come with us."

"Where?"

"You'll find out when we get there. Now listen to me very carefully. You will carry two of these haversacks. You can sling them on your shoulders. You will remain connected to me by this rope, and I will pull you down if you try to escape – in which case I will kill you. But if you behave yourself, we will set you free

70

when we reach our destination, and you can return here. Do you understand me?"

"If you take me with you, I can never return."

He raised his eyebrows. "It will not be very far."

"You do not understand. The Nazis will think I helped you to escape, and they will put me in a camp – if they do not shoot me."

"Shit!" he muttered. He hadn't thought of that. "What about your family?"

"I have no family."

"No children?"

"I have no children."

"But you have a husband."

She blew a raspberry.

"Hm," he commented. "Well, Jutta, the choice is yours. You can opt for being strangled, here and now. Or you can come with us and take your chances."

"If I come with you, and we reach your destination, will I not be a prisoner of war?"

"I don't think I can guarantee that. I'll do what I can, but you may wind up entirely on your own."

"It is better than being dead," she remarked.

It was now entirely dark. They left the little wood and made their way south. The ground was rising and the going was hard, especially as they had to ford several fast-rushing streams cascading down from the heights.

"I think you are going to Italy," Jutta remarked.

"Don't think," Harry recommended.

By midnight he was exhausted, and they had to stop to allow him to rest.

"You are not well?" Jutta asked, sitting beside him. Her own strength was considerable, and she did not appear the least tired.

"I am wounded," Harry said.

"Where?"

"In the leg and back."

"They have been attended to?"

"Yes."

"When?"

"What's it to you?"

"I was a nurse before I got married. I may be able to help you."

"It was dressed . . ." He had to think for a moment. "Yesterday morning." He looked at his watch: ten to twelve. "Actually, this morning."

"Then the dressing will need changing."

"Why should you want to do that?"

She smiled, most attractively. "We are on the same side, now, eh?"

"It's a point of view. But you can't do anything at this moment; it's time we were moving. You can look at it when it's daylight."

She shrugged.

"What's she on about, sir?" Lawton asked.

"She wants to dress my wounds."

"Some people have all the luck," he commented.

Slowly Harry pushed himself to his feet. "Let's move."

The land grew ever steeper.

"You reckon our friend knows anything about abseiling, sir?" Lawton asked. "This could well come to that."

Harry had a better idea. "Do you know these mountains?" he asked Jutta the next time they stopped. "Living so close."

"I have been here. When we were first married, my husband and I used to go camping. This was before the *Anschluss*."

"You weren't in favour of the *Anschluss*?"

She gave a quick smile. "I was not asked."

"But your husband was."

"My husband is a Nazi."

"And you are not."

"It is not good to ask questions like that, in the new Germany. It is even less good to answer them."

"Point taken. We need to find somewhere to hide, by dawn."

She nodded. "I will find somewhere."

"Good girl. What will your husband do when he returns and finds you gone?"

"I do not think he will return before at least this coming night. Even if he is released from his duties, he will use the opportunity to remain in town and drink at the bar." She made a face. "He would rather do this than come home to me."

"The man clearly needs his head examined," Harry commented, and switched to English. "Looks like you did the right thing after all, Lawton. This young woman is very much on our side."

"Glad to be of service, sir."

"What are you saying?" Jutta asked.

"I am telling him that you are going to help us."

"I do not trust him."

"That's a case of the pot calling the kettle black."

"What is this pot and kettle?"

"I'll explain it some time." He got painfully to his feet. "Where is this hiding place?"

"Four, five miles."

"Then let's move."

"If I am to help you, will you not untie my wrist?"

Harry considered, then did so. "Just remember, if you attempt to run off, I shall have to shoot you."

"I can see this is the start of a beautiful friendship," she remarked.

Harry found her fascinating. Actually, he found most women fascinating, but this one, in her good humour and startlingly imperturbable acceptance of this complete – and apparently irrevocable – upheaval in her life, was amazing.

Unless – and this was most likely – she had already been considering abandoning a husband she clearly did not love and a regime she opposed, but had not quite made up her mind to risk it – until they had stumbled into her life and made her decision for her.

But soon his thoughts regarding her were overtaken by pain and exhaustion as they continued to climb higher. Jutta certainly knew the best way up the mountain, and they never had to use their ropes; but the mere fact of having to climb was a strain on his wounded leg, the pain from which seemed to be spreading right through his body. But at last she said, "There!"

She was pointing at a darker darkness in the mountainside, and they discovered it was quite a deep cave.

"No bears?" Lawton asked.

"We'd smell them," Harry said. "What we do need is water."

"There is a stream a little higher up," Jutta said. "Send your man to fill the canteens, while I look at your wound."

Harry gave the instructions, and Lawton went off with the canteens. Harry was grateful to be able to lie down while Jutta removed his equipment, pants, underwear and bandages. It was quite light outside by now, although it remained gloomy in the cave. She peered at the wounds.

"This is not good," Jutta remarked. "Did all the pellets come out?"

"No. There's one still in there."

"It should come out."

"I believe it's a cutting job. Don't tell me you were also trained as a surgeon?"

"No."

"Then it'll have to stay put."

"You have antiseptic?"

"In the haversacks."

She found one of the first-aid packs, sorted through the various contents. Presumably she couldn't read English, but she seemed to know what each one was.

"Lie on your face," she said. "This will sting."

"Get to it," he told her.

It did indeed sting, and in the middle of it Lawton returned.

"Having fun, are we?" he remarked.

"Anything out there?"

"An aircraft, but circling high. How are you, sir?"

"How am I?" Harry asked Jutta.

"You will live," she said. "If you have a good day's rest. And if that pellet comes out sometime soon. There are sedatives here. I think you should take some and rest as much as possible. You are running a fever."

"How far from here to the border?"

"Perhaps five miles. But it is rough country. You must rest."

"I'm apparently to be sedated for a while, Lawton," Harry said. "Take charge until I wake up."

"Yes, sir," Lawton agreed.

Jutta administered the pills, and Harry leaned back with a sigh. "What's the real problem?" he asked.

"Gangrene," she said. "We are not living in the most hygienic of circumstances. But we will cope, providing we get you to some proper care before our own supplies run out. You say there are people waiting for you across the border?"

"It's not quite as simple as that. We have to locate them first."

She made a moue. "You rest. We must get the fever down."

Harry slept heavily, for all the hard ground on which he lay, and was only awakened by a sharp noise. For a moment he did not know where he was, but the returning pain of his wounds swiftly reminded him. Then he supposed they had been discovered by the Germans. He sat up, expecting to die on the instant, and saw Lawton and Jutta wrestling on the floor. The soldier had taken off his battledress and his drawers, and the woman's dress had been thrown up above her waist; her own drawers were draped round one ankle – Harry had an unforgettable vision of white legs intertwined. Jutta gasped and tried to strike at Lawton's face with her nails as Lawton held her wrists and pressed his body against hers.

"Lawton!" Harry snapped. "Stop that."

Lawton's head raised, and Jutta's turned, at the sound of his voice. They could see him quite clearly as it was now bright daylight outside; he reckoned it was not yet noon – he could only have been asleep for a few hours.

"Get off that woman," Harry said.

"Give over, sir," Lawton protested. "She's a bleeding Kraut. A fucking Nazi. They killed Green and the lieutenant."

"She didn't," Harry reminded him.

"They're all the same to me," Lawton said. "No you don't," he snapped as Jutta made another violent effort to get up. He released one of her wrists to slap her across the face, and she gave a little gasp as blood dribbled down her chin.

"Get off that woman, Lawton," Harry said. "That is an order."

"Don't push your luck," Lawton said. "I'm in charge here. You're a bleeding cripple, Major. You ain't worth a damn. If I hump you over the rest of these mountains it'll be an act of charity."

"And I will have you shot for mutiny."

"In that case, I won't bother, eh? It'll be great. The only survivor. I'll probably get the VC, just like you. And no one will ever know."

Harry realised the man had definitely cracked, from a combination of both the stress of the past few days and now his lust for the woman. He would have to be kept under restraint until they reached Italy and he could be placed under arrest – and that would require force. He looked left and right for his equipment, with its revolver holster, but Lawton realised his intention and was too quick for him; he quickly let go of Jutta's other wrist to rear back on his knees, still straddling the woman, and reached for his own weapon, which was close at hand.

"Just simmer down, Major."

Harry subsided; his holster was another two feet away.

"Although I don't know why I'm bothering," Lawton said. "You may as well die now as later."

He levelled the revolver and Harry drew a deep breath, but in that moment Jutta came to life and gave a gigantic heave of her thighs. Lawton uttered a strangled exclamation and half fell off her, his shot going wild and smacking into the wall of the cavern.

Harry rolled with desperate urgency, reached his holster, drew the weapon and fired in virtually the same movement – as he had been trained to do. He was a superb shot, and the bullet struck Lawton between the eyes before the latter could even level his gun again. He fell backwards without a sound, blood and brains flying. Jutta pulled herself out from beneath him, but even so blood splashed on to her bare legs.

For several seconds the sound of the firing reverberated around the cavern, drowning even the noise of their panting breaths. Then Harry said, "Check outside."

Jutta pulled down her skirt and crawled to the cave mouth, remaining there for several seconds while she looked left and right, up and down. "There is no one to have heard," she said. She came back into the cave, knelt beside him. "Are you hurt?"

"Not more than before. And you?"

76

"Just bruised."

"There is blood on your face."

"And in my mouth." She wiped her lip with the back of her hand. "I am sorry."

"Believe me, so am I. Did he . . . ?"

She shook her head. "He would have done, had you not woken up. He was very strong."

"I must ask you to forgive him. We have been under a lot of stress."

"As I must ask you to forgive me. I caused his death."

"I don't follow that."

"If I had not been here . . ."

"Or at the farm? You mean, if you had not been born. That covers too much territory."

She sighed. "What are we going to do?"

"Start walking again tonight."

"And him?"

"He can stay where he is. Someone will find him someday, or we can send back for his body after the War. I'll take his papers."

"You mean you will report this?"

"Yes," Harry said. "This was not a murder. It was a military execution."

Jutta shuddered. "Cannot we just never speak of it?"

"No," Harry said. "It is my duty to speak of it."

"And I?"

He grinned. "It may be a means of getting you out of Italy and into England. You are an eyewitness of what happened."

"You mean I will have to appear in court?"

"A military court, yes."

"And after? They will send me back here?"

"Hopefully not. Certainly not until after the end of the War and the end of Nazism."

"I can never return to Austria."

"So you keep saying. But with the Nazis gone . . ."

"There will still be my husband."

"Ah. Well, I will see what I can do."

"Ah," she said in turn. "Now you must rest. There is still a lot of walking to do."

Part Two
The Lady

I heard the old, old men say
All that's beautiful drifts away
Like the waters.

William Butler Yeats

The Invalid

"There's a visitor to see you, Major Curtis." Matron herself insisted on being in charge of her resident hero; besides, the sick man had been kept incommunicado since his arrival and even had a sentry on the door of his private ward. "Colonel Bannon."

"Ah," Harry said. He had been anticipating this, not altogether happily. But at least if the fever that had taken hold of him in Italy had left him weak as a kitten, being at home again had brought his strength flooding back. His only wish was to get out of hospital – so far as he knew even his parents did not know if he was alive or dead . . . and after so long they had to fear the worst.

Matron held the door for the brigadier, and Bannon nodded at her somewhat nervously. She simpered, and closed the door behind her.

Bannon stood beside the bed; he was a big man with a long nose. "You're a sight for sore eyes."

"I've felt better," Harry said. "How's it going? Everything I hear is a bit garbled."

Bannon glanced out of the window; it was February, and the hospital grounds were covered in snow. "We've had our downs, but there have been more ups. You heard about that business in the Ardennes?"

"What they're calling the Battle of the Bulge. Bit of a do, was it?"

"Not really. It was a last throw of the dice, but it had everyone in a flap for a while. Since then, though, it's been total collapse. The Russians are poised to take Berlin, and our people are well into Germany."

"So when do I get out of here? Or do I miss the end of the show?"

"I'm afraid you probably do, as it should all be over in a month at the outside. That's too soon for you."

"I'm as fit as a fiddle."

"Not according to your present medical report. The quacks seem to think you contracted malaria in Italy."

"Absolute rubbish."

"You must admit you were pretty ill. That's why it took us so long to extract you. And the sickness itself, bouts of delirium, high temperature . . . Those are indicative of malaria."

"Peter, I was wounded."

"Flesh wounds. Nothing serious. And they had been well looked after. Tell me about this woman."

"I have nothing to tell you."

"So you said in your report. I assumed you were being discreet."

"Well, I wasn't. I can tell you that she was an Austrian hausfrau who wanted to be rid of her husband. She was virtually kidnapped by Lawton, and agreed to lead us over the mountains into Italy. She was a trained nurse, and she looked after me – without her I could well have died. By the time we contacted the partisans I was in a state of collapse and running a high temperature; there was still one of those shotgun pellets in my back. I think I passed out, more or less, for several days. When I came to, she was gone."

"Surely the partisans knew what had happened to her?"

"Not really. She had gone east with some group. Unfortunately, I wasn't well enough to follow it up at the time." He sighed. "Shame. She was a nice girl. And as I said, I suspect she saved my life."

"Yes," Bannon said drily. "However, she was present when Lawton bought it."

"You could say she was the reason he bought it, although he had been showing signs of insubordination well before that."

"Yes. Pity. That she disappeared in possession of such information, I mean."

"What difference can it make? What happened is in my report."

"Yes. I'm afraid we have decided to suppress that report.

That's why you have been kept incommunicado until we were quite sure you were well enough to understand your orders without any fear of another lapse into delirium."

"You've lost me," Harry said. "I reported exactly what happened, throughout the mission. I also made certain recommendations."

"Ah, yes. Victoria Crosses for both Manning and Green. I'm sure they deserved them. Unfortunately, their relatives are not going to get them. As far as history is concerned, your mission never happened."

"Say again?"

"Well, you see, Harry, it was one almighty cock-up. This was not your fault. You carried out your assignment with your usual panache and expertise. The fault lay with our intelligence, which reported Hitler's departure from Berchtesgaden just too late to abort the mission. Now, obviously, assassinating enemy heads of state is not something that can be condoned by everyone. Had your mission succeeded – while of course we would have hailed Hitler's death as a positive move towards victory – we would yet have left the exact details a mystery."

"What you mean is, you didn't really expect any of us to come back."

"Well . . . it seemed unlikely."

"I'm sorry to have disappointed you," Harry said.

"My dear fellow, we are delighted to have you back. It's just a tragedy that your companions didn't make it. However, as the mission was in fact a failure, to allow any publicity regarding it to emerge would merely make us look very bad, on both counts – having the idea in the first place, and failing to succeed in the second."

"Cheer me up," Harry said. "But there's one small factor you've overlooked. The Germans know all about what we attempted."

"Yes, but they are keeping very quiet about it as well. They're in no hurry to admit that such a raid could have been carried out so deep into their territory, and they know as well as we do that had Hitler been in residence, he would have been killed."

"My dear Peter, there are some things you just cannot hide. We all but destroyed the man's house."

"It's been rebuilt, very quickly – and despite the crying need for the labour and materials to be used elsewhere. There is even a rumour that Hitler intends to flee Berlin and return there, with all the SS men he can summon, to fight to the last bullet. So we may have to destroy it all over again. However, at the present time, both governments have come to the same conclusion – to pretend for as long as possible that it did not happen."

"So three good men lost their lives for nothing. Not even a recognition of their gallantry," Harry said bitterly.

"According to your report, there were only two good men."

"They all performed magnificently on the mission. It was bad luck that Lawton cracked up afterwards."

"Maybe," Bannon agreed. "But the fact is that while you exercised your rightful authority in executing him for mutiny and rape, or at least attempted rape – both crimes which carry the death penalty in wartime – were that to come out it would both put the kybosh on our attempt to keep the whole thing secret and cause all manner of questions to be asked. There would have to be at least an inquiry – at which you would be the only witness – or perhaps more than that if it was felt that you had exceeded your authority."

"You seem to be forgetting that I actually shot Lawton in self-defence."

"Unfortunately, in the absence of your Austrian friend, we have only your word for that. I'm not disbelieving you, Harry. I've known you too long, and I have no doubt at all that everything you stated in your report was the exact truth as you recall it. Sadly, not everyone is as privileged as me. So there you are. This entire incident will be regarded as never having happened."

"And the others who were party to it? Brigadier Martin, Air Vice-Marshal Hartman, Captain Forester . . . not to mention my two reserves?"

"They have all been sworn to secrecy. Should any one of them break their oath, not only will their claims be totally dismissed by the War Office, but they could well find themselves in prison."

"And what happens to me?"

Bannon stood up. "Get well, and report for duty as soon as you are. I will now allow it to be released that you were wounded and taken seriously ill while carrying out an undercover operation, but are on the road to recovery. This news will be sent to your parents, and they will be allowed to visit you."

"Thank you."

"You have also been promoted to lieutenant colonel. It'll be gazetted in a day or two."

"Again, thank you."

"Well, the fact is that you should get another gong. Even a bar to your VC, certainly to your DSO. But unfortunately . . ."

"The whole thing is being hushed up."

"There is also the business that there is no corroborating evidence as to actually what was done and by whom. I'm sure you understand how the Army works."

"I've been in it long enough."

"Yes. Well . . . Oh, by the way, Captain Forester sends you her best wishes. In view of your long association, I invited her to come down with me today, but she declined. I presume you know she is getting back together with her husband?"

"She did mention that she'd seen him," Harry said.

"Yes. Well . . . I must be getting along." Bannon went to the door, and there checked. "Strictly off the record, Harry, did you . . . ah . . ."

"No I did not."

"Not your type? Or the fact that she was a Kraut?"

"Jutta was not a Kraut. She was an Austrian and an anti-Nazi. She was also an extremely good-looking woman. Just to put your mind at rest, I did not kill Lawton either out of jealousy or to have her for myself."

"Good lord! The thought never crossed my mind."

Commanding officers, Harry reflected, never did make good liars.

"However," he added. "I am not saying I wouldn't have had sex with her if I hadn't been so damned ill – as it was, though, the thought never really crossed my mind."

"Dashed awkward situation," Bannon agreed. "Especially as

she was dressing your wounds all the time. She must have seen quite a lot of you."

"She did."

"Well . . . ships that pass in the night and all that. One last thing. Throughout your report you refer to her as Jutta."

"That was her name."

"But she must have had a surname."

"Her name was Jutta Hulin," Harry said.

He wished he could be sure how much he remembered of her was fact and how much fever-induced imagination. In the gloom of the cave she had been no more than a shadow – clearly strong and well-endowed in every possible direction, handsome of feature and with that delicious sense of humour. That evening, as he remembered, she had left the cave to bathe in the stream and had returned naked, revealing a body as compelling as the rest of her – a glowing portrait of large breasts and slender thighs, long legs and powerful muscles. But any possible relationship had been out of the question with Lawton's body lying only a few feet away, and he had in any event been drowsy with the sedatives she fed him.

The next day they had arrived in Italy. But by then his awareness of what was happening had been completely shrouded in the fever that was taking hold of his body. That could not possibly have been malaria; there were no anopheles mosquitoes in the Austrian Alps. The temperature had been a result of his wounds – which were more serious than he had supposed – and the exhaustion. His main memory of that last night's march had been an unending and recurring thirst – and the woman feeding him water, a constant shadowy saviour.

Once across the border they had had to hole up for three days while he cautiously used his radio. Then surely would have been the time for them to get together – but by then he had become even weaker. And then the partisans had come, eager hands to take care of him. And Jutta had simply disappeared. Which presumably meant that he had not interested her in the least as a human being, much less as a man. He had provided a means and a reason for fleeing her home, and as his aide she had gained an entrée into the Italian resistance – to find some new protector and escape further to the south and into the arms of the advancing British and American Armies.

He supposed that, should he ever find the time, he might be able to track her down; but should he sacrifice the time? Had she wanted his company, she would have stayed – at least long enough to make sure he recovered.

The experience, coming immediately after his brush-off from Belinda, had quite put him off women. Except, when he got out of here . . . It was over a year since he had last seen Deirdre, and then *he* had faded from *her* life without so much as a goodbye. Even if she was not happily married by now, she was another woman who would certainly not wish to see him again.

For the first time in his career, he was obsessed with the sense of total failure – at least when in command. He had been too junior to feel the slightest responsibility for the disasters that had led to Dunkirk. His first command, the raid on Ardres, had been a triumph; again he had been too junior to have been able to do anything about the St Nazaire catastrophe. Since then, Algiers, Spetsos, even the raid in Lisieux just before D-Day had been a success, however costly. Now he had failed utterly. Perhaps the fault had been with the others, but he had still once again lost his entire squad; the disaster was compounded by his actually having to shoot one of them.

"If this extreme depression continues," said Dr Chartwell, "I'm going to have to send you to the psychiatric ward. You're going to have to have a psychiatric session in any event before you leave here, and if the boffins see in you what I do, they could well put you away for a while."

"Like hell," Harry growled. "When *do* I get out of here?"

"Another couple of weeks, if you perk up a bit."

"Two *weeks*?"

"Well, you've been here three already."

"And before then more than four months in Italy. I'm getting rather fed up with military hospitals. I'd bet I've spent more time in dumps like this than any other soldier in the British Army."

"On and off, you're probably right."

"In another two weeks the War will be over."

"Let us fervently hope so. Don't you think you've seen enough of this war to last you a while . . . like a lifetime? I'll be in again tomorrow. Do try to cheer up, old man. How old are you?"

As if he didn't know that already. "Twenty-three."

"Twenty-three years old. And a colonel. And you've *survived*. What more do you want from life?"

"Tell me something. Do I really have malaria?"

"Yes, you do."

"And we're waiting for it to clear up, is that it?"

Chartwell pulled up the chair and sat beside the bed. "Malaria never clears up."

"Say again?"

"It is the biggest killer in the world. Nowadays we can contain it with drugs. But once you have it, you have it."

"Are you trying to tell me I am never going to be fit again?"

"Depends what you mean by fit. For the rest of your life, you are going to suffer from recurrent attacks of ague and high temperatures. These will not last more than two or three days at a time, and they will decrease as time goes by. They will never, under normal circumstances, be life-threatening. Just a bloody nuisance, because, you see, you will never know when an attack will come on. You will just suddenly feel like death and your temperature will shoot up. As I said, there is no cure that I or any other doctor can promise. We can prescribe drugs like Atabrine, which will alleviate the situation, but really, the best way of handling it is to go to bed and sweat it out."

"You are telling me my Army career is over."

"Of course not. When you're not having an attack, you'll feel as fit as a horse – and be as fit as one too. I have patients suffering from malaria who play rugby, box, play tennis, cricket, soccer, take part in athletics . . ."

"But they don't climb Mount Everest."

"Is that what you're thinking of doing?"

"Come off it, Doc. You know what I mean. There is no way you could recommend anyone who might be stricken down for three days without warning to undertake, much less command, a mission behind enemy lines."

"No, I could not. But if the War is really going to be over in two weeks that will cease to be a problem."

"Do you seriously suppose there will be no more wars?"

"Isn't that what they're saying?"

"That was what they said after the last one."

"Well, look at it this way. You are a lieutenant colonel. When you leave here you'll have your own battalion. Battalion commanders are not as a rule required to lead seek-and-destroy missions behind enemy lines."

"But you will have to put in my record that I have malaria."

"I will put in your record that you have suffered an attack of malaria. That is the best I can do, Harry."

"But everyone will know it's in my blood for good."

"Anyone who know anything about medicine, yes."

"And you expect me to cheer up," Harry said bitterly.

John and Alison Curtis came down the next day. John Curtis was a recently retired bank manager, who had just managed to get into uniform in the Great War but had never actually reached France. He had been too old to serve in the Second, save as a member of the Home Guard; even then, living in Worcestershire as he did, he had been nowhere near any possible front line. He viewed current events vicariously through the eyes of his two sons. Paul, the eldest, was in the Navy. Harry had been the more successful in terms of medals and rank – but he had also been the most often in hospital. Yet the mere fact that he was alive meant it had been a good war for the Curtis family.

"You look terrible," Alison said, having kissed him.

"You're seeing me at my best, compared with a few weeks ago."

"They tell us you have malaria."

"I believe I do."

"You caught malaria – in France?" Alison was well read.

"As a matter of fact, no. I had to go to Italy on a mission."

"I thought that blighter Mussolini had drained the Pontine Marshes," his father said.

"I believe he did. But there seems to have been some other bits he overlooked."

89

"At least it's better than being wounded," his mother said.

"Oh, I managed to pick up some of that as well. Some lunatic fired a shotgun at me."

"And hit you where?" John was anxious.

"In the back."

"You were shot in the back?"

"Can happen."

"Harry . . ." his mother said severely. She was well aware of her son's amorous proclivities.

"I promise it wasn't an irate husband," Harry said.

"Well, anyway, it's good to have you home," John said. "You are coming home?"

"I imagine so, briefly, when they let me out of here."

"They say the War is going to be over soon," Alison said. "When are you going to set the day?"

"Ah . . . I'm sorry to say Belinda and I have broken it off."

"Oh, Harry!" Alison was less perturbed than she pretended; she had never really cared for Belinda.

"You never let us know," John complained.

"Well, it actually happened just as I was leaving for Italy, and things were rather rushed. Then I got ill . . ."

"What caused the break?" Alison asked.

"She decided to go back to her husband."

Alison stared at him with her mouth open.

"Women are like that," he explained. "Some women," he added hastily.

"I will never understand modern morals," John remarked.

"Then what are we going to do with you?" Alison asked. "You know Yvonne got married?"

"Never." Now that was a relief. Yvonne Clearsted was a childhood sweetheart who had always been his parents' choice as a daughter-in-law. They had actually been engaged, briefly, and had shared a bed, once. But they had always been totally incompatible – even if their parents had been jointly unable to see it. "Looks like I'm on the shelf."

Harry loved his parents deeply, but he could never escape the feeling when in their company, and even more when at the family home in Frenthorpe, that he had inadvertently strayed into another world. It was a world he had only ever known as a child and a teenager, and it had been deliberately maintained as it had been in 1938 – no doubt in the certain expectation that he would one day wish to return to it, take a job as a bank clerk like his father, and settle down to being a proper human being. Thus his room was kept exactly as it had been on his last day at school, before setting off for Sandhurst. And as always, the huge old Newfoundland, Jupiter, was there to wag his tail and bark joyously at the homecoming of one of the young masters.

Situated where it was – a reasonable distance from Worcester itself, and nowhere near any possible industrial target – Frenthorpe had not ever been bombed; the nearest the War had come to it, apart from the newspapers and wireless, had been the irritating business of ration books and coupons. But even that now promised to end soon.

Naturally, there was a round of parties to honour Harry's homecoming: as a VC he was the village's most celebrated resident. And as usual, his mother managed to unearth a few pretty girls, who gaped at the hero and hung on his every word. He did not suppose he was more than a year or so older than any of them, but he felt like their father.

He also had the unhappy business of writing to the families of the three dead men: Manning's mother, Green's father, and even Lawton's ex-wife – in the last case telling a white lie as he related how gallantly her late husband had died facing the enemy. In all previous instances like this he had made a point of visiting the families personally, but now that six months had passed it seemed pointless to renew their grief except by a brief letter of condolence.

His sole desire was to get back into uniform as quickly as possible, but the local doctor – who had been given a file by Chartwell, and who he had to see every week – was reluctant to give him a clean bill of health until he was absolutely sure.

Still, he reckoned even the medical men could not stop him getting on with his life. Despite his reflections when he had been in the depths of depression, he telephoned Inquiries to obtain Deirdre's phone number, but they didn't have it.

"I know she had a telephone," he pointed out.

"Did she live alone, or share?" the woman at Inquiries asked.

"She shared with another girl."

"Then the telephone must be in the other name. What was it?"

"Damnation. I can't remember."

"But you have the address." She seemed determined to be helpful.

"Yes, I do."

"Give it to me, and we may be able to sort something out."

"Half a mo." He hunted through his wallet – which had remained safely with Battalion throughout his absence from the country – found the piece of paper, and read the Hammersmith address over the phone.

"If you'll just wait a moment," the woman said.

Harry waited, listening to various voices in the background and sundry clicks and thumps. Then a different voice came on the line.

"Are you the gentleman who is inquiring about a telephone number for Miss Deirdre Hale?"

"Yes, I am. What's up?"

"May I ask your name?"

"By all means. Lieutenant Colonel Harry Curtis, First Commandos."

"I do apologise, Colonel Curtis, but I must ask – are you related to Miss Hale?"

"Sadly, no. Or, not yet."

"I see. I am most terribly sorry."

"About what?" Lead balloons were gathering in his stomach. "What's happened?"

"We do not actually have a phone listed in Miss Hale's name, Colonel Curtis. But I have to tell you that the address you gave us – the entire block of flats – was destroyed by a flying bomb towards the end of last year."

Harry stared at the phone in disbelief. Not again! The first woman he had ever imagined himself to be in love with had been killed by a bomb – but that had been back in the blitz of 1940.

"Colonel Curtis?"

"Were there no survivors?"

"Well, I'm afraid that isn't our province. But I am sure you can find out."

"Yes," Harry said. "I suppose I can. Is it possible for you to tell me whether it was destroyed in the day or at night?"

"I can find out for you. Would you care to call back?"

"Ah . . ." Do I want to call back? he wondered. The fact that during the day she would have been at work was not really relevant; she could easily have been out at night as well. Besides, did he really wish to know for certain that she was dead? If she was alive but had been forced to move away because of the destruction of the block of flats, she was still lost to him . . . until and unless she obtained a telephone number in her own name – and that was not likely to happen before the end of the War. And if he did not *know*, then he could suppose she was still alive, that one day they might run into each other again. He could live in a dream.

Harry Curtis, VC, DSO, MC, the man who had always survived because he could look at the facts of life or death squarely in the face and act with total ruthlessness, whether it involved man or woman.

There was a joke.

The Proposal

I t was the beginning of April when Dr Philpott at last wrote
out a report to inform Harry's superiors that he was fit to
resume duty.

"I should point out," he remarked, gazing over his pince-nez
and across his desk, "that I am only doing this because I have
known you all my life, and I know how anxious you are to get
back into uniform."

"Are you trying to tell me that I am *not* combat fit?" Harry
asked, waiting to hear the dreaded word malaria.

"No, no," Philpott said. "Physically you are just about a
hundred per cent. Even that slight deafness you accumulated a
couple of years ago seems to have cleared up. Although I'm not
saying that it won't come back again, given time. No, it's this
continued depression that is bothering me."

"I'm not in the least depressed, Doctor, except by being stuck
up here when there are so many important things going on. Sign
that paper, and I'll be as happy as a schoolboy."

Philpott sighed, and signed the paper.

"You won't be going back to France?" Alison Curtis asked
anxiously. "I mean, you've been wounded three times. They can't
send you back, can they?"

"They can't *send* me back," Harry agreed. "But they can't
refuse me if I volunteer."

"Harry!"

Harry kissed her. "Even if I volunteered, there's not a lot
happening in France at the moment. It's all in Germany. I've
never been to Germany. I might never have the opportunity
again."

"Harry . . ."

"I don't think they are going to have the time to send me anywhere before the shooting stops," he told her. "I'll be in touch."

London was far more badly damaged than he had expected. Of course he remembered the scars of the Blitz and 1941, still exposed in their craters and shattered buildings. It was the recent damage – that caused by the Buzz Bombs and the V-2 rockets – that was surprising and depressing.

But the Commando headquarters remained untouched and familiar, save for the young woman behind the desk in the upstairs office.

"You're new," he remarked.

"Yes, sir," she replied, taking in both his rank badges and his ribbons.

"What happened to Captain Forester?"

"Captain Forester has been discharged, sir."

"Honourable or dishonourable?"

"She is married, sir."

"I think you mean, remarried."

"Yes, sir. Did you know Captain Forester well?"

"We had a nodding acquaintance. Is the brigadier in?"

"Not at this time, sir. He is in a conference."

"When do you expect him?"

"Not until this afternoon, sir. He spoke of going out to lunch after the conference finished."

"There's a nuisance. I'll have to come back. Will you tell him that Harry Curtis called?"

"Harry . . ." she gulped. "Colonel Curtis? *The* Colonel Curtis?" Once again she looked at his medals. "You are. Sir."

"It does happen to be my name," Harry agreed. "You mean you've heard it?"

"Oh, yes, sir. Everyone has heard of Colonel Curtis."

"I'm not sure I like the sound of that."

But on reflection he rather thought he did. This young woman was at the moment like a piece of butter. And having given her a second look, he decided that she was well worth it. Statuesque was the word that came to mind, for even seated behind a desk and wearing a khaki tunic it was obvious that she was tall and had a very full bust. Her hair was golden, presently caught up in a tight bun but suggesting length and all manner of glories when it was released. She looked terribly well-groomed, and there was not a ring on her finger – and if her features were a trifle bold they were certainly compelling.

He had no desire to become involved with any woman at that moment, certainly not emotionally and he wasn't even sure about physically – although he had not had sex since that disastrous evening in Caen with Belinda, nearly a year ago. But he did not feel like having a lonely lunch; he was basically too lonely as it was.

"However," he said. "As you seem to know me, and I have now met you, would you care to have lunch with me."

"With you, sir? But . . . can we? I'm a lieutenant and you . . ."

"I am a colonel – who has got where he is by never doing what he was expected to do, and always doing what he was told he could not do. However, I feel I should warn you that I am an absolute cad where women are concerned."

"I don't believe that for a moment, sir," she said, standing up and revealing that she was indeed statuesque – he reckoned that she was about five eleven. "Captain Forester spoke very highly of you, both as a man and a soldier."

"And she should know. Did she also tell you that when it comes to women my intentions are usually strictly dishonourable?"

"No, sir, she did not mention that."

"It's true."

"You used the word usually, sir. May I accept your invitation?"

She knew a little restaurant quite close to the office, where she was apparently a regular customer; they were given a corner table and fussed over.

"Do you know, I don't even know your name," Harry confessed.

"Cynthia, sir."

"I assume you have another one?"

"Bromwich, sir."

She looked rather anxious, as if there was a reason for him recognising it. He didn't.

"Well . . ." He raised his wine glass. "Here's to Cynthia Bromwich."

She raised hers in turn. "And here's to Lieutenant Colonel Curtis."

"What a mouthful. I think, when we're so completely off duty as we are now, you should call me Harry and I will call you Cynthia. Right?"

"If that is what you wish, sir."

"Now," Harry said. "I gather that you have replaced Captain Forester as Colonel Bannon's secretary."

She nodded.

"How long have you been in the job?"

"Three months."

So Belinda had taken off just before Christmas, while he had still been in Italy waiting to be extracted . . . and only known to be still alive to a few privileged people. Belinda would have been one of those.

"For those three months," he remarked, "I have been totally out of action. Yet you seem to know all about me."

She flushed. "I've read your file."

"Just mine?"

"Well, no. But yours was the most interesting."

"I see. How long have you been in the Commandos?"

"Three months. I had to undergo some preliminary training."

"So they picked you out of the ATS to replace Forester. How long have you been in the Army?"

"Three years."

"You go in threes. May I ask how old you are?"

"Twenty-four."

"Snap."

"I knew that."

"So . . . you joined up in 1942, when you were twenty-one. What did you do before that?"

She shrugged. "Not a lot. Rode horses and things."

"You mean you were a stable girl?"

"You could put it like that."

"And what persuaded you, after three years at war, that it was time to do your bit?"

"I had to wait until I was twenty-one, you see," she explained. "I wanted to join up earlier, but Daddy wouldn't let me."

Harry raised his eyebrows. "I didn't know girls nowadays paid that much attention to what Daddy says. Or did he own the stables?"

"As a matter of fact, he did. Still does."

"And you're hoping to inherit them, one day."

"Well, yes."

"Point taken. And has Daddy forgiven you?"

"I think so. He's really rather sweet."

"I'm glad of that. Would you like to share a bed with me?"

It was her turn to raise eyebrows. "Just like that?"

"I know. My approach has often been criticised. The fact is, I'm feeling rather low. I have just broken up with a long-standing girlfriend who I actually intended to marry, and another old friend has simply disappeared – for all I know she may have been blown up by a bomb. I have spent the last six months in and out of hospitals, and I appear to be missing the end of the War. I am in the midst of what you might call a right royal fuck-up."

"Isn't that the tale all men tell, when they . . . well . . ."

"In my case it happens to be true."

She gazed at him for several seconds, fork poised. Then she said, "Yes, it is, isn't it. Am I supposed to replace these missing women?"

"I thought you might be prepared to alleviate a sagging spirit."

"Would you be mortally offended if I asked for time to think about it?"

"Is that a polite way of saying thanks but no thanks?"

"It's a polite way of saying I'd like to think about it. I don't like rushing into things like that without due consideration."

"You aren't a . . ."

"I am not a virgin, Harry. But I do like to choose my men. And frankly, up to ten minutes ago I had never considered you at all."

"There's a put down."

"Not at all. As I said when we first met, you are a colonel and a famous man. I'm a humble lieutenant." She looked at her watch. "I think we should be getting back."

They arrived at the office at the same moment as the colonel.

"Hello, hello," Bannon remarked. "Getting to know each other, eh?"

"We lunched together, sir," Cynthia explained. "I hope you don't object?"

"Not in the least, but you want to be careful with this fellow. Every time he goes on a mission he gets entangled with a fresh woman."

"But not all of them are in my file," Harry suggested.

"Our cabinets aren't big enough. Come in, Harry. Come in. It's a treat to see you looking so well."

Harry glanced at Cynthia before following his old friend into the office, but her face remained expressionless.

"Have a pew," Bannon invited, seating himself behind the desk.

Harry sat down. "I'm to give you this." He placed the envelope containing the medical reports on the desk.

Bannon did not open it. "What do you think of our Cynthia?"

"If she's as efficient as she is good-looking, you're on to a good thing."

"Oh, indeed. Plus the cachet."

"What cachet?"

"My dear fellow, didn't you know? She's the Earl of Brentham's only child."

"Good lord!"

"You weren't rude to her?" Bannon was anxious.

"I don't think so." I merely asked her to go to bed with me, he thought. "I thought she was the daughter of some horse trainer."

"Well, she is, in a manner of speaking. Not that the earl actually trains his horses, but he has a lot of them."

"But . . ." Harry began to remember things. "The Earl of Brentham. Isn't he as nutty as a fruitcake?"

"My dear Harry, such a description may be applied to you and me, but when it comes to an earl the word is eccentric. One could go so far as to say, extremely eccentric."

"Didn't he once ride a horse up the steps of the Palace of Westminster?"

"Indeed he did. It has never been determined whether, at that moment, he thought he was Caligula or had merely forgotten to dismount."

"Is this eccentricity hereditary?"

"You're thinking of the beautiful Lady Cynthia? So far she's given no evidence of it."

"So, how should one address the young lady?"

"In polite society? Lady Cynthia, or my lady. In uniform, however, she is Lieutenant Cynthia Bromwich. She insists on this."

"I'll try to remember," Harry murmured. "Now, Peter, what have you got for me."

"Ah. Yes. Let's talk about this malaria." As he still hadn't opened the envelope, he had to have been in touch with Chartwell.

"As I said before, a load of rubbish," Harry explained. "As you know, I was seriously ill in Italy, running a high temperature and that sort of thing. The fact is, I still had one of those shotgun pellets in my back, and it was festering."

"But it was taken out and you were given antibiotics, yet the fever persisted," Bannon pointed out.

"I don't have a fever now," Harry argued. "Nor have I had one for several weeks."

"There was also talk about depression."

"Of course I've been depressed. I'm always depressed when I'm confined to barracks, or whatever. Give me a command, or a mission. Get me out of here. And I'll stop being depressed."

"Hm," Bannon commented. "You know the show is just about over?"

"So I gather. In Germany, at any rate. But that doesn't apply to the Japanese, does it?"

"They're expected to hold out a while longer," Bannon conceded. "But as far as our people are concerned, it seems to be a matter of hard slogging through the Burmese jungles."

"I'm quite prepared to take my share of that."

"With malaria? It's endemic in that part of the world."

"Then I'm not at risk, am I? If I already have it."

"There is also the matter of those three stripes on your arm."

"Come off it, Peter. There are many men still on active service who've been wounded at least three times."

"And lastly," Bannon said, imperturbably. "There is the matter of rank. You are no longer a lieutenant, or a captain, or even a major. I can't just find a vacancy in one of our battalions and slot you in. You have to have a command, and at this moment I have nothing to give you."

"Are you saying that I am unemployable?"

"Of course I am not, Harry. You are probably the most brilliant British soldier to emerge from this war. It is simply that I do not, at this moment, have a job for you. At least, of the sort you would like and obviously have in mind. You just have to be patient. There is also the point that once the shooting stops, there is going to have to be an immediate appraisal of the position and size of the armed forces. I mean to say, we cannot keep several million men and women in uniform indefinitely. We couldn't afford to pay for them, certainly once we return to peacetime accounting. Now, obviously, a large percentage of those will wish to get out and pick up their lives again . . ." He paused, hopefully.

"I am not one of them," Harry said. "I have no other life to pick up. I went from Sandhurst straight into the Guards and then to France. But even if there had been no war, I had intended to make the Army my career."

"Oh, quite. What I meant to say was that at this time there is no possibility of raising new Commando battalions for you to command."

Which wasn't what he had intended to say at all, Harry knew.

"I will of course hunt like mad and see if I can find you a position commensurate with your talent and experience – and wishes," Bannon went on. "But it may take me a week or two. In the meantime, have you ever thought of lecturing?"

"Lecturing? Lecturing who? And on what?"

"There are a great many men and women who have been called to the services, and have not yet been sent overseas. They would benefit greatly from listening to your experiences, and especially your survival techniques."

"With respect, Peter, you have just told me that the Army is going to be demobilised just as rapidly as possible. None of these recruits you would like me to talk to will ever see active service."

"I wouldn't say that. The system last time was first in first out, and I don't see that changing. And I happen to know that it is the intention of the Government to maintain national service for the foreseeable future. I'd like you to think about it, and I'll draw up a list of possible dates and places. I take it you can be reached at your parents' home?"

"Yes," Harry said disconsolately. "That's where I can be reached."

"How did it go?" Cynthia asked.

"I have a feeling I've just been given the push," Harry said.

"You? That's not possible."

"I always thought so. But only as long as the War lasted. Now it's just about over ... What do you do with a dedicated murderer? Oh, by the way, Lady Cynthia, I should apologise for my advance at lunch."

"You're not supposed to use that title," she admonished. "And you're not going to tell me you're afraid of it."

"I've never really thought about it," he confessed. "Having had little to do with blue blood in my time. I've shaken hands with the King, when I got this." He tapped the VC ribbon. "And with Lord Mountbatten. And my last battalion commander was a lord. But that's about it."

"What makes you think they were different from anyone else?"

"I don't think I ever did . . . think that they were different, I mean. As I said, it's not something I have ever given much attention to. On the other hand . . ."

"Taking one of their scions to bed is a serious matter."

"It is," he said seriously. "I suppose as much as anything else, I have spent most of the past five years fighting to preserve English history and the pomp and circumstance that goes with it. Which means the aristocracy. Bannon tells me you're an only child.

Doesn't that mean that when your old man pops off you'll be the Countess of Brentham?"

"Sadly, no. Earldoms are a male preserve, except insofar as their wives are called countesses, and they can bear that for life. As for the earldom, they will find one of my cousins and install him."

"Does that mean you'll be out on your ear?"

"No. I'll have to be content with being a lady, but I will have all of Daddy's loot – as much of it as we can salvage from the Death Duties, anyway. So you see, you won't be committing lèse-majesté or whatever it was that was bothering you."

"Did you say, won't?"

"Didn't you expect me to?"

"Well . . ."

"That was before you found out who I was. But I haven't changed, you know. I still have two eyes, a nose, two lips and a chin. I have two arms and two legs, two tits and two hams, a belly button and a pudendum. I even have four fingers and a thumb on each hand, and five toes on each foot. You can count all of those if you like."

"Where and when?"

"Obviously not here. His nibs is likely to pop out of his office at any moment. You live in Worcester, don't you?"

"My parents live in a suburb. I don't have a place of my own."

"Frenthorpe," she said.

"That's right."

"I have a place in Worcestershire. Or rather, Daddy does. Only a few miles from Frenthorpe. Do you have transport?"

"I'm afraid not. Do we really want to involve Daddy at this stage?"

"Oh, he won't be there. He and Mummy are in Scotland. I'll pick you up. Friday evening at six. I have the weekend off."

"You sure you want to do this?"

"Yes."

"Why?"

She made a moue. "Let's say, I've never slept with a VC."

They were still gazing at each other when the door behind them suddenly opened. "Still here, Harry?" Bannon asked.

"Great stuff. You'll never believe what just came through on the radio. Hitler's dead!"

"Wowee," Cynthia said. "With respect, sir. Does that mean it's all over?"

"Well, nearly, I imagine. Admiral Doenitz has been appointed Fuehrer. And their armies are still in the field. But I imagine Doenitz will be seeking peace as quickly as he can. I think this calls for a drink."

He led them into the office and poured three whiskies.

"To victory!"

They drank.

"Now, do you know what, Cynthia? I am going to throw discipline to the winds and give you a great big kiss. I have wanted to do that since you first came through that door."

"Be my guest, sir," Cynthia said, wrapping both arms round his neck and raising both eyebrows at Harry. When she was released – looking somewhat crushed and breathless – she asked, "Is Colonel Curtis also allowed the privilege, sir?"

"I don't see why not."

Harry took her in his arms. She kissed delightfully, moving her body against his. "Friday at six," she whispered, when she took her mouth away from his to touch his ear.

"Have you heard the news?" Alison Curtis was a bubble of excitement. "And the Russians are saying that Berlin has fallen. Your father and I opened a bottle of champagne."

"Well, let's open another one now," Harry said. It was just past six. In exactly two days time . . . what? Did he really suppose that Cynthia Bromwich was going to be different from any other woman he had known, simply because she came from the top drawer? Or was he, despite it all, turned on by that mere fact? And did it even matter, in the context of the enormous events happening around them – and looming in front of them.

But he did not really wish to think about peace right now . . . What might follow, certainly for himself, was too incalculable. Equally, he could not avoid a sense of bitterness. Hitler was dead, a suicide, apparently. With Eva Braun. Thus Manning,

Green and Lawton had died entirely in vain; they had not saved a single life, and they had sacrificed their own.

But that went for so many missions and forays and attacks in this war.

Thinking like that was an aspect of the depression into which he had sunk since that disaster at Berchtesgaden. He needed to be positive – for example, he would never have met Jutta if not for that mission. Was that of the least importance? She had implanted herself on his mind and his memory, just as Deirdre had done, and then she had disappeared again, just as Deirdre had done. Unlike Deirdre, however, he had never actually touched her – however often she might have touched him!

So now he was going to attempt to lose himself in the arms of a young woman who, however well-bred, seemed entirely to have adopted wartime morals. He didn't suppose he could possibly succeed, although it promised to be at least interesting.

Next morning the news arrived that Field Marshal Jodl had surrendered all the German armies in the north to Field Marshal Montgomery. John Curtis served champagne with lunch.

"Any moment now," he declared.

"I shall be away for the weekend," Harry said.

"Oh," his mother said. "That's a shame. What happens if Germany surrenders?"

"I'll come back. There's a promise."

"Official business, is it?" his father asked.

"Semi," Harry said.

He had become so used to lying to them about his job and his missions it was like second nature. But his parents exchanged knowing glances.

"Well," Alison said. "Take care."

Rather to Harry's dismay, while Cynthia Bromwich was refreshingly punctual, she turned up driving a Lagonda.

"This'll get the neighbours talking," he remarked, as he slung his kitbag in the back and sat beside her.

"Why? I'm in uniform. I could be driving you anywhere, for a secret meeting."

"I thought that's what you were doing," he commented.

"Trouble is, Army drivers don't normally have the use of a car like this. Is it yours?"

"It's one of Daddy's. And you worry too much about what people say." She waved at the elder Curtises standing in the doorway, and drove off.

"I can see that you don't," he commented.

"Not in the least. Listen, I am yours for the next seventy-two hours. You *are* going to enjoy them?"

"I'm certainly going to try."

"Me too."

They drove out of the village and along a country lane. When they were out of sight of any house, she slowed the car. "Permission to take off my cap, sir."

"Permission granted."

She stopped the car, threw her cap in the back.

Harry did the same. "Permission to unfasten your hair, Lieutenant."

"Permission granted, sir."

Carefully Harry pulled out the various pins, and the golden locks tumbled past her ears and over her shoulders, absolutely straight. "It really is a shame to have this up," he said.

"Regulations," she pointed out. "But as it's down . . ." She put her arms round his neck and drew him against her for a kiss. Harry's hands drifted over the front of her tunic, and she gave a little shudder.

"Don't you like that?" he asked.

"I love it. Let's hurry."

They drove for another couple of miles, and came in sight of tall chimneys situated on top of a tall house; the house spread to either side in a variety of wings.

"It's always puzzled me who owns this place," Harry remarked.

"Daddy does." She swung through the wrought-iron gates.

"Good lord! You mean you've been living this close to me and I never knew it?"

"Well, like I said, we don't use it very often. I grew up mostly in Scotland and Devon, or the London flat."

"How many houses does your father have?"

"I'm not sure. Five or six, if we include the one in Cannes. But we don't actually know what condition that's in – or even if it's still standing."

"Poor you," Harry commented as the car wound its way down a long, tree-lined drive.

Cynthia glanced at him. "I didn't have anything to do with accumulating all this, you know."

"But you'll be happy to inherit."

"Whatever we can save from the taxman, yes. I'm beginning to think you're a Socialist."

"As the War began before I was old enough to vote, I have never had the time to take the least interest in politics."

"Great. I have the time to educate you properly." The car drew to a halt before a wide terrace, reached by a flight of stone steps almost as wide. Immediately the front door opened and a butler and a footman appeared.

"Oh, shit," Harry muttered. What the hell had he got himself into.

Cynthia got out. "Good evening, Perryman," she said. "You received my message?"

"Of course, my lady."

"This is Colonel Curtis."

"Welcome to Bromwich Lodge, sir."

"It's a pleasure to be here," Harry said as he got out of the car, not at all sure that he was telling the truth. He reached into the back for his bag and realised Cynthia did not have one.

"Charles will look after that, sir," Perryman said.

Harry looked at Cynthia, who was regarding him with an amused expression. "Let's have a drink," she said.

Perryman hurried to open doors for them, and Harry found himself in a large and high-ceilinged hallway studded with potted plants, suits of armour, and paintings. The butler opened a double door on their right and showed them into an even larger drawing room – a mass of upholstered settees and chairs, more pictures and various bric-a-brac on the incidental tables, the whole dominated by a magnificent Adam fireplace.

"As weekend cottages go, this has got to be the best," Harry remarked.

"Daddy doesn't like it," Cynthia said. "I think he means to sell it, as soon as the War is over."

"Does he have a buyer?"

"Oh, he'll find one. It'll become either a hotel or a nursing home or something. Thank you, Perryman."

She accepted a glass of champagne, and Harry did likewise.

"What time would you like dinner, my lady?"

"Early," Cynthia said. "I'm ready for bed, and I'm sure Colonel Curtis is too."

Perryman's expression did not change. "Would eight o'clock be satisfactory?"

"Seven thirty would be better."

"Of course, my lady."

"You can leave the bottle, and close the door," Cynthia instructed.

"Of course, my lady." Perryman obeyed.

"He seems able to take everything in his stride," Harry commented. "Or is this a regular occurrence?"

"Jealous?"

"I think I could be."

"I'm so glad. Actually, you are the first man I have ever brought here."

"Then I am flattered. Is there a reason?"

"Yes, there is. I will tell you later. Would you like to top us up?" Harry obeyed, while Cynthia sat on the settee and crossed her knees. "Sit beside me," she said. Again he obeyed, and she brushed her glass against his. "As always, you and me," she proposed.

He drank. "As always, I have a feeling that there is a lot going on I don't know about."

"I would not like to have any secrets from you."

"Fair enough. You seem to know all of mine already."

"If the colonel was telling the truth about the women, I obviously don't. Whether you want to tell me about them is up to you. I will tell you about me, but after dinner. Is that all right?"

"You mean I might leave without eating? I'm really quite hungry."

"So am I," she said. "But not for food."

She unbuttoned her tunic, and put her arms round him. "Would you like to undress me?"

"I can't think of anything I'd rather do. But . . . here?"

"Dinner won't be ready for another half an hour, and Perryman won't come in before then. You've time for a good feel."

"And you want that?" He still couldn't believe this was happening.

"Yes," she said. "I want that, very much."

He pulled down her tie, unbuttoned her shirt. She was doing the same to him – to his surprise, not very expertly. She was not wearing a brassiere, and his hands encountered only hard nipples and soft flesh. She stroked his chest and threw her leg across his; he caressed her stockinged thigh and then her hip beneath her drawers, while she moaned gently and kissed him. Then he was lying on his back while she squirmed on top of him, but, oddly, she made no attempt to release his pants although she had to feel his erection – just kept kissing him almost savagely, her hair flopping about his face while he cupped her bottom. He did not, however, drag on her drawers, as he did not know if she was ready for that yet.

Apparently she was not, for suddenly she rose to her knees and got off him, cheeks flaming as if this was the first time she had ever done anything like that. She stood with her back to him, looking into the mirror over the mantelpiece while she buttoned her blouse and straightened her skirt and stockings.

"I got carried away," she muttered, using her hands to smooth some order into her hair.

"Snap."

She turned to face him. "You were very kind. Very gentle."

He was tempted to remind her that he hadn't actually done anything yet, but decided against it.

"Dinner will be ready in five minutes," she said.

The meal was, from Harry's point of view, in keeping with the rest of the evening so far. The dining room was as large as the whole downstairs of his parents' house; the oak table was at least twenty feet long, and the walls were lined with various sideboards laden with decanters and silver. They sat at opposite ends of the table, hardly able to communicate without shouting, while Perryman served them. The meal itself bore no relation to the norm in rationed England, and the wine – even to Harry's untutored taste – was excellent.

"Did you put the heating on upstairs, Perryman?" Cynthia asked.

"As soon as I got your message, my lady."

"Thank you." She smiled down the table at Harry. "We do try to save fuel, where possible."

He tried to imagine this remarkable creature existing in an ATS barracks – sharing a communal bathroom, standing to attention, going on long jogs with those splendid breasts trembling beneath her singlet – and found it impossible, although enjoyable to attempt.

They finished their dessert. "Would you like a port with your coffee?" she asked. "Or would you rather go straight up."

It was difficult to be certain from the other end of the table, but he was sure she was nervous.

"I'd rather go right up," he said. Adding, quite untruthfully, "It's been a long day."

Although he suspected it might be a long night.

"Then let's." She got up. "That was very good of you, Perryman."

"Thank you, my lady. Breakfast at the normal time?"

"I haven't decided yet. I'll ring when I'm ready."

"Very good, my lady. Goodnight, sir."

Feeling distinctly sheepish, and very much the kept man, Harry nodded. "Goodnight, old fellow."

He followed Cynthia up the stairs and emerged on to a carpeted corridor, off which there opened several doors. She chose the second on the left, and led him into a very large bedroom with a generally gold motif, from the wallpaper via the chandelier to the carpet. Even the eiderdown and pillow slips were the same colour – as he didn't doubt were the sheets – and through the open door to the en suite bathroom he saw that the fittings there matched too, including the toilet cistern. For a moment he wondered if she had chosen this room to impress him, then rejected the thought; it would never have entered her mind.

Cynthia crossed the room and opened wardrobe; Harry saw that it was filled with clothes, presumably hers.

"You said you were here for three days?" he asked, closing the door.

"Sadly, yes. Oh, you were thinking of these. I leave clothes in all of our houses. Saves me having to pack."

"Ah. Silly of me." His own suitcase waited on a rack by the door.

Cynthia took out a hanger from which was suspended a white satin nightgown and turned to face him, holding it in front of her. "Is this all right?"

"It's very lovely. If you must."

"Oh." Her mouth made an O. "I never thought of that."

"It's just that I never use nightclothes."

"Quite. How stupid of me. Well . . ." She licked her lips, and now she was definitely trembling. "What would you like to do first?"

Harry began to have a distinctly uneasy feeling. There was something wrong with this scenario, which should have been so magnificently right. He could only suppose – and hope – that she was as overwhelmed by his reputation as she had first appeared.

"We could have a bath," he suggested. It was the best way he knew for two people to get to know each other, or even to resume an old acquaintance, he thought, remembering Belinda in Caen – but that was not a memory he wished to resurrect. "If there is enough water."

"There's lots of water," she said. "Would you like to go first?"

"Isn't your bath big enough for two?"

Her mouth made another O. "You mean, get in together?"

"Haven't you ever done that?"

She shook her head, cheeks crimson.

"But you have no objection?"

He thought she did, but she said emphatically, "Oh, no. It sounds rather fun."

"Then you run the water, and I'll shave. I don't want to scratch you all up."

"No," she agreed. "No. You mustn't do that."

She was in a state of total confusion, which seemed to grow as he undressed. Returning from switching on the taps, she stood by the bed watching him, and his uneasiness returned; it was difficult to accept that she had ever seen a man strip before.

"My God," she said.

"I always get this way when in a bedroom with a beautiful woman. Don't all your boyfriends?"

"I was referring to the scars," she said. "They're *everywhere*."

"I suppose they are. Do you find them off-putting?"

"Of course not. I'm just wondering how you survived."

"I think a lot of people have done that. But most of them were German."

He went into the bathroom and shaved, watching the doorway in the mirror. She didn't appear for several minutes, and he had to switch the water off himself. Then she slowly filled the doorway, naked and with her hair tied up on the top of her head. For a moment he couldn't move; she was just about the most perfectly shaped woman he had ever seen, with the large high breasts, wide thighs, and long slender legs of a Venus de Milo – and she had arms!

"You don't like me," she suggested, cheeks still flaming.

"Like is hardly the word." He went to her, put his arms round her, held her close; she shivered again at his touch. She seemed happier when he kissed her, sliding his hand up to the nape of her neck. Then, very tentatively, she slid her own hand down to touch him, before pulling her head back to stare at him, mouth open.

"You're very welcome," her assured her. "But I think we need to have that bath before we get out of control."

She licked her lips, stepped into the bath, and slowly lowered herself. He sat opposite her, against the predictably gold-plated taps, his legs outside of hers. Carefully not looking at him, she began to soap herself.

"Give it to me and I'll do your legs," he said.

Another quick flick of her tongue. He ran his hands up and down the smooth flesh, up as far as her thighs, while she held her breath – as if wondering how far he was going to go. But he let her complete herself, preferring to watch her, before regaining the soap for himself.

They did not speak as they towelled and then returned to the bedroom. Now she was shivering again, although the room was delightfully warm.

He frowned at her even as he sat beside her on the bed and kissed her. "How long is it since you have done this?"

As a reply she fell back across the bed, taking him with her. There was so much he wanted to do with her, so many parts of her he wanted to caress – but he was allowed no time. Her legs were parted and wrapped round him, and after the build-up he was spent in seconds.

He raised himself on his hands. "Old rough and ready. We'll do better next time."

Only then did he realise that she was both moaning and weeping.

"Was it that bad?"

Her legs relaxed and fell back. Harry got up, meaning to go to the bathroom, but remained staring at the sheet.

"Oh, shit!"

"I'll be all right," she muttered. "It wasn't so bad."

He sat on the bed. "You told me . . ."

"I lied." She rolled on her face, and he had the strongest temptation to spank her, and not from any erotic impulse. He had, as usual, been completely taken in by a woman.

"In the name of God, why?"

She rolled on to her back, arms and legs flung wide. "I wanted it."

"Why? You're—"

She sat up. "Please don't say it. Yes, I'm an earl's daughter. You spotted it from the beginning. That makes me different. I don't want to be different, Harry. I was the only virgin in my squad during training. The others thought it was great fun. We'll get you laid, they said. I went out on so many dates, to so many dances, but they could never resist the temptation to tell my partner, she's an earl's daughter. And they all retreated so fast you'd have thought I had leprosy. I don't suppose I was all that sorry. Most of the time. They were a sorry bunch. But I still wanted it to happen, with the right guy. And you . . ."

"You thought I was the right guy."

"I still do. Look . . ." She stretched across the bed to hold his hand. "You have nothing to blame yourself for. Everything that has happened I wanted to happen. I made it happen."

"You'll regret it. As for blaming myself . . . For God's sake, Cynthia, I have just deflowered the daughter of—"

"Please don't say it. You have to think of me as a woman. With whom, I hope, you have just had a pleasant ten minutes."

"Of course I have. But . . ."

"And with whom you are going to spend an even more pleasant weekend."

"You mean you want me to stay?"

"Of course. I want you to fuck me morning, noon and night."

"And when you get pregnant?"

"That's my worry. Please come to bed, Harry. I want to sleep in your arms."

Remarkably, he did sleep, in her arms. But the enormity of what he had done hung over him like a cloud, and was still there when he awoke.

"We need to talk," he said.

"After," she countered.

This time there was less pain and no haste. He could stroke her to his heart's content, and she could stroke him – still tentatively, uncertain if there were any forbidden territories. Then they bathed, and she rang down for breakfast. It was brought up by Perryman, who never changed expression at the sight of his mistress in bed with a man.

He also brought up *The Times*, which indicated that the War might be over at any moment.

"We made it just in time," Cynthia said. "I did, anyway."

"I promised to be with my parents, when it happens," Harry said.

"Of course. I've love to meet them."

"They're . . . well, I suppose one would describe them as very ordinary middle-class people."

"I said, I'd love to meet them. They're your parents."

"I'm sure they'll enjoy meeting you. But . . . well, you're taking this very much in your stride. Hear me out," he said

114

as she was about to interrupt. "I understand it was something you wanted to do, and I hope I have measured up. But the ramifications . . ."

"I said, I'd take care of a pregnancy."

"I was thinking of what happens when the duke of somewhere or the earl of somewhere else comes courting, woos you and wins you, and on his wedding night discovers you are not a virgin."

"It won't be on his wedding night," she said. "I'll make sure he finds out well before."

"Which will make it the easier for him to break the engagement or whatever."

"If he is that small-minded, I wouldn't want to marry him anyway."

"Your parents won't be too happy about that."

"I'm over twenty-one."

"They can still take umbrage."

"And cut me off without a penny? Daddy would never do that. I'm his only child."

"You seem to have it all thought out."

She drank coffee and stared down the bed. "There is another and even more simple solution."

"Tell me about it."

She turned her head. "That you marry me."

Courting

H arry nearly choked on his coffee. "Marry you? Me?"

"You mean you're not the marrying kind. The colonel told me you were engaged, down to quite recently."

"Yes. I am the marrying kind, as it happens. I was engaged to your predecessor."

"Captain Forester? But . . ."

"Yes. She decided to return to her husband."

"With *you* available? The woman needs her head examined. I would regard it as a great honour to be your wife, Colonel Curtis."

"That's a very sudden and certainly premature decision. You hardly know me."

"I know all about you, from your file. And I will get to know you better, over the next ten, twenty, thirty, forty, even fifty years. I am looking forward to it. As you will get to know me."

"But – you can't possibly be in love with me. Not on the strength of a file and a couple of days . . . and a couple of fucks."

"How many days and fucks does it take to fall in love? What you mean is, you are not in love with me."

"What I mean is, if you think you are in love, it's with an idea – the great warrior, the famous hero, and even, as you have read my file, the great lover. None of those are true."

"Let's itemise them," she suggested. "If you are not a great warrior, how come you have spent the entire War going on secret missions behind enemy lines, always successfully, and always returning – if not in one piece, certainly in pieces."

"Not all were successful," he argued, aware that he was being outmaneuvered.

"Item two: if you are not a great hero, how do you account for

116

that chestful of medals you wear? They can't all have been accidents."

"As a matter of fact, they were."

"As for being a great lover, you can't possibly be a judge of that. The fact is testified by the number of women who have apparently been happy to climb into bed with you. That includes me. I'll admit I don't have too much experience, but I think you're a great lover. I certainly have no desire to try anyone else."

"That attitude will almost certainly change. You're judging me entirely on my war record. When the shooting stops, you will very rapidly find me a colossal bore. If the shooting has really stopped, it will be a matter of garrison posts scattered all over the world – or merely rotting at Aldershot."

She raised her eyebrows. "You mean to stay in the Army?"

"I'm a professional soldier. I'm not trained to do anything else. I'm not even trained to be a human being, only to kill other human beings."

"What a tremendous concept."

"You're incorrigible. Okay, let's get down to the nitty-gritty. As I said, I come from a lower middle-class background. I have absolutely no money apart from my salary, and no prospects of receiving any by inheritance. There is no possibility of my being able to support you in the manner to which you are accustomed."

"Can't I support myself?"

"I don't think that's really me."

"All right. Be a male chauvinist pig. We'll live on your salary."

"With Papa bailing us out whenever we get into debt."

"I shan't touch him for a penny."

"Bu you will eventually inherit his fortune."

"So we'll be able to afford a new car and give our children a proper education."

He tried another tack. "What about all the social events you usually go to?"

"I'll drop those as well if you wish me to."

"Oh, for God's sake." He held both her hands. "Why, Cynthia. Why?"

"Because I want to be your wife."

"Just like that."

"But you don't want me. Don't you love me even a little? Couldn't you?"

"You are a very beautiful and loveable person, Cynthia."

"Then won't you give it a whirl?"

He knew he was fighting a losing battle. He had never been proposed to before, and he simply didn't know how to handle it. "Warts and all?"

"Every single one."

"There are an awful lot."

"If you're thinking about women, don't worry about it. If an old flame crops up and you want to go off and shag her, I won't complain. As long as you come home again."

"You would complain, you know. But not all of them were lovers. There is a woman in Holloway Prison who has sworn to kill me, as nastily as possible."

"Good lord! Whatever did you do to her?"

"I don't think I ever actually touched her. But back in 1942, when I was on a mission to Algiers, I found it necessary to execute her sister to prevent her from betraying us. Yasmin came to England after me, but she was arrested for killing another of the executioners before she could get to me."

"Why wasn't she hanged?"

"Clever defence, I suppose."

"But . . . if she's been sent up for life . . ."

"We must hope the sentence means what it said. But you have to know about these things."

"Yes, I must. Thank you for telling me."

"But it hasn't changed your mind."

"Of course not. They taught me how to shoot when I was training, as well as unarmed combat. I'll be your back-up. When we're married."

What am I doing? he wondered. I hardly know this girl, except for the fact that she has an identified pedigree going back several hundred years, while I cannot trace my ancestors more than a couple of generations; that she has access to more money than I can ever have dreamed of – the prospect of her renouncing her inheritance was extremely remote – and that she has spent her life moving in circles I have never even considered.

And that her motives were at the least suspect. Perhaps she had convinced herself that he was her dream man . . . That was extremely unlikely to last. But the fact was that marriage to Cynthia Bromwich promised to be extremely exciting, and he was going to need something exciting when the shooting stopped.

And, of course, he had made it happen, by so carelessly inviting her out to lunch and then to bed – without a clue as to what he was getting involved in, and without, as usual, caring. Hoist by his own petard, indeed. But what a magnificent petard!

"You'll have to tell me what we do first," he said.

"Well, it can't be official until you've spoken with Pa, and asked for my hand."

"And when he kicks me out?"

"Then we'll elope. But I really would like to keep it sunshine and light. I'm going to speak to him first, just to sort things out. Would you like to tell your parents right away?"

"No," Harry said. "I don't think we should tell my parents until yours have given the nod."

"All right," she agreed. "Mum's the word. Now, as we're engaged, unofficially, let's make love."

Germany surrendered on the Tuesday. Cynthia was due back at work that day, but when she telephoned Bannon he said she could have another day off, as all London was celebrating in any event. So they drove over to Frenthorpe.

"This is Lieutenant Bromwich," Harry told his parents.

Both were obviously taken aback by the spectacular blonde looks presented to them, although Cynthia had resumed her uniform and put her hair up to look suitably anonymous.

But not quite anonymous enough. "You're the lady who picked Harry up on Friday," Alison said.

"Yes, ma'am. I'm his driver," Cynthia explained.

"Bromwich, Bromwich," John Curtis said. "That name is familiar."

"There are a lot of us," Cynthia said.

"What a racket," Harry commented, listening to the pealing church bells and the shouts from outside.

"What a day," his father said.

"Let's all go down to the pub," Harry suggested, watching Cynthia to see how she reacted.

"Brilliant!" she said. "I do like pubs."

Suitably pummelled and inebriated, they returned to the house for lunch.

"Then I must be off," Cynthia said. "Duty calls."

"Are you sure you're up to it?" Alison asked.

To Harry's pleasure and relief his mother was obviously taking to her son's latest conquest . . . Even if she couldn't yet know that it was a conquest.

Cynthia giggled. "You mean, am I sober enough to drive."

"Well . . ."

"I'll go with her," Harry said. "I can catch the train back."

"Tonight? Do you think they'll be running?"

"Good point. I'll spend the night in town and come up tomorrow or the day after. Things should have calmed down by then."

"I think that's an excellent idea," Cynthia said. "Sir."

Needless to say she was using her parents' London flat, which had escaped the bombing and which, although a fraction the size of the Worcestershire house, was furnished in an equally breathtaking style. There was even a resident maid to see to their creature comforts.

But although this new and so foreign lifestyle was growing on him, Harry had an ulterior motive for staying in town for a few days; he wanted to see Bannon, both on account of his career and his marriage. Possessing field rank, as he now did, he needed no one's permission to get married – but Cynthia was still enlisted and she certainly did.

"Harry!" Bannon squeezed his hand. "Hard to believe it's all over, eh?"

"Very," Harry said.

"Sit down, man, sit down." Bannon seated himself. "So what comes next, eh?"

"Is your idea that I should take a lecture tour still on?"

"I think we can put that on hold right now."

"Brilliant," Harry said. "Don't tell me something has come up? Like a command?"

"Ah . . . in a manner of speaking. There's quite a lot to be sorted out. At this moment, no one seems to have any idea how long we shall have to maintain forces in Germany, but it does appear as though it may be for some considerable time. Equally, no one has yet determined just how large those forces will have to be. There is even some talk of each of the three great powers, as well as perhaps France, having to occupy parts of the country on a more or less permanent basis, until a peace settlement can be agreed and a decision made as to what actually is going to happen. Some people want Germany broken up into small states, others have other ideas."

"What you are saying is that the wartime army strength is to be maintained."

"Not exactly. There will be large-scale demobilisation, beginning almost immediately. But the Army will be kept at considerable strength for the foreseeable future. For this purpose, as I mentioned when last we spoke, National Service is being maintained, also for the foreseeable future. However, first things first. I must ask you this question: do you still intend to continue your Army career or do you wish to go on the list for demobilisation?"

"I wish to stay in the Army."

"I thought that would be your decision. Right. Now, as you can imagine, the Commandos are one of the units which are to be maintained at full strength, not only because they proved their value during the War, but because they're all volunteers and as such may be presumed to wish to continue Army life. Each man will of course be given the opportunity to retire if he so wishes, but we do not anticipate there will be a great number, and in any event the brigade will be kept up to strength. There is also a possibility that we may be merged with our sister regiment, the Royal Marine Commandos. However, that is not my province. My requirement is to maintain a flow of recruits to the brigade. Now, as I have no adequate field command to offer you at this moment, I would like you to take command of the Scottish training centre. I'm sure you remember it well."

"You wish me to train recruits," Harry said, slowly.

"This is a most important task, Harry. And I can think of no one better suited to carrying it out."

"And I'll be so far from any possibility of action that if I have a malarial attack it won't matter."

"That's true enough. But it is simply a temporary posting until you can have a battalion of your own. And you simply have to get it through your mind that there isn't going to *be* any more action. That part of your life – of all of our lives – is over. And we should all thank God for that."

"I will do that," Harry said. "Well, as my active service days appear to be over, I intend to get married. With your permission, Peter."

"Get married? What a splendid idea. But why are you asking my permission?"

"Because the woman I am marrying requires it. Although I imagine she will be one of those applying for an early discharge."

"Do I know this fortunate young lady?"

"Indeed you do. She's in the outside office."

Bannon didn't immediately connect. "Well, bring her in, Harry. Bring her in." Then the penny dropped. "You don't mean . . .?"

"Yes, I do."

"Good God! But . . . she's the—"

"I know who she is."

"And you proposed marriage? So quickly? And she accepted?"

"About face. She proposed marriage, and I have accepted."

Bannon leaned back in his chair and scratched his head. "You've spoken to the earl?"

"Not yet. There's been no opportunity, as Cynthia's leave was up. I would like you to give her some more leave so we can sort things out."

Bannon gazed at him for several seconds. "I don't want to come across as a Dutch uncle, Harry, but . . ."

"She knows quite a lot about me, Peter. All the bad parts, anyway."

"I wasn't thinking of the past. Any man is due a few peccadilloes before he marries. It's afterwards that they can become serious. If you go and let down an earl's daughter . . ."

"I have no intention of doing so."

"Well, you would say so in the first flush of love, wouldn't you?"

"She seems prepared to trust me."

"Well, she would also in the first flush. I think you had better ask her to come in, and I hope you and I have known each other long enough for you not to take offence at anything I might say to her."

"Be my guest." Harry got up and opened the door. "Would you come in, please, Lieutenant Bromwich."

Cynthia had actually been walking up and down, as she knew what he had wanted to see Bannon about. Now she gave him a quick look, entered the office, and stood to attention.

"At ease, Lieutenant," Bannon said. "Harry, a chair for the young lady."

Harry placed another chair before the desk.

"Please sit, Cynthia," Bannon invited.

Cynthia obeyed, and Harry sat beside her.

"This is all a bit sudden, isn't it?" Bannon asked.

"How long is a piece of string, sir?"

"Yes," Bannon remarked drily. "I gather you have not yet spoken to your parents about it?"

"As you say, sir, it has been rather sudden."

"Therefore you have no idea what their reaction may be?"

"I am twenty-four years old, sir. They have to accept my decision as to whom I am going to marry."

"Your father, shall we say, walks the corridors of power at Westminster. You do understand that if he does not like the idea, and you persist, it may have an unfortunate effect on Harry's career?"

Cynthia looked at Harry.

"I am prepared to accept that risk," Harry said.

"And does Lieutenant Bromwich know where your next posting will be?"

"She doesn't, as I have only just found out for myself," Harry pointed out.

"Do tell," Cynthia suggested.

"Colonel Curtis is going to take command of one of our Commando training centres in Scotland."

"Brilliant. I love Scotland. Mummy and Daddy have a home in Ayrshire. They're up there now."

"This camp is somewhat further north. A rather bleak place. This is necessary, you see, if the men are to be adequately trained."

"I think you are trying to frighten me, sir. You are not going to succeed."

Bannon sighed. "Well, you make a damned handsome couple. I gather you'd like some additional leave to go up and see your parents?"

"That would be very helpful."

"Then you have it. Would I also be right in assuming you wish to be demobbed as soon as possible?"

"Yes, thank you, sir."

"You understand it won't be tomorrow. I may, however, be able to have you transferred to Scotland. I am assuming there is no, ah, urgency about the marriage?"

"If I am pregnant, sir, there is no way we can know for at least another month."

"Yes." Bannon looked extremely embarrassed. "Very good. You go off tomorrow. Will you be accompanying her, Harry?"

"No," Cynthia said. "In the first instance, I'd rather see my parents alone."

Bannon looked at Harry; it was not like him to take a back seat.

"In this instance, we play it her way," Harry said.

"Very good. But you are required to take up your posting immediately."

Harry nodded. "I'll just stop off in Frenthorpe to bring my folks up to date."

"Do they know about this?"

Harry grinned. "Not yet."

"I see. Well, I'll wish you both the best of luck. I'll expect you back here the moment your, ah, business is completed, Cynthia."

"It should not take more than a couple of days, sir."

"I'm giving you a week. Just in case it doesn't go quite as smoothly as you hope."

"I'll telephone you at the camp," Cynthia said. "You'll have transport?"

"I'm the commandant," Harry pointed out.

"Sounds tremendous. Well, when I call, you'll come down and meet my folks."

"Still confident?"

"Oh, yes. Daddy loves soldiers, and medals, and heroes. You're just up his street."

Still confident, he thought, as he sat in the train on its way to Worcester and the Frenthorpe stop-off. He wished he was. Instead, he was aware of a feeling of total unreality. No doubt almost everyone in England – everyone in the world – was feeling vaguely the same way. Certainly all around him people were clearly suffering from shock, some wandering around in a daze, others hugging and kissing each other, a great deal of alcohol still flowing . . . Six years of the most bitter self-destruction the world had ever known had ended. No more would death rain from the sky on defenceless civilians. Or even on defendable soldiers, he mused. No more would ships be torpedoed without warning.

Why, he realised, Paul would be coming home too. He would have to be best man at the wedding.

Harry did not think he was being arrogant in supposing that the sense of unreality was greater for him than for most people. If he had seen far less of the grim business of day-to-day fighting than the average soldier – save for a few weeks in France just after D-Day – he had put his life on the line on more occasions than most. He could remember them all as if they had happened yesterday. The beach at Dunkirk and his first wound. His first ever raid, on the Lofoten Islands outside Narvik, when they had expected such bitter resistance and encountered almost none – and where he had first met Veronica. The airborne raid on the communications centre at Ardres, when he had been taken prisoner for the first time – however briefly. The raid on St Nazaire, which had turned out such a disaster. The raid on Algiers, perhaps the crowning triumph of his career – but which had involved him with Yasmin Le Blanc's vengeance. The raid on Spetsos, which had so nearly cost him his life. The drop into occupied France to prepare the way for D-Day – so costly in lives. And then the business at Berchtesgaden, again so very costly.

Why, he thought, I have killed my last man. How ironic that the last man he had had to shoot had been one of his own.

And now? He would spend his time training men to commit acts of murder, mayhem and unlimited destruction, training which everyone hoped – and quite a few seemed to believe – would never have to be put into practice. While he personally would be embarking on a roller-coaster ride which would take him . . . where?

He was honest enough, at least with himself, to know that this whole business had very little to do with Cynthia herself. He had asked her out to lunch and then to bed in a mood of almost savage resentment against fate itself for having lost Deirdre on top of Belinda on top of the dream that had been Jutta Hulin. He had not really expected her to accept, certainly not once she discovered who she was. She had surprised him, again and again and again. His first reaction was that she was merely a member of the amoral aristocracy of whom one read in the newspapers. When he realised she wasn't, he had been seriously concerned. He had only once in his life before taken a virgin to bed – and Yvonne Clearsted had been after him for years.

But this woman . . . He could not doubt that when he had accepted her invitation to spend a weekend together, she already had marriage in mind. To a man she had only just met – but had spent three months reading about, and perhaps dreaming about? However flattering that might be, it yet indicated a high level of romantic instability.

Yet he had gone along with her. He had offered her all of his warts, while seeking to discover none of hers. There had to be quite a few, and some could promise catastrophe. Of course there would be those who would say that he had been unable to resist the heady combination of beauty, wealth and nobility suddenly dropped into his lap, quite literally. And he would have to admit that those factors were important. But not in themselves. They were important because of the part they had played, and would continue to play, in the sheer excitement of possessing, and being possessed by, Cynthia Bromwich. Of living up, day in and day out, to the image she had of him. Of developing, no doubt, an advanced case of hubris.

He wondered if he could do it, and what her reaction would be to his failure? So there it was. Events had stripped him of his life's blood, the thrill of combat, the adrenalin-inducing uncertainty of whether he would kill or be killed on every mission. So he was seeking to replace that with the excitement of marriage to a blue-blooded young woman who obviously possessed a strong manic streak – he should find out how many of her ancestors, apart from her father, had gone over the top, either politically or morally.

He supposed she would tell him herself, if he asked. Certainly her father's eccentricities were well known.

John and Alison were in a state of euphoria when Harry told them he was not even returning overseas but was going to be stationed in Scotland for the foreseeable future.

"But that's tremendous," John said. "We'll be able to see so much more of you. Do you know that Paul is coming home as well? He's a commander."

"There's something to look forward to. I imagine we'll have a great many notes to compare."

"Now you'll be able to settle down," Alison said, concentrating on what she regarded as the important issues. "Find some nice girl, get married, and raise a family."

"I think that's a splendid idea," Harry said.

His parents looked at him in surprise; they had not expected enthusiastic agreement – or any agreement at all.

"You're sounding as if you have already made a choice," John suggested.

"Well, straws in the wind."

"Will you tell us who?"

"Would you mind awfully if I didn't, for a day or two? She hasn't actually said yes, yet."

They were obviously disappointed. "I just hope she isn't another of those beastly Army women," Alison said.

"Why, Mother, I thought you liked Lieutenant Bromwich."

"Well, she seemed very pleasant. But one can't help wondering, with all that training, and sort of, well, free-and-easy lifestyle, whether they are really suitable as wives and mothers."

"Any more than I am really suitable as a husband and father," Harry grinned.

"Now, Harry, that's not what I meant." Alison frowned. "It's not her, is it?"

"Who?" Harry asked, quite aware that his mother was referring to Cynthia.

"Well, that Lieutenant Bromwich."

"As a matter of fact it is."

"Oh, good lord! Harry! You haven't . . ."

"We spent last weekend together, yes, and decided to tie the knot."

"You said she hadn't said yes."

"I'm sorry. What I meant was, she has to check with her parents."

Alison snorted. "Aren't you good enough for them?"

"I'm good enough for her, Mother. Which is what matters. She is just doing the proper thing."

"Well, she certainly is a looker," John said. "And I'm still sure I know her name. Bromwich. I really must try to remember. Oh, by the way, a letter came for you yesterday. Judging by the various postmarks, it's been following you around half the world."

Harry took the envelope, frowning. His address, care of the Brigade, was written in English, and the return address in the top left-hand corner indicated that it was from someone named MacLeod, in Johannesburg.

"I don't think we know that name," Alison remarked. "Would it be one of your people?"

"Not in South Africa," Harry said, and slit the envelope.

Dear Major Curtis,

As I have no home address for you, I can only hope this letter will reach you.

I wish first of all to apologise for leaving you so abruptly and without a farewell. I do not consider that I abandoned you, as you were in very good hands. But in our conversations while crossing the mountains you indicated an uncertainty as to whether or not you would be able to assist me once we reached, or were rescued by, your army. I understood very well that your hands would be tied and your desires frustrated by that red tape which pervades any army. Discovering an opportunity to leave the partisan encampment, and thus be totally dissociated from you and be merely a refugee, I decided to take it. Thus I hope you will forgive me.

My aspirations worked out very successfully, once it was discovered that I was a trained nurse. I was put to work, and I feel I pleased my superiors; I was given the opportunity to apply to join various batches of nurses who were being sent to parts of the British Empire, and thus found myself in this delightful place.

I had only been here a month when I received news that my husband was dead. You will appreciate that I could not be grief-stricken about this, and when, shortly afterwards, Dr MacLeod proposed marriage – he works in this hospital and we had been dating for some time – I decided to accept and attempt to achieve some stability and perhaps even happiness with my life. Sadly, I am not very good at picking husbands. But as you English say, I have made my bed and must now lie on it. For the rest of my life?

I wish you to know that I will never forget those three days we spent in such intimacy. My only regret is that you were too ill to appreciate them properly yourself. So I must be content to remember you in my dreams and wish you every fortune in your career.

With much love,
Jutta MacLeod

"Well?" Alison asked.

"As you suggested, an old comrade-in-arms," Harry said.

He retired to his room to read the letter again. Very little of it, at least as regards her recounting of events, rang true. They had reached the partisans in the middle of August, and it was now getting on for the middle of May. That was nine months. From what he had read and heard on the radio, the refugee and Displaced Persons camps were still choc-a-bloc, with processing taking place very slowly. And the wives of known Nazi supporters were at the bottom of the list. But if she had concealed the fact that she was the wife of an Austrian Nazi, how had anyone known to inform her that he was dead?

During those three days, when he had only been half conscious, he had recognised that she was a very cool, very positive, and very devious young woman. That had not made her any the less attractive. Now . . . He re-read the letter a third time. There could not have been a more open invitation for him to ride to her rescue, with the promise of everything she possessed at the end of it. Perhaps he owed it to her; she had certainly saved his life. And the temptation was quite enormous; his pain and fever-shrouded memory of her revealed her almost as a goddess. Had she really been as beautiful and desirable as he wanted her to be?

But to think like that was madness. As everyone constantly reminded him, the War, the freedom from restrictions of morality or ethics that governed normal lives, was ended. He had to put the wild romanticism that had carried him for five years behind him, and settle down to being that human being he still did not understand. As for guilt, if she had saved his life, he had equally saved hers – by giving her the opportunity to escape collapsing Nazidom.

Besides, he was engaged to be married, just about, and on the point of entering a word of wealth and social prominence he had never really believed to exist.

He folded the sheet of paper, replaced it in its envelope, and stowed it in the top drawer beneath his socks and ties. A last memory of the glory that had been.

The Wife

H arry had no intention of carrying the matter of Jutta any further, but remarkably, when he left the train in Fort William, on the platform he encountered an old comrade – the pair had never actually been friends.

"Charlie Harbord!"

"Harry Curtis!" Harbord took in Harry's badges, and added, "Sir."

Harbord was a major, a big heavy-set man who had once been in the Commandos. They had last seen each other during the escape from St Nazaire, during which Harry had saved Harbord's life under fire – the event for which he had received the Victoria Cross. That had been three years previously. Harbord had been very badly wounded, and although he and Harry had regained England it had been clear he would never again be a combat soldier. But here he was, in uniform, and looking very fit.

"Still seeking glory, I see," he remarked. He had always had a waspish tongue.

"It's a living," Harry said. "Or it was, down to a few days ago. But what are you at, in this neck of the woods?"

"Just passing through, really. I'm in Intelligence now."

"Are you. That must be interesting."

"It is. I say, old man, I'd appreciate it if you'd let me buy you a drink. I never did have the chance to, well, at least thank you in person for the French business."

"Why not?" Harry agreed. There was a command car waiting, and the camp was only a few miles north of the town. He told the driver to relax, and accompanied Harbord across the street to a pub. "So, how's the War been treating you recently?" he asked as he drank his pint.

"Nothing dramatic, like your stuff. But as you suggested, interesting."

"What exactly do you do?"

"Mine is mainly investigation. Prisoners-of-war, and now, of course, DPs. You'd be surprised how many of those – especially if they happen to be German – are actually Nazis. They of course would use the word 'were', and claim they were coerced."

"Hm," Harry said, the germ of an idea beginning to roam around his mind. "What about the Nazis who have stayed behind?"

"Oh, we're working on those too. Again, of course, everyone claims to have been coerced. But it's early days yet. We'll get there."

"What about Austrians?"

"Oh, indeed."

"Well, let's see. Suppose I were to give you the name and some information about an Austrian Nazi, do you suppose you could trace him? Find out whether he's alive or dead?"

"I'm damned sure I could. Given time."

"His name is Hulin, and he farmed not far from the village of Fusch in the Austrian Alps. He was married to a woman named Jutta."

Harbord produced a notebook and wrote down the name. "I shouldn't think that would be difficult. Have you got it in for this chap?"

"I've never met him. It's his wife I'm interested in."

"Ah. *Cherchez la femme.*"

"That's exactly it. She saved my life."

"A Nazi?"

"She wasn't; that was her husband. Anyway, I was wounded and somewhat helpless. She got me out into Italy where we linked up with partisans. I was pretty done up by then, and not really aware of what was going on. When I came to, she'd gone."

"Interesting," Harbord commented. "Tell me, what were you doing in Austria?"

"This and that."

"I see. Well, as I said, I'm pretty sure we can trace the

husband. But if she didn't go back to him and just became a nameless refugee, that's a tall order."

"She's in South Africa. Johannesburg. Married to a Dr MacLeod."

Harbord raised his eyebrows. "If you know all this, why do you need me?"

"I would like to know how she got there, and just what her relationship with MacLeod is."

Harbord nodded. "There's been quite a lot of that. Attractive women desperate for a new life, offering themselves in marriage to anyone who can get them out of the refugee mainstream in a hurry. I take it this woman is attractive."

"Extremely so."

"Well, from what you have told me, if this MacLeod really is a doctor in a Johannesburg hospital, tracing him and finding out something about his wife won't be a problem. And then?"

"I should be very grateful if you would let me have the information. I am particularly interested in how Frau Hulin got to South Africa."

"*Cherchez la femme*," Harbord said again. "Well, old man, it will be a pleasure to do this for you. There is just one thing: suppose I turn up something illegal in the lady's various perambulations."

"Such as if Hulin is alive and well and living in Austria, while his wife is alive and well and living in South Africa . . . and married again."

"It's a strong possibility. But there are other possibilities as well."

"If I had not raised the matter, you would never have heard of these people."

"True."

"So, can't you find out what you can about them, and then forget that you ever heard of them?"

"As long as there is nothing really nasty involved."

"Such as?"

"Such as if this Hulin turns out to have been a high-ranking Nazi officer. I would have to follow that up."

"There is no chance of that."

"Or if his charming wife turns out to be a Mata Hari re-incarnation."

"There is absolutely no possibility of that, either," Harry assured him.

Harry attempted to put the whole thing out of his mind. He thought that when Harbord came back to him, he might well reply to Jutta's letter, perhaps warning her that various aspects of her previous life were known, and bringing her up to date on her husband's whereabouts and any actions he might have taken about her. It would be a way of keeping in touch with that last relic of his wartime past.

Settling in at the training camp was hampered by the expected telephone call. He received an enthusiastic welcome from his staff as well as the recruits. The staff had all heard of him and his exploits, and had lost no time in communicating the status of their new CO to the new boys, while to his pleasure he discovered that his adjutant, Captain Stephenson, and his batman, Corporal Todd, had served with the battalion in France.

"Do you reckon there'll be anything more for us to do, sir?" Stephenson asked somewhat anxiously – older than Harry, he had not had the opportunity to acquire rapid promotion or any medals.

"Everyone fervently hopes not," Harry said. "But it's our business to prepare these lads for it, just in case."

He inspected the camp – a formality, as he had spent a good deal of time here over the past five years – and the men, and was pleased; they looked much fitter on the whole than those he had first trained with, and were, if anything, even more enthusiastic.

But really picking up the threads, and putting some of his own ideas on training into practice, had to wait on the phone call.

It came the day after he arrived.

"For you, sir," said Orderly Room Sergeant Howorth. "Do you wish to take it? It's a woman."

"I'll take it," Harry said, and picked up his receiver. "Curtis."

"Would you like to come and see us?"

"When?"

"How about today. With a view to spending the night."

"You mean I'd be welcome?"

"Was there any doubt?"

"I've been called away on business," Harry told Captain Stephenson. "I'll be back tomorrow."

"Yes, sir. Do you require a car?"

"And a driver," Harry said. Having joined up immediately out of school, and having been fairly busy since, he had never had the time to take driving lessons.

When the driver, Private Rawlings, arrived, Harry handed him the address.

"That's the Earl of Brentham's Scottish home, isn't it, sir?"

"That's right," Harry said.

He left the driver and Todd to their own thoughts; he had sufficient to keep him busy.

It was really going to happen, or so it seemed. After so many false starts, he was actually going to get married. Or at least, engaged. But he did not suppose Cynthia Bromwich was the sort of woman to renege – or allow him to do so – certainly not once the engagement was announced; that would mean to be humiliated, and she would never accept that.

Thus he would be married. To a woman he did not love. Cynthia had accepted that, but she still wanted him as a husband. Marriage, like all of life to someone like her, was a great and amusing game she played with her friends. See what I've got! And in fact, given the accelerating egalitarianism that was sweeping the country as the aristocracy lost both its money and its prestige with every generation, there was no more prestigious catch than a VC – save perhaps for a royal prince, and at this moment unmarried royal princes, at least of the British House, were non-existent.

She also had the reassuring confidence that they would fall in love in the course of time: she had the beauty, the sexuality, the allure of rank, and the money that went with it; he had the looks, the sexuality, the allure of fame, and the reputation that went with that. Besides, she and her ancestors had always lived in a society where arranged marriages were the norm rather than the exception; that she had arranged her own was an aspect of her forceful personality.

He sincerely hoped she was right about the future. Perhaps she was, from her point of view. So why was he doubting? He could not possibly suppose he was in love with Jutta Hulin – or MacLeod, as she was now calling herself. She was a dream, an eternal pin-up to be kept on the inside of one's bathroom door – save that as he didn't have a pin-up, her memory would undoubtedly fade.

Belinda? He had never loved Belinda: he had been seeking security. Yvonne Clearsted, or Veronica Sturmer? The first, definitely not. Veronica . . . she had always been too ambivalent, about so many things. Deirdre Hale? She too was a dream, with more substance because he had, once, held her in his arms. But perhaps for that reason the dream of Deirdre was less compelling than the memory of Jutta.

The fact was, he had never actually been in love with anyone, and Cynthia was certainly the most enthusiastic as well as the best bet. He needed to get on with it.

Another butler – looking remarkably like Perryman – and another footman were waiting to take Harry's bag.

"I need beds for my driver and batman," Harry said.

"Of course, sir. Halliday will show you where to park the car, Mr . . .?"

"Rawlings," Rawlings said.

". . . Rawlings, and then he will bring you and Mr . . .?"

"Todd," Todd said.

". . . Todd, into the servants' hall. If you will come with me, Colonel Curtis."

But Cynthia was already waiting for him, having heard the sounds at the front of the house. "Harry!" She held out her hands.

She was wearing a dress, and her hair was loose; it was the first time he had seen her out of uniform and not naked. She was certainly a lovely woman.

Now she drew him against her for a kiss. "Mumsy and Daddy are in the small drawing room," she said. "Wilkinson, you'll serve champagne."

136

"Of course, my lady."

She held Harry's hand as she drew him into the hall, which was even larger and more crowded with suits of armour, antique weapons, potted palms and paintings than the house in Worcestershire.

"Don't be nervous," she said.

"I am not nervous," he replied, unsure whether or not he was lying.

A footman waited before a pair of double doors, some twenty feet down the hall and at the foot of a large staircase. These he now opened as Cynthia and Harry approached.

"If this is the small drawing room," Harry whispered, "where is the big one?"

"Upstairs, of course."

"Ah, silly of me."

He followed her into the large, over-furnished room, and paused as the couple seated by the fireplace rose and turned to face him.

"Mumsy and Daddy, Lieutenant Colonel Harry Curtis," Cynthia announced. "Harry, Mumsy and Daddy."

Harry advanced again, suddenly remembering that he had quite forgotten to find out the correct way to address an earl or a countess.

"Curtis, eh?" The earl spoke in a bark. He was a big man with very little hair on his head but compensated for that by wearing a walrus moustache. How he came to be the father of someone like Cynthia had to be one of nature's great mysteries. "I knew a fellow called Curtis once. Rode for me."

Harry decided to settle for simplicity. "No relative, I'm afraid, sir."

"You're awfully young to be a colonel," the countess remarked.

Whatever her husband's shortcomings in looks, the Countess of Brentham was very definitely Cynthia's mother – tall, blonde and statuesque. Her features were a trifle ravaged, either by alcohol or by having lived most of her life with the earl – or very probably a combination of both.

"The fortunes of war, ma'am," Harry said.

"I told you all about it," Cynthia pointed out. "Do come in, Wilkinson."

The butler entered, bearing a tray with a champagne bottle and four flutes.

"Celebrating, are we?" the earl inquired.

"Oh, Daddy!" Cynthia said. "Harry and I are going to be married. Remember?"

"What does a colonel earn nowadays?" the earl asked.

"Not a lot, I'm afraid, sir."

"And you're staying in the Army?"

"Yes, sir." Harry did not intend that there should be any argument about that.

"Good fellow."

Harry was totally surprised.

"Do you love her?" the countess asked.

"Very much," Harry said. A white lie, surely.

"She says she loves you. Do you believe her?"

"Yes, ma'am, I do."

"Well, then, you may pour, Wilkinson."

The butler, who had been hovering, obliged, and the earl raised his glass. "My congratulations."

The countess embraced Harry, and her husband shook his hand.

"There," Cynthia said when she and Harry were alone after lunch. "Wasn't that easy?"

"It was certainly surprising," Harry agreed.

As Harry had imagined would be the case, John and Alison Curtis were at once surprised and over the moon. They immediately travelled up to Scotland to be formally presented to the earl and countess. Though they were a little overawed, the meeting appeared to go off very well. Meanwhile the news was leaked to the press, who had a field day with it: "Earl of Brentham's daughter to marry war hero!"

It had been agreed that the marriage would not take place until after the defeat of Japan. There were sufficient details requiring sorting out to make the delay almost essential – such as where they were going to live.

Harry's quarters at the training camp, while amply big enough for two – previous commandants had been married – were not really of a very comfortable, much less luxurious, standard. The countess came for a visit, and issued a monumental sniff. Whereupon it was decided that one of their wedding presents would be a London flat, so that whenever Cynthia grew tired of a spartan existence she could retire to civilisation.

The earl, of course, was all for having Harry moved to the War Office, but this Harry refused to contemplate – at least by the pulling of strings. "I must be doing something worthwhile," he explained to his future father-in-law.

However, he did go along with the family's efforts to have Cynthia demobbed as quickly as possible, and this was accomplished in the summer. Harry did not feel it would be conducive to discipline for her to share his quarters before they were married, but they managed to spend occasional discreet weekends together at a nearby hotel; he reckoned this was all to the good, as it assisted the process of getting to know each other.

It was also embarrassingly necessary to buy her an engagement ring. "I'm terribly sorry," he said. "But that's as much as I can afford."

Cynthia held out her arm and surveyed the rather small diamond solitaire. "I think it's *lovely*," she declared. "I shall wear it always."

She remained enthusiastic and loving. Her only irrationality had to do with money. Her father, having discovered Harry's salary, determined to continue and indeed increase the allowance he had been paying her since she had joined the Army; this tripled their joint income. He could not complain of her desire to party wherever and whenever possible, even if – having been in the Army and at war since the age of eighteen – it was an aspect of life in which he had never indulged and knew nothing about. He accepted he would have to learn, just as he accepted Cynthia's desire to show him off to her friends; thus whenever he had a proper leave they went down to London together to attend some bash or other, and he allowed himself to be fawned over by admiring females – nearly every one of whom possessed a title.

As these jaunts to London meant that they could share the

Brentham town flat as well as go flat-hunting for themselves, he actually found them enjoyable, although quite as exhausting as a Commando field exercise. They also helped him to pursue what had become his principal short-term aim in life: to make himself fall utterly and irrevocably in love with Cynthia.

He understood that this was not a course of action that would appeal to any psychiatrist – but then, very little of what he had done in his brief career could possibly bear psychoanalysis. Loving Cynthia was necessary, and it should have been easy. She had absolutely everything going for her, from her magnificent body, to her flowing hair, to her total abandonment in bed, to her utter disregard of convention. She was amazingly erudite, having had the best of governesses – probably knew as much military history and as much about military procedures as he did himself – and withal possessed a charming sense of humour and a wicked laugh. She was totally generous, and never had a bad word to say of anyone, and to both his pleasure and relief she seemed to enjoy the occasional weekend in Frenthorpe, making fast friends with Paul when he came home to be demobbed.

So why did he still have reservations? Possibly because he had the feeling that he was a new toy, plucked off a shelf in a shop and loved with the adoration of a child. An adoration that couldn't possibly last.

Far more difficult, and perhaps a contributory factor to his general feeling of malaise, was coming to terms with being at peace. No doubt almost every man and every woman in uniform found this difficult after so long at war. Suddenly to have to replace wanton destruction and in many cases wanton waste with a miserly hoarding of what resources were left and still available would by itself have been a traumatic turnaround. In the case of the front-line fighting man, the awakening every day having no longer to wonder if it was to be his last – or even more disturbing, how many men he would have to kill that day – was yet more difficult. And in the extended case of the spearheads – men who had been thrown behind the enemy lines to kill and be killed in the name of furthering the Cause – it was well-nigh impossible.

He supposed he was one of the lucky ones, in that the severance was not complete. He was still in uniform, still a

Commando, still training men for the next battle, should it ever come. Yet he still had nightmares. He had never been aware of fear during the War itself. Now he knew fear, in retrospect, of what he had been, what he had done.

Moods like that made the comfort of Cynthia's arms the more necessary, the more consoling.

Letters of congratulation poured in, most of them envious. Yvonne Clearsted – she was now Yvonne Robinson – wrote to say how happy she was for him; the paper was almost turning green before his eyes. Belinda Forester wrote waspishly – especially when referring to her replacement. Even the Greek girl Harry had rescued from Spetsos, Zoe Konikos, wrote – but hers was a genuine letter of congratulation.

In the late summer, he also heard from Harbord:

I think I can claim a fair measure of success.

Johann Hulin is living peacefully and farming in the Austrian Alps. Predictably, he claims to have been forced into joining the Nazi movement. He reported his wife missing in August of last year, but with the collapse of the Reich very little was done about it. Hulin seems to have advertised for news of her, and on obtaining no response, he has applied to have her declared legally dead. This is still before the courts, and very probably they will make him wait the full seven years. However, he has accumulated another woman, who lives with him on the farm. Presumably he means to marry her in the course of time.

Now for the wife. Jutta Hulin, as you know, joined up with the Italian partisans, and either with or without their help made her way south. Arrested, presumably because Italian was clearly not her mother tongue, she was placed in a DP camp, but because of her nursing background was put to work in the local hospital. There she met a South African doctor named MacLeod, an army surgeon. When the Italian front collapsed, MacLeod applied for demobilisation, to return to Johannesburg and resume his career. With him went his new wife, Jutta Hulin. You will of course note that this marriage took place before she went to South

Africa, not afterwards. The marriage is thus bigamous, but that is known only to her, you, and me; I very much doubt that she ever told her new husband about it.

So there it is. Your Jutta may have been a naughty girl, but she has done nothing worth pursuing, from my point of view. I'm sure you agree. I am therefore destroying the file.

Oh, by the way, congratulations on your amazing stroke of luck. You must have been born under a four-leaf clover.

So there it is, Harry thought. As long as her husband never catches up with her, she should live a long and . . . unhappy life? Judging by her letter, MacLeod was not measuring up. Or perhaps measuring up too well. But that could very well be piqued-wife speak. And that had to be her affair. It was his business to measure up to Cynthia's requirements.

Colonel Harry Curtis, VC, DSO, MC and Bar and Lady Cynthia Bromwich were married in Westminster Abbey on the twenty-first of October 1945. It was a splendid occasion, with even a couple members of the Royal Family present, and a huge list of other guests. The happy couple left the church beneath an arch of drawn swords held by officers of the Commando Brigade, and the reception was held at the Savoy Hotel.

As foreign exchange was still a problem, they honeymooned in the Bahamas, before returning to fall into a routine. Cynthia was now out of the Army, and she found life in a remote part of the Highlands very boring. Thus she only spent one week in four with Harry, while he managed one weekend in four in London, where she was refurbishing the flat the earl had bought for them. This was costing a fortune, but Daddy was paying, and Harry was in fact quite happy with the arrangement; Cynthia was an exhausting lover, and when they were together required servicing at least twice a night. This was not altogether a good mix with the rigorous training he undertook daily with his men, nor with the predicted sudden and violent attacks of debilitating ague, which happened about once a month.

He was already feeling the dead hand of boredom and frustration that is a soldier's lot in peacetime, accentuated by the very visible decline of Great Britain as a world power. The nation was on the verge of bankruptcy, rationing continued, every requisition for *matériel* had to be argued over the telephone and even then he received only half of what he required for the proper training of his people. Even worse was the fact that the British Army was still engaged on quite a large scale in various parts of the world, either on policing duties or sitting in western Germany glaring to the east. Neither of these occupations greatly appealed to him, but they had to be better than commanding a training camp, and if the rumours were true that there was every possibility of a war with Soviet Russia in the near future, he wanted to be in the front line.

Apart from training and occupying Cynthia's time he learned to drive a car; very necessary, as Cynthia's wedding present to him was an Alvis coupé, an enormous glitter of a machine.

In the summer of 1946 she announced that she was pregnant. Harry was both delighted and relieved – he had begun to wonder if his wartime activities, and/or his malaria, had done for his virility. Cynthia was also pleased – and, he thought, relieved – and their respective parents were delighted; the earl insisted on doubling Cynthia's allowance, which was embarrassing but not to be refused.

Cynthia found pregnancy irritating, as it soon precluded balls and riding, but her essentially sunny disposition kept her reasonably happy – although she did get her father to pull the necessary strings to double Harry's time off so that he could be with her in London. The pregnancy itself was without problems, and a baby boy was duly born in the spring of 1947. They named him Julian, after some ancestor of Cynthia's.

The arrival of the child further complicated their to-and-fro lifestyle, and early in 1948 Harry reckoned he had done his bit as a training commandant and sought an interview with Bannon, who was now a major general.

"Don't you reckon I've served my time?" he asked.

Bannon gave one of his infectious grins. "You've been a very good boy. We must see about getting you a leg-up. Brigadier Curtis, eh? I'll bet that'd please the little lady. Not to mention father-in-law. He's been dropping some pretty heavy hints around Whitehall."

"I'd rather have a battalion somewhere."

"What, abandon Lady Cynthia?"

"If it was Germany, we could virtually keep up the same arrangement as we have now. And if this rumour about the Russians acting up over Berlin is true, that's where I'd like to be."

"Forget it, Harry. If there is to be a showdown over Berlin, it'll be settled by a nuclear exchange."

"You can't be serious."

"That is current perceived thinking. We certainly haven't the men or the equipment to match them on the ground – even with you in our front line, if you'll excuse a very bad joke. But I agree you've been at the camp long enough. Have you ever thought of a secondment? Just as a temporary measure, of course."

"Secondment to what?" Harry was immediately suspicious; he had no desire to return to the Guards and square-bashing in front of Buckingham Palace.

"Ah. Well . . ." Bannon looked embarrassed. "Technically, it would be a kind of police work."

"Would you mind repeating that?"

"Actually, it's just up your street. Malaya."

"I've never been there."

"But you were anxious to go, back in '45, as I remember."

"That was to fight the Japanese."

"This could be to fight the Communists."

"Come again?"

"To put you in the picture, briefly, most of the underground resistance to the Japanese occupation between 1942 and 1945 was organised and carried out by the Communists. They were very bold, very ruthless, and they suffered horrendous casualties. But they were still there when Japan surrendered, by which time they had created their own agenda: running the country. Now of course this was not what we and, we believe, the vast majority of Malayans had in mind – the majority of the Communists are Chinese. Particularly this was the case with the European, mostly British, rubber growers, who were anxious to get back to the peninsula and resume their business activities just as soon as they could. This they have largely done, protected by such troops as we had available, and by the Malayan Police Force.

"But over the past couple of years our people have inevitably been whittled down, partly owing to economy, and partly because it was supposed that the crisis was over; the Communists seemed to have disappeared. Now it has turned out that they hadn't disappeared at all, but were just taking stock of the situation, and biding their time. Over the past couple of months there have been several attacks on the more isolated rubber plantations, and people are becoming a little agitated about it. Frankly, the police cannot cope, and as most of the veterans who fought under Bill Slim have been recalled and demobilised, our forces there are mainly green conscripts who really know very little about either the jungle or guerrilla warfare, which this situation may well develop into. They need someone both to train them in irregular tactics and to lead them when they have been trained, at least until they can develop a command structure of their own. A circular looking for suggestions arrived on my desk a couple of weeks ago, and I immediately thought of you. I was actually going to send for you when you requested this interview. Interested?"

"No," Harry said.

"Reasons?"

"Firstly, while I may know something about guerrilla tactics, I know absolutely nothing about the jungle. Secondly, what you are really suggesting is that I cease training future Commandos in order to train conscripts; my visit here is to get out of training. Thirdly, I am quite the wrong man for the job. My entire career has been devoted to taking life or teaching others how to do that. I presume that you have no desire to see me roaming around the Malayan Peninsula shooting from the hip. And fourthly, and most important, Cynthia would throw a fit."

"Don't you think she might enjoy it?" Bannon suggested mildly. "Exotic country and all that."

"To my wife, there is only one place in the world worth living in, and that is London. Anyway, there is no way we could contemplate taking Julian, and equally, no way she would contemplate leaving him behind. Even for a limited tour."

"Ah. Well, I suppose you know best. And your other arguments are pretty valid. Mind you, I am sure you could overcome them if you were to put your mind to it. But I am certainly not going to twist your arm. We'll see about getting you a place in town, although I must warn you that sitting behind a desk could be even more soul-destroying to someone like you than training other blokes to do our job. Meanwhile, you'll have to carry on in Scotland until we can find a suitable replacement."

Harry reflected that this was the first time he had ever refused an assignment. But protecting a few rubber planters could not be in the same class as attempting to win a war. He did not even mention the proposal to Cynthia, but he did tell her he had been promised both a transfer to town and a promotion, and she was delighted. His transfer duly came through during the summer, but the promotion was only a half rank to full colonel; he concluded the powers that be had not forgiven him for refusing Malaya.

Cynthia was furious, and wanted to speak to Daddy, but Harry dissuaded her. He was more interested in what was happening in Europe, where the Russians had undertaken a full-scale blockade of Berlin. The British and Americans determined to call their bluff by supplying their half of the city by air, but no one could doubt that the single shooting down of a western aircraft, whether by accident or design, would begin World War III. It was impossible to hope this would happen, but Harry could not prevent the adrenalin flowing.

But the Russians eventually climbed down, and the uneasy status quo of the Cold War was resumed. Harry discovered that Bannon was absolutely correct in his estimation that the War Office could be a soul-destroying place. His principal pleasure now was playing with Julian, as the baby became a little boy. But as he approached his twenty-ninth birthday in the late summer of 1950, he could not help but reflect that the truly important part of his life had been completed by the time he was twenty-five – and that a vast period of nothingness stretched in front of him.

One morning, when he was lying in bed with a considerable hangover after a particulary heavy party, Cynthia returned from the bathroom to lie beside him with her head on his shoulder. This was unlike her, as she was usually an early riser, eager to get on with the day. On the other hand, a great deal of champagne had flowed the previous night.

"Happy, darling?" she asked.

"Oh, yes," he said. At that moment, he was.

"May I ask you a question?"

"Of course."

"Have you ever seen, or heard, from any of those women you knew during the War?"

"What do you mean by ever?" he asked.

She raised herself on her elbow. "What do *you* mean by ever?"

"Well, several old friends wrote to me to congratulate me on my engagement, five years ago."

"But have you seen any of them? I mean, shagged any of them?"

Harry opened his eyes. "Of course I haven't. I'm your husband."

She kissed him. "That's very sweet of you. You'll remember that I did give you permission to get together with any of them, if you wanted to."

"And that was very sweet of you, my darling. But it's not my scene. You're my woman, now and always." Except perhaps in my dreams, he thought.

"You do say the loveliest things." She rolled away from him to lay on her back. "Of course, the permission cuts both ways."

Harry frowned, and turned his head to look at that superb profile. "You'll be telling me next that you're having an affair."

"I would never do something like that without telling you first, Harry."

"Do you think I'd want to know?"

"But you have to know. There can be no secrets between us."

Harry raised himself on his elbow. "Just what are you trying to tell me?"

"That I wish to have an affair."

Part Three
The Tiger

Follow a shadow, it still flies you,
Seem to fly it, it will pursue.

Ben Jonson

A Voice from the Past

S lowly Harry lay down again. He was not at all sure of his feelings. He was not at all sure he wanted to be sure of his feelings – he might do, or say, something stupid.

It was her turn to rise on her elbow. "Now, you mustn't be angry or middle-class about this," she said.

"I am middle-class, darling," he pointed out. "Lower middle-class."

"Nonsense. You have left those roots behind you. I want you to understand."

"Do you think that's possible?" He simply had to treat this situation in as matter-of-fact a fashion as she was doing.

"Of course it is. There has been a tradition in my family, oh, for hundreds of years, that it is a wife's first duty to bear a son for her husband. Once she has done that, she is free to indulge as she chooses. Did you not know that?"

"I have read of it. But that was about a hundred and fifty years ago. Regency times, Regency morals."

"That is what certain historians and sociologists like to think. We do not have to think like them. Now listen, there is no need to be concerned about scandal. There won't be one. I am going to take a holiday in the West Indies. I will go alone because you cannot get away from your Army duties. I will be gone about a fortnight, then I will come back. Baby will be looked after by Nanny. As for what I do on my holiday, that is my business."

"If it is to be that secret, why are you telling me?"

"Because I do not wish us ever to have secrets from each other."

"I see. Am I allowed to know the name of the man? I presume you have already met him."

151

"You're angry."

"Of course I'm angry. I'm bloody furious. You're my wife. And now you say you're going off to play the—"

"Please don't say it, Harry. One should never say things one might regret."

They gazed at each other, then he rolled over, threw her on her back, and mounted her. Neither of them was really ready for it, but she did not fight him, although he thought he might have hurt her.

"Well," she said when he was spent. "I hope you feel better."

"No," he said.

"Well, relieved at any rate. I am going to come back to you, you know. I'm your wife. And besides, I love you."

"But not that much."

"Of course I do. It's just that a girl needs to flap her wings every so often. You'll see, it'll make me appreciate you more."

"And suppose you get pregnant?"

"Of course I'm not going to get pregnant. My name isn't Oxford."

"What do you mean by that?"

"Back in the Regency, there was a woman called Lady Harley. Her husband eventually became Earl of Oxford. She was supposed to be the most beautiful woman in England. She did her duty, and had a child by her husband. Then she had six more, each by a different father; they called the family the Harleian Miscellany. Byron was one of her lovers, but I don't think they had a child together."

"Very amusing."

"It's a true story. But I suppose they didn't know much about protection in those days. I do assure you that the only children I am going to have will be by you. Now I must bath."

"You haven't told me the name of the bloke."

"I don't think I should do that, right this minute. You're liable to go and beat him up, or something." She kissed him and got out of bed.

Harry tried to think. There was so much to think about, and he was so close to an explosion of jealous outrage.

His wife, who, like Lady Harley, could well qualify as being the most beautiful woman in England – all of that warm splendour, going naked into the embrace of another man, who would caress her breasts and her bottom, kiss her mouth and put his hand between her legs . . . He did indeed want to do something drastic – but what?

Act the conventional outraged husband and sue for divorce on the grounds of adultery? He didn't suppose Cynthia would waste her time defending the suit. And where would he be then? Dare he admit, even to himself, that he had got used to the utterly luxurious lifestyle to which he had been introduced, and would hate to give it up? More important, given the earl's influence behind the scenes, it would probably mean that his career would come to a full stop. And most important of all, it would mean cutting himself off from Julian; even if he won the divorce case he couldn't doubt that the Bromwiches would make sure they retained custody of the child.

Well, then, go out and have an affair of his own, as he had been invited to do? His problem was that he had not thought of another woman since the letter from Jutta MacLeod – and that was five years ago now. When he thought of the number of women he had known, in the most Biblical of senses, during the War . . . But he had determinedly turned his back on all of that with the advent of peace.

In any event, he could not just lie here, or sit at his desk, with the knowledge that Cynthia was sharing a bed with another man.

A possible, if no doubt temporary solution did occur to him that morning. He could do nothing about her immediate plans, but when she returned, they needed to get away from her friends and family for at least a little while, so that they could both think and get things straight in their minds. And it needed to be somewhere far removed from London . . .

He went to see Bannon. "As you suggested might be the case, boredom is well on the way to doing what the Germans couldn't over five years of honest endeavour."

Bannon nodded. "Who'd be a soldier in peacetime? You're not wanting out, are you? You will make brigadier, in not more than a year or two, I promise you."

"I am not the least bit interested in whether or not I become a general, Peter, or even Chief of the Imperial General Staff. I want to do something. I've been reading the papers. It seems to me we're not making a lot of progress in Malaysia."

"Progress?" Bannon snorted. "We have a full-scale insurgency going on. However, rather belatedly, we're taking steps to do something about it."

"You mean, strengthening our forces?"

"We have a problem with that. We are trying to improve the efficiency of what we do have."

Harry nodded. "I regret turning that job down a couple of years ago. Is it still going?"

Bannon frowned at him. "You serious?"

"Yes."

"What about wife and child?"

"I assume they'd be perfectly safe in somewhere like Singapore?"

"Ye – es. Singapore, I understand, is a delightful spot. Very civilized. But . . . it's not Mayfair."

"I'm sure she'll get used to it."

"Of course. However, the fact is Harry, time waits for no man."

"You mean the job has been filled."

"I'm afraid it has."

"Anyone I know?"

"I don't think you could have met him. Mike Calvert."

Harry whistled. "Heavy stuff."

"Well, this is heavy business. He's absolutely qualified for the job. As you may know, he was one of Wingate's commanders with the Chindits in Burma during the War. Probably Wingate's most brilliant commander."

"I've read about it. Didn't they use to call him Mad Max?"

"I think they still do call him Mad Max. He's an Asian equivalent of yourself. And he is already a brigadier."

"So I'm out-ranked and probably outclassed, in that part of the world," Harry said. "Do you suppose he'd be interested in an assistant?"

"You wish to go to Malaysia and work under Calvert?"

"Sounds like it might be rather fun."

Bannon stroked his chin. "You know . . . it might work. If we gave it enough publicity, hell, the Commies might just surrender on the spot if they realised they were up against you two. But . . . we'd have to square it with him. It would be a catastrophe if there were a personality clash."

"I don't see why there should be. I've always got on pretty well with my superior officers, don't you think?" He grinned at his superior officer. "But I entirely understand that you have to check with him. I would like to make an official application for the posting."

"Right. The idea is growing on me. I'll see to it right away."

"How long do you expect it to take?"

"Well . . . a few weeks."

"Do you think you could make it three, or just under?"

Bannon raised his eyebrows. "Reason?"

"It's just that Cynthia feels she needs a break and is going out to the Caribbean for a couple of weeks. I'd like to know what's happening by the time she gets back."

"You mean you're not going with her?"

"Lying on a tropical beach isn't really my scene. I'm going to babysit."

"Oh. Right. Well, I'll see what can be done."

Mike Calvert was delighted to be offered the assistance of one of the most famous fighting men produced by the War.

"He wants you just as soon as it can be done," Bannon said. "I'll have to arrange for someone to take over from you at the Office. That done . . . how soon can you leave?"

"Just the moment Cynthia gets back," Harry said.

He didn't doubt there was going to be a scene when she did, but he was intrigued to discover how she would handle it. He was equally intrigued to discover how he was going to handle her return.

He considered it best not to meet her plane, just in case she was travelling with her companion of the past two weeks, and instead remained at the office until she telephoned to announce that she was home.

"Oh, splendid," he said. "I'll be right over. We have a lot to talk about."

"Ah . . ." For a moment she was uncertain. No doubt she had not expected him to be so cheerful. "Yes. I'm sure we do."

She had just bathed and was wearing a dressing gown; Julian was out walking with Nanny.

"That has got to be about the most exhausting flight in the world," she complained. "I have never been able to sleep on an aircraft." She held out her arms for an embrace, which he gave her willingly enough.

"At least your next long trip will be by sea," he said.

She pulled her head back. "Are we going somewhere?"

"Singapore."

She gazed at him for several seconds, while her hands slowly slipped from his shoulders. "I have not the least desire to go to Singapore."

"To tell you the truth, neither have I. But . . . duty calls."

Cynthia stepped away from him and sat on the bed. "You are being sent to Singapore?"

He nodded. "I am being seconded to the forces there. We seem to have an emergency on our hands."

"How long is this business supposed to take?"

"How long is a piece of string? Until one comes to the end. That is, until the emergency is officially over."

"Hasn't it already been going on for some time? Weren't you offered this position two years ago?"

"That's right. I declined it then because we were newly married, and Julian had just arrived. But I really don't think I can use that excuse again."

"You mean Julian and I were an excuse?"

"You were a reason for not obeying a command. It's not something I mean to make a habit of."

"If this 'emergency' has been going on for two years already, it could go on for several more."

"I'm afraid it could. Although we shall try to end it as rapidly as possible."

"Will there be home leave?"

"I'm sure there will, from time to time. Subject to the situation, of course."

"Which means, as long as there is an emergency, there won't be any. I really do not think it would be a good idea for you to accept this posting, Harry."

"I already have accepted it. And it'll be fun. You'll love Singapore."

"You expect me to go as well?"

"Well, of course. That's what I meant when I said you'd be taking a long sea voyage."

"And Julian?"

"He'll come with us. It's not as if, at his age, it'll interfere with his schooling."

She stood up, took off her dressing gown and began to dress, slowly. "I am not going to Singapore," she said. "Neither is Julian. My God, that is virtually the end of the earth. Rain and bugs and disease. It is out of the question."

"Oh," he said. "I am very sorry about that. Well, it looks as if we shall have to be separated for a while."

She turned to face him. She had put on her knickers and was fastening her bra. "Harry, I have asked you to refuse this assignment."

"And I have explained that I cannot."

"You mean that you *will* not."

"Darling, I am a fighting soldier. You knew that when you married me. Now I have been ordered to return to the front line – even if I do not imagine there will be much fighting involved. I am certainly not going to decline."

"I could ask Daddy to have the order rescinded."

"That would make me very angry indeed."

"I see. You mean you wish to go."

"Darling, I have to go. That is what I have been trying to tell you for the last ten minutes."

"Leaving Julian and me behind."

She sat at her dressing table and began brushing her hair.

"I have no desire to leave you and Julian behind. I have made all the necessary arrangements for you to come with me."

"And I have said that I do not wish to go."

"Well, I suppose in this day and age I cannot force you."

"What exactly does that mean?"

"That as I said, it looks as if we are going to be separated for a while."

At lunch she said, "I think I'll take Julian up to Scotland for a visit with Mumsy and Daddy. There is no need for you to come."

"I see. Do you wish me to be here when you come back?"

"That is up to you. This is your home. When are you intending to leave for the Far East?"

"At the end of next week."

"Then I must try to be back by then, to say goodbye."

Cynthia did not call him on her arrival in Scotland, but, predictably, two days later the earl rang up. "Harry, my boy!" he boomed.

"Good morning, sir. I assume Cynthia and Julian arrived safely?"

"Oh, yes. Oh, yes. What's all this about you going off to the Far East?"

"Duty, sir. It's to do with this Malaysian insurgency problem."

"Isn't that rather like sending a sledgehammer to crush a nut?"

"There appear to be a great number of nuts, sir."

"Ha ha. I suppose you know that Cyn is deucedly upset."

"I am sure she'll get over it."

"I don't know. She's a damnably determined girl. She regards what you are planning to do as desertion."

"With respect sir, she knew she was marrying a serving officer, who intended to continue serving. If every member of the Armed Services were to be charged with desertion by his wife on being ordered overseas, where would we be?"

"Well . . . harrumph . . ."

"I also think you should know, sir, that I wished Cynthia and Julian to accompany me, and indeed have made all the necessary arrangements for her to do so. If she continues to refuse, I think *I* am the one entitled to accuse *her* of desertion."

"I say, steady on, old man."

"I am just painting the whole picture, sir."

"Harrumph. And you are going. I mean, that is definite."

"That, sir, is definite." Harry said.

John and Alison were also concerned, but in the first instance at the idea of Harry returning to active service.

"Just a few Commie rebels," he explained. "It shouldn't take very long, and it certainly won't be dangerous."

"Still, the Far East . . . What does Cynthia think of it?" Alison asked.

"She thinks it stinks."

"Still, I suppose she'll get used to it."

"She's not coming."

Both his parents gazed at him.

"As I said, she thinks it stinks. I can't force her."

"But . . . how long will you be away?"

"It could be as much as a year."

"You'll have home leave?"

"I shouldn't think so, till it's done."

"You intend to be separated from Cynthia, for a year?" John asked. He was a man who liked to marshal his facts.

"It looks like it."

"But of course she can come out to see you from time to time," Alison suggested.

"I don't think she means to do that, Mother."

"Are you trying to tell us that your marriage is breaking up?"

"Let's keep our fingers crossed," Harry said.

Peter Bannon pulled his nose. "You can always change your mind."

"I am not going to."

"This could turn out badly. I mean, the Bromwiches are no people to upset."

"For me to surrender now would mean that I would become even more of a toy poodle than I have been for the last five years."

"A toy poodle? You?"

"Me. So, I shall not be needing those other berths."

Bannon sighed. "You do realise that this business may take a little while."

Harry nodded.

"And you reckon she'll be waiting for you when you come back?"

"Now that I really couldn't tell you."

Bannon sighed again.

"I have the list here, sir," Todd said. "Anti-malaria inoculation, anti-tetanus inoculation, smallpox vaccination . . . They start tomorrow."

"What about the tropical gear?"

"That arrives tomorrow too, sir. I must say, I'm looking forward to this."

"That's because you're not married," Harry suggested.

"Well, of course it makes it easier, sir. I can understand how distressing it must be to leave the lady behind. And the boy."

"Yes," Harry said. "Joe, I want a woman."

"Sir?"

"I wish to have sex. I have not had a woman for over a month, and I'm feeling lonesome. Will you arrange it, please?"

Todd gulped. "Here, sir?"

"No. I don't think that would be a good idea."

"Yes, sir. I know of a very good house . . ."

"Not that, either," Harry said. "Would you believe that I have never been to a brothel, Joe? I would like you to arrange the woman, and book us into a discreet hotel somewhere. And Joe, I do not wish to contract syphilis or even the clap. She must be absolutely clean."

"Yes, sir. Have you any preference as regards nationality or colouring?"

"Yes," Harry said. "I would like her to be English, as small as possible, and with black hair."

He had no idea what Todd had told her, but the young woman was very nervous. She was already in the room when Harry arrived, opening the door at his knock and peering at him anxiously.

He was wearing civvies, and he knew she would only have been given his first name. "I'm Harry."

"Oh. Yes. Mr Todd told me." She stood back and allowed him to enter. Her hair was certainly black, although her eyes were blue, so possibly she had dyed it. For the rest she fulfilled his requirement of being as opposite to Cynthia as was possible; she was hardly more than five feet tall, and very slender.

"Just how old are you?" he asked, wondering what Todd had landed him in.

"I am twenty, sir."

"And this is your business?"

"I look after gentlemen, sir."

"I see. Well, let's have a look at you."

She had taken off her coat and was wearing a dress and a cardigan, stockings and high-heeled shoes. "Mr Todd said you'd pay me twenty pounds for the night, sir. And for the room."

"What's your name?"

"Leila, sir."

"Well, Leila, let's begin with a little honesty. Mr Todd has already paid you twenty pounds for your services, and he has already paid for the room."

She bit her lip. "Mr Todd is a friend of yours."

"He is my servant," Harry said.

"Oh, aye. You're a toff, then. I could tell it the minute you walked through that door."

"Well, then, let's be with it."

She gave a little simper and proceeded to undress. But already he knew it was going to be a disaster. Presumably their initial exchange hadn't helped, but he realised that it wasn't going to work in any event. He was still too angry. As he watched her attractively slender body uncovering itself, he knew only an urgent desire to hurt her, beat her, make her cry . . . because he had not been able to make Cynthia cry. And while he had once ordered the execution of a woman, he had never knowingly harmed one for the pleasure of it.

She stood by the bed, hesitating.

"Oh, get in," he said. "Have a good night's sleep." He took out his wallet and extracted a five-pound note, which he unfolded and laid on the bedside table. "Buy yourself a good breakfast."

She was already beneath the sheets. Now she sat up as he went to the door. "You do not like me?"

"I haven't made a decision either way. But I do not *want* you, tonight."

He closed the door behind him.

"Singapore," said Captain Loxton. "There's no finer place on earth."

Harry hoped he was right. It had been a long and thoroughly miserable voyage. His identity had very rapidly become known to the other passengers, and their attention had been as cloying as it had been unwanted. Their approaches had varied, through open hero-worship – as he wore his uniform to dinner his medals and ribbons were there for everyone to see – to a conspicuous satisfaction: "Now we'll show the buggers" – to a determination on the part of the unmarried women, and some of the married ones as well, to have at least a flirtation with the famous soldier.

But by the end of the voyage he had gained a reputation for being taciturn and even antisocial. He was quite willing to admit this was entirely deserved: he was feeling distinctly antisocial.

His brief meeting with Leila had entirely summed up his present position – even if he reckoned twenty-nine was a little early for either the male menopause or a mid-life crisis. The fact was that he, who had lived high, wide and handsome as regards women for all of his adult life, had suddenly run into a brick wall regarding the fair sex. Apart from dreams, the only woman he wished to have sex with was his wife. But he couldn't be sure what would happen the next time he did find himself in bed with her, if that was ever likely to happen – she had not returned from Scotland in time to bid him farewell, which meant that he had not been able to say goodbye to Julian either.

He had forced this situation: in the first place in the hopes that she would accompany him, and that they would be able to resume their romance far away from what he considered the pernicious influences of London society; and in the second that if she refused, she would be the one in the wrong, as he was merely obeying orders – even if he had instigated the issuing of the orders himself. So perhaps he had been successful there; only time would tell. But for the moment he had never felt so wretched in his life.

Thus from his vantage point on the liner's bridge, where he was welcome whenever he wished to escape the attentions of the other passengers, he watched the mainland taking shape behind the myriad islands guarding the Sembilan Strait. The only salvation he could think of was to get to work just as rapidly as possible.

There was land everywhere now. The ship had indeed been close to land ever since she had entered the Strait of Malacca twenty-hour hours ago, with the mountains of Sumatra rising five thousand feet to starboard, and the tangled jungle of Malaysia becoming ever more visible to port.

His war having been fought in and around Europe, and not having travelled extensively with his parents, this was by far the longest voyage he had ever undertaken. It should have been as enjoyable as it would be unforgettable. On this voyage he had seen the Mediterranean for the first time from sea level – and at peace. The Red Sea and the Indian Ocean had all been strange to him, as had Bombay for a brief stopover, and the storm they had encountered south of Ceylon. At least he had not been seasick.

Now he was in the part of the world made famous – to Englishmen – by Stamford Raffles, and equally that unique part of the world which had been the only sizeable part of the British Empire to be lost to an enemy.

"You won't believe this, Colonel, but five years ago this town was a wreck," Captain Loxton said.

There was still a lot of building going on, Harry estimated, judging by the numbers of cranes to be seen, but he didn't know whether those were carrying out repairs or a sign of burgeoning prosperity. "Did you know it, before the War? Before the surrender?" he asked.

Loxton nodded. "The ship I was on then visited regularly."

"And has it changed? I mean apart from the destruction."

"And how. Back in 1939 it was a white man's paradise. Chota

pegs in the club, white-jacketed waiters, natives getting out of your way on the pavements, cute little Chinese girls waiting to be picked up . . ."

"But they're back in control now, aren't they? The whites, I mean."

"Well, yes, they are. But not in the same way. You'll find Chinese and Malays, the more wealthy ones, in the clubs now. You'll find their sons and daughters playing on the next tennis court. I suppose that's inevitable, and it's progress; these people are looking for home rule. But there's more to it than that. They'll never forget the surrender of February 1942. Down to that day, no matter what happened, no one in this part of the world ever doubted that the Brits were the greatest soldiers, the greatest conquerors, the world had ever seen. When you think that something like a quarter of the world's population, principally here in south-east Asia, were kept in order and obedience by a fraction of the UK's population . . . say one million soldiers and administrators and their wives and children making six hundred million toe the line . . . and then, just like that," he snapped his fingers, "eighty thousand odd front-line British and Commonwealth troops surrender to roughly the same number of Japanese. Talk about the world being turned upside down. Even people like me, British born and bred, have got to ask ourselves, where's the spirit gone? You know, Colonel, just about two hundred years ago, Admiral Byng didn't surrender his fleet or any part of it; he merely failed to relieve the Minorca garrison. He was shot. There was a nation just about to embark on empire. Only seventy years ago Marshal Bazaine was put on trial and convicted for surrendering Metz to the Germans – and that at a time when his country was already virtually defeated. But General Percival was patted on the back and told, bad luck, old chap. And he virtually, in a couple of hours, proved to the world that Great Britain was not only a misnomer, but that we were no longer capable of empire."

"You feel strongly about it," Harry remarked.

"So do a lot of people. That's why so many people, me included, are happy to see someone like you coming out here to put things right."

"If you mean my job is to put things right for the Brits, Captain, I'm afraid you're going to be disappointed. I'm here to put things right for the Malays. Hopefully."

The liner anchored off, and was immediately boarded by customs and immigration officers, as well as a horde of reporters, all anxious to take photographs of Harry and fire questions at him.

"I'm afraid I have nothing to tell you," he said. "I am here to learn, and to assist Brigadier Calvert in any way possible. Come to me in a month's time, and I may be able to tell you something worthwhile."

"Will Lady Curtis be coming out to join you, Colonel?"

"Not at this time. As you may know, we have a small child, and we feel that he and his mother are better off in England."

"If I may say, sir, you handled that very well," a voice behind him said.

Harry turned and surveyed the somewhat languid young man, who wore a little military moustache to go with his khaki uniform – which included the ubiquitous shorts regarded as best wear by the British Army in the tropics, and which Harry had not yet adopted – and the three pips of a captain on his shoulder straps.

"Cantrell, sir. I'm on Brigadier Calvert's staff. The brigadier instructed me to meet you and see to your, ah, comfort."

"The brigadier being where?"

"Kuala Lumpur, sir. We'll go up there tomorrow, unless you wish to spend the day in Singapore."

"I wish to join the brigadier just as soon as possible," Harry said.

"Very good, sir. Shall we go ashore?"

"Don't I have to go through customs?"

"Oh, good lord, sir, you're a British Army officer. Can your man look after your gear?"

"If you'll tell him where to take it."

Cantrell gave Todd instructions, and the two officers went ashore through a forest of barges and lighters and native boats.

"Is it always this busy?" Harry asked.

"Always, sir."

"And always this hot?" Harry wiped his neck with his hand-kerchief.

"I'm afraid so, sir."

They arrived at the hotel – thankfully set some distance back from the waterfront – and Harry was shown to an air-conditioned room, which was a relief.

"Now, sir, what would you like to do with the rest of the day?" Cantrell asked.

"I think I would like to have a look at the place," Harry said. "And not just to rubberneck. After three weeks at sea my legs need all the work they can get."

"So give me some idea of the situation," Harry suggested, as the two officers strolled through the old city. It had rained recently, heavily, but now the skies were clear and the heat was sucking the moisture up as a thin mist.

"Frankly, sir, it's a bit of a mess. Up-country, these brigands control a lot of territory. The locals are of course terrified of them – and with reason, given some of their crimes. This means obtaining information is next to impossible, and so is identification. In any village we visit there could be a dozen terrorists, but there is no way of telling who they are when they're in the midst of a whole lot of other Malays or Chinese. There is also the fact that there is a huge body of sympathy for them, and not only in the country. There is considerable support right here in Singapore, as well as in Kuala Lumpur, and in other centres like Penang. You never really know when you meet someone, in the best social circles, whether or not he or she is a secret sympathiser. I'm not saying all of these people are actually Communists. A lot, perhaps the majority, are actually confused nationalists who want the British out so they can run their own affairs, and believe the Commies are their best bet to accomplish that. They really have no idea what they would be letting themselves in for if we *were* to pull out."

"But I assume there is no question of that?"

"I can't answer for the politicians, sir, but the Army certainly isn't thinking of it."

"I'm glad of that," Harry said. "I'd hate to have come all this way for nothing. What do the resident Brits think of it all?"

"Well, sir, I'd have to say that morale is pretty low, even here in Singapore – and this is a long way from any open skulldug- gery. The rubber planters up-country are virtually living in a state of siege, and you can't blame them. Only last week a plantation was overrun and the manager and his wife, as well as one of the staff, were murdered. And we're talking about nasty stuff, especially where the women are concerned. But what is really bothering them is the feeling of uncertainty, of not know- ing what is going to happen. They'll happily stick it out if they feel we – both the Government and the Army – are determined to win this little war. But of course, their fate if we were to pack it in, whether for reasons of economy or political pressure, doesn't bear thinking about."

"I take your point."

"Still, sir, we must look on the bright side. Do our bit. Stiff upper lip and all that. That's what dos like tonight are all about."

"You've lost me," Harry said.

"The reception, sir. At Government House. You're invited."

"Me? I've only just got here."

"Ah, but they knew you were coming. You do have a shell jacket?"

"I do," Harry said. "But I have not the slightest desire to wear it right now."

"You can't refuse an invitation from GH, sir. Terribly bad form."

Harry sighed.

Wearing a shell jacket involved not only wearing his ribbons, but the medals as well. He was relieved to discover that he was not the only male guest with a chestful – but no one else came near in quality.

"Our hero," said the governor, shaking Harry by the hand. "Take good care of him, Cantrell."

"I shan't leave his side for a moment, your excellency. Ma'am."

The governor's lady was stout and wore pearls and was

everything a colonial governor's wife should be. That she was old enough to be Harry's mother did not inhibit her from giving him a roguish smile. "Enjoy yourself, Colonel Curtis," she said. "Circulate. We shall have a talk later."

"I shall look forward to it, ma'am," Harry said, and followed Cantrell into the throng. As the captain had suggested would be the case, it was a very mixed bag indeed, although all the male guests – be they Chinese or Malay or British – wore dinner jackets and black tie, and all the women were also in Western garb. All seemed anxious to meet the famous British soldier, and the introductions and compliments flowed around his head along with Cantrell's warning that any one of the locals he was meeting could be a member of the Communist movement – someone he might, one day quite soon, have to arrest and perhaps hang.

This was a new experience; he had not actually met any Germans or Italians before the outbreak of the War, and thus he had gone into battle against them with total impersonality.

"How long do we have to stay?" he muttered at Cantrell.

"Well, at least an hour."

"An hour?"

"One should actually stay for two, sir. But I shall explain to the Governor's ADC that you have a long and tiring journey tomorrow and need a good night's sleep."

"Good thinking."

"I could also perhaps throw in something about your being a bad sailor, who really suffered on the voyage out."

"Throw in whatever you like," Harry said. "Just get me out of here. If I have to meet many more people my arm is going to fall off."

"There are just a few left, sir. You wouldn't want to disappoint the ladies, now would you?"

Harry followed the direction of his gaze to where a small group of women were sitting together, sipping their champagne and no doubt gossiping. They all appeared to be British, or at least, Caucasian.

He sighed, and accompanied the captain across the room.

"Why, Captain Cantrell," one of the ladies said. "I thought you were never coming."

"Everything comes to she who waits," Cantrell pointed out. "Ladies, may I present Colonel Curtis, First Commandos. Mrs Arkwright, Miss Lund, Mrs Payne, Miss Llewellyn, Miss Halliday, and Mrs Reed."

"Colonel Curtis and I already know each other," Jutta said.

The Affair

Harry had been endeavouring to avoid looking too closely at any of the women, and was thus utterly surprised. But if his memory of Jutta's face had rather faded, composed as it was of fever-ravaged images, he could never have forgotten her voice – even though, in contrast to when they had last met, she now spoke English with apparent fluency.

"How exciting," remarked one of the other women enviously. "Do tell."

"I think he was doing something top secret at the time," Jutta said. "So I do not think I should."

Harry gazed at her. He found it difficult to believe that she was actually sitting in front of him. But now he could take in the shoulder-length auburn hair, the softly contoured but still strong features, the full figure that fitted neatly into the ankle-length pale blue cocktail frock, the high-heeled sandals . . . Again in such strong contrast to his vague memory of her. "Quite a surprise," he said. "But a very pleasant one."

"And for me," she said.

"Well," Cantrell said. "I'm sure you have lots to talk about. Now, Colonel . . ."

"You're absolutely right," Harry said. "Mrs Reed and I do have lots to talk about. You'll excuse us, ladies?"

The remainder of the group exchanged glances. "Of course," someone said.

Harry spotted a vacant table and chairs in a nearby corner. "Let's sit over there."

Jutta got up and crossed the room without a word.

Harry turned to Cantrell. "Perhaps you'd be good enough to find us a couple more drinks," Harry suggested.

"Ah, yes, sir," Cantrell said. "We were going to leave early."

"We may well do so," Harry said. "Just fetch those drinks, there's a good fellow."

Cantrell departed. Harry smiled at the women, and followed Jutta.

What was he feeling? What was he doing? Suddenly treading on air. With what in mind? He had no idea. But she had a lot of explaining to do. Jutta Reed? She was certainly wearing both an engagement and a wedding ring.

She sat down and crossed her knees. He sat beside her. "Until five minutes ago, I did not believe in coincidences."

She smiled. "There are no such things, actually."

"Explain?"

"Your name has been in all the papers recently, how you were coming to Malaysia to help Mike Calvert deal with the Communists. Great Britain's most famous soldier. So I made a point of being in Singapore when your ship docked; I knew there would be a reception for you."

"And you're sufficiently in with the Government House crowd to be sure of an invitation."

"No, no. I doubt they have ever heard of me. But the way things work in the colonies, you see, is that you merely have to call at Government House, sign the Visitors' Book, and leave your card – and you are invited to the next soirée."

"Regardless of who you are? Or who you might be?"

"I think they have the good, old-fashioned point of view that if you have a printed card you must be all right. You're looking very well. When last I saw you, you were very ill."

"And you saved my life."

"Oh . . ." She shrugged, delightfully. "I was saving my own as well, you know. Did you get my letter?"

He nodded. "It offered more questions than answers. Now there are even more. Such as, what happened to MacLeod?"

"We got divorced, when I got together with Patrick."

"Reed?"

"Yes. He's a rubber planter. A wealthy man. Or his parents were, before the War. Since he took over, it's been a matter of rebuilding. But we're getting there."

171

"Where are you situated?"

"In the north. Up from Kuala Lumpur."

"Isn't that Communist country?"

"So they say."

"But you're not scared of being murdered in your bed."

"They'd have a difficult time getting in. Patrick has turned our place into a fortress."

"And you love him madly."

Her gaze was cool. "He has been very good to me."

"Unlike friend MacLeod."

"He beat me."

"I gained the impression, from your letter, that he might. I'm sorry I never replied."

"Why should you? You had your own life to live. And your own beautiful and aristocratic wife to pursue. Which one is she?"

"She is not here. As I think you know, if you have read about my appointment in the newspapers."

Jutta wrinkled her nose, another delicious gesture.

"The reason I never replied to your letter," Harry said, "was because I was still angry that you abandoned me like that."

"I left you in good hands."

"I wasn't thinking of that."

Then what was he thinking of now, he wondered? However much he wanted – needed – to hold this woman in his arms, he had absolutely no right to re-enter her life and perhaps disrupt what appeared to be at least a comfortable marriage.

On the other hand, he reminded himself, it was she who had chosen to re-enter *his* life.

"I think we found a certain empathy," she said. "Created by circumstances, of course. But nonetheless real. It would be nice to think it still existed."

"Yes," he said, and looked up as Cantrell appeared with two glasses of champagne.

"You will inform me, sir, when you are ready to leave," the captain said, obviously put out by this unexpected turn of events.

"Yes, I shall," Harry agreed, and waited for him to retreat into the throng. "I have to go up to Kuala Lumpur tomorrow."

"Why, I am going up as well. Perhaps we could share a compartment."

"You mean you're going by train?"

"Yes. Why?"

"I imagine I'm going by car."

"Oh. Well. Perhaps . . ."

"I can offer you a lift."

"Are you allowed to do that?"

"I'm a great believer in doing anything I choose."

"That must be a very pleasant position to be in."

"Then will you accept? There is so much I want to talk to you about. We haven't even scratched the surface."

"I know. Of course I will accept the lift. But . . . do we have to end the conversation now?"

"I suspect people are beginning to notice that we are having rather a long, private chat."

"But you are about to leave."

"You mean you will have dinner with me?"

"It would be a great pleasure," she said. "If you tell me where you are staying, I will come to your hotel in half an hour's time."

Harry was still not sure what he was doing, what he wanted to happen. There could be no question of what he wanted to do. The thought that after all of these years she might wish it too was overwhelming.

And Cynthia? She had predicted that this situation should arise, purely for her own satisfaction. She had even predicted who it might arise with, without understanding that one of the "old friends" to whom she had so casually referred might turn out to be the one woman he would rank above her. A woman he hardly knew.

As Cantrell was prepared to remind him.

"Mrs Reed is to join us for dinner," Harry said, as they returned to the hotel. "Or rather . . ."

"Of course, sir," Cantrell said. "I shall have dinner elsewhere. May I ask, sir, how well you know the lady?"

"I have known her for six years. Well, in a manner of speaking. Why do you ask?"

"Six years," Cantrell mused. "Then you knew her in South Africa."

"I have never been to South Africa," Harry said. "You still haven't told me what's on your mind."

"Well, sir, if Mrs Reed is an old friend, I would rather not say."

"And I would like you to say."

Cantrell gazed straight ahead. "She has something of a reputation, sir."

"As what?"

"Well, sir, you perhaps know she has married twice?"

"Ah . . . yes."

"As I mentioned, it was in South Africa, and there was a very sticky divorce."

"Sticky in what way?"

"You name it, sir. Wild parties – orgies, if you like – wife-beating, affairs . . . There was even talk of an attempted murder."

"Who attempted to murder whom?"

"I believe the husband – he was a doctor named MacLeod – attempted to murder Mrs Reed. He found out she was having an affair, you see."

"Did the case ever come to court?"

"Yes, it did. MacLeod is now serving a ten-year prison sentence. In a South African gaol. Nasty. But the fact is, most people seem to think Mrs MacLeod, as she then was, was lucky not to go to gaol herself."

"Why?"

"Well, sir . . ." Cantrell flushed. "The man she was having an affair with, he wasn't, well . . ."

"Ah," Harry said.

"He wasn't black, sir. He was what is known as a 'Cape Coloured'. Under the new apartheid laws, that's illegal."

"But she got off."

"No, sir. She fled the country. With this chap Reed, who happened to be there on a visit."

"You mean she's wanted in South Africa?"

"Well, I don't think she'd be wise to go back."

"Anyway, now she's married to this fellow Reed, all's well that ends well."

"Well, sir, there's those who say she only married him for his money."

"That's not a crime. Lots of women do it. And quite a few men," he added thoughtfully. "Thanks very much, Captain. Oh, by the way, I've invited Mrs Reed to have a seat in our car up to Kuala Lumpur tomorrow morning."

Cantrell gulped.

Harry waited in the hotel bar, having booked a table for dinner, sipping a whiskey and soda – something of a relief after all that champagne. He had given Todd the evening off, and did not anticipate an interruption. He had no idea what he was getting himself into, but he was looking forward to it. As he had deduced almost from the moment of their first meeting, Jutta was a woman who both took life as it came and was prepared to take control of it whenever possible. Nor was she averse to sailing close to the wind.

She remained the most exciting woman he had ever met. And if she was disappointing in bed, that might be the only way of getting her out of his system. But he did not think she was going to be disappointing in bed. The disappointment would be if she did not want to go to bed with him.

She was punctual, entering the bar and causing heads to turn.

"Scotch?" Harry offered.

"That would be very nice."

They gazed at each other.

"Do I gather you have been leading an exciting life since last we met?" Harry asked.

"Ah. Someone has been whispering in your ear. I doubt my life has been as exciting as yours."

"You'd be surprised. Since we last saw each other I have not heard a shot fired in anger. I have been totally desk-bound. Which is why I'm here. Utter boredom."

"Even when married to the Countess of Brentham?"

"She's not actually the Countess of Brentham, nor will she ever be."

"And you have fallen out of love with her."

"Faults on both sides. And you?"

"I told you. Patrick has been very good to me."

"Peccadilloes and all? Or doesn't he know about them?"

"He knows most of them."

"But not about hubby number one."

Jutta raised her eyebrows. "Isn't he dead? I thought he was dead."

"He's very much alive. But, having heard nothing of you, he has applied to have *you* declared dead."

"That is the best thing."

"But you're not dead yet. It's a seven-year business. There are two to go."

"Ah. May I ask how many people know about this?"

"Just me. The man who investigated it for me has destroyed the file. At my request."

"So you have me in your power, all to yourself."

"What an entrancing thought. Let's eat."

They sat opposite each other.

"You are very handsome, in your uniform," she remarked.

"And you are very beautiful. In anything."

She made a moue. "I cannot believe you found me beautiful, in the mountains."

"I seem to remember I was pretty scruffy myself. But you . . . I remember you coming up from bathing in that stream as if it were yesterday."

"I did not know you were awake."

"And in your letter, you suggested that you might like to see me again. But I suppose that was a long time ago."

"Six years is not very long. I did wish to see you again. That is why I am here tonight."

"And Patrick? Is there an arrangement, or is this just something you want to do?"

"It is something I want to do. Something I have wanted to do since those nights in the mountains. Would it worry you if there *was* an arrangement?"

"I might be relieved. I would not like to get you into trouble."

"I will not get into trouble."

"Well, then . . . coffee?"

"Yes, please."

They retired to the lounge.

"Will you stay?" Harry asked. "Or would you prefer to go somewhere else?"

"I will stay. Will I be able to see you again, after?"

"I would hope so. But I'm afraid I know nothing of the set-up in Kuala Lumpur, or up-country."

"We have a house in Kuala Lumpur," she said. "I go there about once a fortnight, for shopping. Patrick does not usually come with me."

"Sounds a pretty good set-up. But you do understand that I am here to do a job."

"And for you, the job always comes first. I understand that, Harry. I think the best thing to do is for you to give me a telephone number I can call whenever I am going into town. Then, if you can make it, we will meet. If you cannot make it, well then, there is always the next time."

"You have an organising mind. Is this your training as a nurse?"

"And as a farmer's wife, perhaps."

"Do you still practice as a nurse?"

She shook her head, and finished her coffee. "Shall we?"

He supposed in her own way she was just as masterful as Cynthia. But, in his own way, he was happy to go along with that – at least at this stage of their relationship.

They went upstairs together. The hotel was full, and if the much-decorated soldier and the very attractive woman caused heads to turn, no one attempted to stop them. Harry unlocked his bedroom door and allowed her to enter, then hung the Do Not Disturb sign on the door and locked it.

Jutta stood in the middle of the room, for the first time looking just a little uncertain. Harry stood against her, took her in his arms, and kissed her mouth.

"I have wanted to do that since the first time I saw you," he said.

"But we have kissed before. I kissed you, the night before we reached Italy." She smiled. "You do not remember."

"Sadly, no. What else did you do?"

A faint flush. "I . . . touched you."

"I must have been in a sorry state not to remember that. Are you going to touch me now?"

"If you would like me to."

"I would like you to."

She unbuttoned his jacket. "All these medals."

"Let's get rid of them."

She took off the shell jacket, laid it across a chair, then slid the braces from his shoulders. She then unbuttoned his shirt and laid it beside his shell jacket.

"Shoes first," he commanded, and sat down.

She knelt at his feet to take off his shoes.

"Now yours."

She sat on the carpet and raised her leg. He slipped the sandal from her foot, while looking up the sweep of stocking as her skirt fell back. She lowered her leg and raised the other. This time he slid his hands up the silk, caressing, until she swung her leg away and knelt again, this time between his legs, to unbutton his pants. Then she stood up to draw them right off.

"My turn."

She turned her back on him, and Harry stood up to unbutton the back of her dress and slip the sleeves from her arms. She gave a little shimmy, and the dress slid past her thighs to gather round her ankles. She stepped out of it, and waited for him to lift her slip over her head. He sat down to admire the splendid contours of her body while she knelt again to remove his socks. He reached behind her to unclip her brassiere and softly held her breasts, feeling them swell into his hands.

She gave a little sigh. "You are so very gentle," she said. "Are you also gentle, when you kill?"

"I doubt it," he said, disappointed. "Is that important to you?"

"The contrast is important. Most of the men in my life have been violent. I think they have lacked your confidence."

Happiness restored, he held her close while he slipped his hands into her knickers, both to caress her buttocks and to slip the silk down past her knees. She was doing the same with his drawers.

Had he ever known such rapport, such a feeling of mutual understanding, mutual anticipation, combined with a mutual lack of apprehension of something going wrong? He supposed it would be a cruel, but entirely just twist of fate, that he should finally find the woman he could love above all the others – after they were both irretrievably married to other people.

Was anything ever irretrievable?

"Have you any children?" he asked, when she lay with her head on his shoulder.

The act itself had been almost irrelevant, compared with the stroking and kissing and just holding that had preceded it. They had been so anticipatory that he had been inside her no more than a few seconds before they had both climaxed; the meeting of the minds had extended to the meeting of the bodies.

"No," she said. "But you have."

"A son."

"I know. You must love him very much."

"Loving him is a complication. There are so many complications."

She raised herself on her elbow. "That depends on what you wish to complicate."

"I would like you to lie here, beside me, for the rest of my life."

She lay down again. "I think I would like that too. But you know, seeing that we met only briefly six years ago, we hardly know each other."

"Someone – I think it may have been Evelyn Waugh – once wrote, or said, that to write convincingly about a country, one had to have lived there for either seven days or seven years. I think we're coming up to both."

"And my South African escapades?"

"I have neither prejudices nor any desire to go there. At least while the present government is in power."

"Snap," she said. "How I wish we could just, snap, and have everything we want."

"Can't we?"

"We would need to be very, very sure. And I do not think we can be sure while we are lying naked in each other's arms. Let us

179

leave it till we can meet again. And think about it in the meantime."

He couldn't argue with that. He had come here to do a job, not to get mixed up in what would be a very messy divorce case.

"Would you like me to leave now?" she asked. "It is coming up to midnight."

"Can't you stay a while longer?"

"Of course, if you would like me to."

"I would like to sleep, at least for an hour, with you in my arms."

She switched off the light, and seemed to fall asleep in seconds. Harry soon nodded off as well, enjoying an immense feeling of well-being – whatever the problems that might lie ahead – and was surprised to find himself suddenly awake. Jutta slept on, still huddled against him. He inhaled her perfume, and then another scent. It was not unpleasant, but it emanated from neither the woman nor himself.

He reacted instantly, throwing himself sideways and rolling off the bed, carrying Jutta with him. She gave a startled shriek as she struck the floor with him on top of her.

In that instant Harry's eyes, becoming accustomed to the darkness, made out the shadow above the bed, striking down with tremendous force. Then he was on his feet; he decided against attempting to reach his service revolver, which was in the wardrobe. Instead he seized the bedside lamp and hurled it. The cord came out of the wall with a click and a shower of sparks, then the missive was crashing against the intruder as he turned for another blow with his weapon, which appeared to be a very large knife. He fell backwards, and Harry threw himself across the bed, trying to grapple with his assailant and get hold of the knife arm, but finding his fingers slipping on the oiled skin.

The overhead light came on as Jutta scrambled to her feet and found the switch. Harry gazed at the man who had attacked him. He estimated he was a Malay, a slightly built man wearing only a loincloth but armed with that knife, which had a large and oddly shaped blade. With this he now lunged at Harry again; Harry fell backwards on to the bed, into which the knife sank once more with horrifying force, penetrating the sheets into the mattress.

The man reared upwards for another blow, and Jutta took command of the situation, picking up the straight chair from beside the breakfast table and swinging it with all of her strength. The chair caught the man on the side of the head; he tumbled off the bed and struck the floor with a crash, the knife flying from his hand. Harry threw himself across the bed to pick it up before standing above the intruder, who was lying absolutely still on the floor.

"Shit!" Jutta commented.

That did seem to sum up the situation, Harry thought, glancing from the body on the floor to Jutta, to the open door, to the garments that lay in the doorway, to the people who were very rapidly accumulating in the corridor, and then back to the body. Because it was now just a body – blood was dribbling from the dead man's head.

"Use my dressing gown," he said.

Jutta apparently also realised for the first time that the doorway was crowded. She pulled the dressing gown from the hook behind the door and wrapped herself in it.

"Colonel, sir?" Todd came into the room, blinked at Jutta, and then came towards Harry and the dead Malay.

"Can you get those people away?" Harry asked.

"Colonel Curtis?" An anxious under-manager.

"This man tried to kill me," Harry explained.

"Good heavens! The police . . ."

"Yes," Harry said regretfully. "They will have to be called."

"Colonel?" Cantrell had appeared, in a dressing gown.

"Bit of a mess," Harry said. "Look, can we have the room cleared? We won't touch anything until the police get here."

"Of course. Come along now, come along." Cantrell ushered the onlookers away from the doorway, closed and locked it.

The under-manager was using the phone.

"Are you all right?" Harry asked Jutta, who had remained standing behind the door, no doubt having decided that was the best way of keeping out of the public gaze.

She nodded.

He went to her, took her in his arms; she was trembling. "You're making it a habit," he said. "Saving my life."

She sighed.

"The police are on their way," said the under-manager, importantly. "May I ask exactly what happened?"

"You may ask," Harry said. "Now answer me one. Is there any sign of that door having been forced, Captain?"

"Looks all right to me," Cantrell said.

"And I locked it before going to bed. Therefore he had a key." Harry looked at the under-manager. "What did you say your name was?"

"My name is Clarke, Colonel. Are you suggesting—"

"I am suggesting you go downstairs and find out how this man got in here," Harry said. "The police will certainly wish to know that."

Clarke gulped. "You won't touch anything?"

"I will touch neither the bed nor the body, Mr Clarke. I certainly intend to get dressed, as does the lady."

Another gulp, and Clarke left the room.

Harry looked at Todd and Cantrell. "You two stay here. Jutta, we'll dress in the bathroom." He gathered up her clothes, took his own uniform from the wardrobe, and closed the bathroom door behind them. "I'm most terribly sorry about this," he said. "At the same time, I have to be glad you were here, or I think I'd be a dead man."

"And before then, we were happy," she reflected. "Harry, I don't suppose . . ."

"I'm afraid not."

"Because I have killed a man."

He nodded. "You have nothing to fear, criminally. It was both self-defence and defence of me, and you couldn't possibly have intended actually to kill him, with a chair. But . . ."

"The publicity." She shivered and hugged herself.

"Will it be very bad for you?" he asked.

"I don't know."

"Didn't he accept all the publicity in South Africa?"

"Yes," she said. "But then I hadn't killed a man. And I hadn't committed adultery virtually in public."

He held her hands. "I will stand by you, no matter what. You know that."

She kissed him. "I did not doubt it, Harry. But it will make trouble for you as well."

He grinned. "Some."

There was a rap on the door. "The police are here, sir," Cantrell said.

Harry and Jutta returned to the bedroom, where there waited a very nervous young police officer, a white man, wearing shorts as part of his khaki uniform. With him were two Malay policemen, one a sergeant.

"Colonel Curtis, sir. Assistant Superintendent Whiteley. This is terrible."

"I agree with you," Harry said.

Whiteley gave Jutta an even more anxious glance. "And this is . . ."

"No," Harry said. "My wife is in England."

"I see. May I ask the lady's name?"

"I am Jutta Reed," Jutta said.

"Reed," the Assistant Superintendent said. "Reed. There is a rubber planter named Reed . . ."

"My husband."

"I see," Whiteley repeated, obviously desperately trying to do so sympathetically. "Can you tell me exactly what happened, Colonel Curtis?"

"Very simply, this man gained entry to my room while Mrs Reed and I were asleep, and attempted to kill me. You will note that the door was not forced, which means he had a key. This can only have been provided by a member of the hotel staff."

"Absolutely, sir. We will look into that."

More people arrived – a doctor and various forensic experts. Whiteley gestured Harry and Jutta to one side of the room; Cantrell and Todd followed protectively.

"Now, sir," Whiteley said. "You say you were asleep when this man broke in."

Harry held up his finger.

"I meant, when he entered the room," Whiteley corrected himself. "You were in bed?"

183

"Bed is where I normally am when I mean to sleep," Harry agreed.

"And the . . . ah . . ." Whiteley checked his notes. "Mrs Reed was also in bed? The same bed?"

Harry began to wonder if the young man was more interested in this aspect of the situation than in the attempted assassination. "There is only one bed, Superintendent."

"Quite so. And what happened when this man attacked you?"

"I attempted to resist him."

"And I hit him with the chair," Jutta said.

"Ah. You admit to hitting him with a chair, Mrs Reed?"

"Of course I do. How else was I to save Colonel Curtis's life?"

"Quite. Did you know the dead man? The one you struck?"

"How was I to know him?"

"You had never seen him before in your life?"

"Not that I remember."

"And you, Colonel?"

"I only arrived in this benighted spot yesterday morning."

"I see. Then do you suppose the motive for the attack was robbery?"

"Not unless it is the custom in this part of the world to kill first and rob after. No, Superintendent, I do not believe the motive was robbery."

"Colonel Curtis is here to assist Brigadier Calvert in stamping out terrorism," Cantrell said. "I am sure you know that, Superintendent."

"Then you regard this as a terrorist attack. Doctor?"

The doctor had been washing his hands. Now he returned from the bathroom, drying them on a towel. "The blow on the side of his head, delivered by the chair, carried such force that he died instantly."

Everyone looked at Jutta.

"I only knew that I had to stop him from killing Colonel Curtis," she said.

"Well," Whiteley said. "I will require statements from you both. I think you had better come down to the station."

"Thank you, but no," Harry said. "We will make the statements here and now. We both have a long journey tomorrow, and I intend to use the rest of the night for sleeping."

"Here?"

"It seems as good a place as any."

"But . . . a man has just been killed here."

"I assume you are going to have his body removed."

"The ambulance is waiting downstairs," the doctor said.

"Then I would carry on, if I were you," Harry said.

The doctor looked at Whiteley, uncertainly.

"Well," the policeman said. "I suppose, if you've finished."

"And perhaps you could have someone clean up the mess," Harry suggested to the under-manager, who was still hovering. He then looked at the police officer.

"Ah, yes, I suppose that would be a good idea. Now, Colonel Curtis, Mrs Reed, statements." He was desperate to regain control of the situation.

"Certainly." Harry and Jutta sat at the table, and a constable produced paper and pens. Harry could tell that Jutta was in an extremely upset state, and not only because she had just killed a man, but she returned his smile and wrote calmly enough.

"There we are," Harry said. "Nothing much, I'm afraid."

The dead body had been removed, and two waiters were busily scrubbing the floor clean.

"As I said, I'd like to get some sleep."

"It's very irregular," Whiteley complained. "But in view of who you are, sir . . . You won't be leaving Singapore in the near future?"

"I am leaving Singapore at dawn tomorrow morning."

"Ah . . ." Whiteley looked at Jutta.

"Mrs Reed will be leaving with me."

"I don't think I can permit that, sir. I mean, a man is dead . . ."

"Are you charging Mrs Reed with murder?"

"Well, no, sir, as it seems to have been self-defence."

"Quite. I will take responsibility for Mrs Reed, and will deliver her to you here in Singapore when and if she is required."

"Ah . . . well . . ." Whiteley looked at Cantrell, hopefully.

"If that is what the colonel wishes," Cantrell said.

"The Tiger," muttered the officer.

185

"What did you say?" Harry asked.

"Ah . . ." Another glance at Cantrell.

"That's what the local papers have been calling you, sir," Cantrell explained. "When they learned you were coming out."

"Great Britain sends its Tiger to Malaysia," Whiteley explained. "I do apologise."

"I regard it as a compliment," Harry said. "Thank you, Mr Whiteley."

The policemen left.

"If there is anything I can do," Cantrell ventured.

"You've been very supportive," Harry said. "I won't forget it. Now try to get some sleep."

"If I may recommend, sir . . ."

"Yes?"

"Well, it might be a good idea to make a slight change to our plans, and instead of leaving at eight as we had intended, leave at six. The press, you understand."

"Good thinking. Can you get hold of our driver?"

Cantrell nodded. "Six o'clock, then."

"Make it five thirty," Harry said. "We have to go to Mrs Reed's hotel to pick up her things."

The door finally closed and locked, Jutta sat on the bed.

"Did you know of this Tiger thing?" Harry asked.

"I read it."

"Then you should be known as the Tigress."

She shuddered. "What is going to happen?"

Harry sat beside her. "I do seem to have this knack of upsetting your life. What would you like to happen?"

She raised her head.

"Oh, quite. But that is going to take quite a lot of doing."

"I cannot possibly . . . well . . ."

"Ask me to divorce my wife. I'll have to think about that."

"Will she find out?"

"Darling, this is going to be in all the Malayan papers within twenty-four hours, and all the UK papers within a week."

"And you will be in the most dreadful trouble."

"I don't anticipate being in any trouble at all. It's you I'm worried about. What will Reed's reaction be?"

"He won't be pleased. I told him I had finished with . . . well, having affairs. I had no idea you were ever going to reappear."

"But you intend to go back to him."

"What else do you recommend?"

He sighed. "Just remember, I am always there, if you need help."

"When you *are* there," she said. "You are here to work."

"Would it help if I came with you to see Reed?"

"No," she said. "Let me see him first."

They looked at each other. "Would you believe I have never killed a man before?" she asked. "No matter how often I have felt like it."

"You were saving my life, as is your habit."

"Yes. I would do that again. Harry . . ." She lay down.

He put his arms round her. "Regrets?

"No regrets," she said. "Only happy memories."

The Plantation

T hey slept in each other's arms and rose at five, while it was still dark. Todd produced some breakfast, keeping an admirably straight face.

"What's it like downstairs?" Harry asked.

"There are some people, sir."

"Any cameras?" Jutta asked.

"I'm afraid so, madam."

"Hardly matters," Harry pointed out. "As they already know who we are." He finished his coffee. "All set?"

Jutta nodded; she was of course still wearing her party frock, and had no hat. Harry had changed into his khaki working uniform. They went down in the lift to find the lobby crowded with policemen as well as reporters and cameramen, and, it seemed, most of the hotel staff. Questions were shouted at them, but they gave no answers, turned their heads away from the flash bulbs, and gained the safety of the command car. Several of the media had cars of their own and followed them to Jutta's hotel, where there was a fresh crisis. The management did not yet know what had happened, but were just becoming agitated at one of their female guests staying out all night. Harry and Cantrell coped with the shouted questions while she ran upstairs to collect her suitcase.

"Whew," Cantrell commented when they were finally driving across the causeway in the cool of the dawn. "Quite a night."

"What time will the news reach Kuala Lumpur?"

"I should think the basics, that you were attacked in your hotel bedroom, are already there and will be in the morning papers. The more responsible editors will seek confirmation of the, er, details, before printing them."

"What do you reckon?" Harry asked Jutta.

"I think I should get home just as fast as possible. We do not have a paper at the plantation, but Patrick listens to the news on the radio."

"You won't make it before this evening," Cantrell said.

"I know." She was keeping remarkably cool.

Harry held her hand and surveyed the country through which they were passing, utterly strange to him but in which he was going to have to campaign. He looked at the jungle, thick to either side of the road and in places encroaching right up to the embankment. He reckoned it would be possible for quite a large body of armed men to be concealed in that bush, within easy rifle shot of the road. But Cantrell did not appear unduly alarmed, and the driver was going as fast as he could – which, however, was seldom more than forty miles an hour, as the road was very bad.

Every so often they drove through a village, scattering chickens and causing dogs to bark, while men, women and children left their houses to gaze at them. Some waved. Others glowered. Then there was a town, and soon another. At the second of these they stopped for an early lunch.

"How soon will we see each other again?" Jutta asked when Cantrell thoughtfully left them alone before resuming their journey.

"That's a difficult one. I'm here to work, and I imagine Calvert already has something for me. But if things get nasty at the plantation, you come into town and I'll take care of it."

"You were going to give me a phone number."

"I will, as soon as I get one. In the meantime, if you need to be in touch, call Army Headquarters; they'll put you on to me. I want to hear from you, anyway, about how things are at the plantation."

She nodded. "What about the inquest?"

"We've a day or two. I have to discuss the matter with Calvert before I can give any answers on that."

"I am in your hands," she said.

"I'm sorry about that."

"I'm not. I would rather be in your hands than anyone else's."

* * *

They reached Kuala Lumpur in the middle of the afternoon.

"How far to the plantation?" Harry asked.

"Only another fifty miles."

"Good road?"

"As good as any."

"Will you make arrangements for Mrs Reed to be taken home, Cantrell?"

"Yes, sir," Cantrell said, a trifle doubtfully.

Half an hour later Harry was shown into the brigadier's office.

"Harry Curtis! This is one of these occasions one never really expects to happen." Mike Calvert was a very big man, good-looking in a forceful manner; his handshake was every bit as strong as Harry's. "Welcome aboard."

"Even if . . .?"

"Even if. At least you got the bastard. Oh, his friends will squeal, but it seems an open-and-shut case. And it announces to the Commies that you're no man to be trifled with."

"It wasn't me who actually did him, you know."

Calvert gestured Harry to a chair, waved his hand, and the Malay orderly left the office.

"Smoke?"

"I don't, thanks."

"I wish I could say the same." The brigadier filled his pipe. "I have only the sketchiest details, so far. Is the lady anyone I should know?"

"I'm afraid she is – Jutta Reed."

"Ah! But you only landed in Singapore yesterday . . ."

"Mrs Reed saved my life during the War, when I was on a mission behind enemy lines."

"The plot thickens," Calvert remarked. "So you knew her fairly well already."

"Fairly. I hadn't seen her since August 1944. But I had kept track of her – although I didn't know she was here."

"And when you saw her again it all came flooding back."

"I'm afraid it did."

"Do you know Reed?"

"I didn't know he existed, before last night."

"Hm."

"Is he likely to be a big problem?"

"To you, personally, I have no idea. In the larger scale, yes. I'm afraid the whole thing rather stinks. How much do you know about what's happening here?"

"Very little. I understand the insurgents are mainly Chinese, or Chinese led, and that they have a stranglehold on the villages."

"Succinctly put. I have to say that I'm surprised, and a little disturbed, that they tried to get at you in Singapore; I had no idea they were operating that far south. You'd better look at this." He got up and led Harry to a large map of the peninsula pinned to the wall. "Their concentrations are mainly here, in these hills, which are known as the Cameron Highlands – from whence they can disperse, when the need arises, into this rather empty and distinctly rough country to the north-east. What we have been doing so far has been standard police procedure. There is a crime, and we go charging after it. There is never any evidence, except perhaps a dead body or two, never any witnesses, and never anyone to arrest – although for all our people know the perpetrators might be standing only a few yards away. So they search the village, and find nothing, post a few notices, and come home. This is the situation we have to overturn."

He returned to his desk.

"I regard this – I was brought in to regard this – as no longer a police matter. It is an insurgency, and our main business is to drive these people out of business. If that means extirpating them, well, they started it. Destroying them is going to be your business. Providing them to you for their destruction will be mine. Are you with me?"

"Certainly. I would say you have the more difficult task."

"I have some ideas. What I intend to do is set up what we shall call 'safe' areas – villages or groups of villages which will be heavily protected. Now I know that with the Commies able to come and go as they choose we are not going to be able to keep them out, unless we fortify every village and stop the people working in their fields, which obviously isn't on. So my second idea is the use of old-fashioned propaganda – only we will call it 'hearts and minds'. We are going to re-educate these people to accept, to believe, that we are the good guys, the hope of their futures, and that if they put their trust in us, not only will we protect them but with their help we will put an end to the insurgency."

Harry pulled his nose.

Calvert grinned. "So it's a long shot. But I've worked and fought amidst these people for the last ten years, all but. We aren't talking about your politically indoctrinated Nazi. All these people want to do is live and die in peace. They believed in us before the War – or at least in our ability to let them do those things. Now, for the last five years or so, they have had the Commies telling them that our day is done, that we couldn't protect them from the Japanese, that we pulled out of India with our tails between our legs, and that we are going to get out of Malaysia just as soon as it can be done. We have to make these people believe that simply isn't true, that Great Britain is just as powerful now as it was in 1939, and that we are here to stay."

"And is that true?" Harry asked.

"Whether it is or not, Harry, you and I have got to believe it – because if we don't, nobody else will. Anyway, that's not your concern. Your business is to kill Commies. My idea is that when they find getting into the villages becoming difficult, and when we begin to glean some more information as to their movements, they will either launch a major offensive or regroup in the Highlands with an offensive in mind. That is when you'll hit them. I am also hoping to lay on some aerial reconnaissance to help us. You with me?"

Harry nodded. "What have I got?"

"Let's call it a battalion. I have raised one force already, what I have called the Malay Scouts. We are now in the process of raising another, which I think could appropriately be called Curtis's Scouts, as you will be commanding them."

"Regulars?"

"Ah . . . not entirely. About half will be local recruits. But these are men who know the country and the enemy."

"Can they be trusted?"

Calvert gave one of his disarming grins. "I'm relying on you to make sure they can be, Harry. This is not a tea party. You have virtual powers of life and death – certainly when you are in the field. Does that cause you a problem?"

Harry thought of Lawton. "No."

"I didn't think it would. As soon as you have completed training – that is, hopefully in a week or so – I'll have you meet your officers and men. We'll also take a recce out to one of the villages we're working on."

But thinking of Lawton had brought Harry's mind back to square one, as it were. "We are about to carry the war to the enemy," he said. "Therefore we have to expect that he will attempt to bring the war back to us."

"That's the idea. It will give us – you – more chance to kill him."

"It will also give him more chance to kill us. Have you any plans for the evacuation of all white people from the bandit area?"

"We have advised it. We cannot force them to leave. But a good number already have."

"But not the Reeds."

"No," Calvert said. "I was going to get back to them. I'm not quite sure how to put this. But I have a sneaking feeling that Patrick Reed isn't altogether on our side. And that probably goes for his wife as well."

"Would you mind saying that again?" Harry asked.

"I know it's not something you want to hear, Harry. But it's been on my mind for some time. Almost since I got here, in fact. As I said, we made a big noise that I was here to stamp out the Communists, and an even bigger noise that you were coming to help me do that. Thus we advised those planters living in the danger areas to evacuate until the emergency was over, and as I said, quite a few did that. Reed didn't."

"Jutta said he'd turned their plantation into a fortress."

"That's true enough. But there hasn't been any fortress around here the Commies haven't attacked and managed to get into . . . save Reed's plantation."

Harry frowned.

"And then, his wife makes a special trip down to Singapore to meet you, and on that night someone tries to kill you. Their intelligence work has to be pretty good to have established where you were staying so rapidly. Would I be out of court to ask if you invited the lady to come to you?"

"Well . . . yes, I did."

"But she did not accompany you from Government House to the hotel."

"No. She said she had to go back to her hotel first."

"You see what I mean."

"With respect, sir, I cannot accept that. You're forgetting that she killed the would-be assassin."

"Yes," Calvert said thoughtfully. "However, I do think you need to tred carefully in that direction. And I am not talking about moral issues."

"I will."

"Right. Now the first thing you must do is get acquainted with the jungle."

"I'd rather meet my people first."

"That wouldn't be a good idea until you're up to it. Don't get me wrong, Harry. Everyone knows you're just about the biggest hero thrown up by the War, and your men will respect you for that. But all men need to be sure that their commanding officer knows what he's about. In Europe, none of the men who followed you had any doubts about that. This is new ground for you. Quite a few of the men you will need already have experience of the jungle. Have you any experience of it?"

"I'm afraid not."

"Thus you'll appreciate that you have to have *some* knowledge of what you are leading your men into before you can lead them into it, if you follow me. You'll have to put in a week's intensive training. This training normally takes several months. Will that be a problem?"

"No, sir."

Calvert grinned. "I didn't think it would. Very good. I'll put you in the care of Sergeant-Major Cullinan. Like me, he's a veteran of Slim's campaigns. What he doesn't know about the bush isn't worth knowing."

"Just the two of us, sir?"

"Your man had better go with you."

"And in the meantime . . ."

"If anything crops up I'll handle it."

"I was thinking of the Reeds."

"You mean, if he comes gunning for you, or if she comes running to you for help? I'll handle that too, if I can. Dismissed, Colonel. Cantrell will show you to your quarters."

Harry stood up. "And the other matter?"

"I will endeavour to have it sorted out. You'll be kept informed."

"Thank you, sir." Harry saluted, not sure if he had actually been made welcome or not.

But then Calvert gave one of his disarming smiles. "I am glad to have you aboard, Harry. Very glad."

The Army had taken over several houses, and it was to one of these that Cantrell drove Harry. There was an armed MP on the door, and security was tight; both officers had to identify themselves. But Todd was already installed in one of the six apartments into which the house was divided.

"Looks a bit of all right, sir," he said. "We should be comfortable here."

"In the course of time," Harry agreed. "We have a few things to do first. Have you ever been in a jungle, Corporal?"

"A jungle? No, sir, can't say I have."

"Then you'd better brace yourself."

Harry spent a fretful afternoon looking at his watch and wondering if Jutta had got home yet, and what sort of a reception she was going to get. It was even more disturbing to realise that he was apparently going to be incommunicado for the next week. He had no doubt that Calvert would handle anything that came up, but then the brigadier wasn't in love with Jutta. It appeared he did not even trust her.

Then what *was* the truth of the matter? As had happened so often in the past, he had led with his chin, and been hit on it. From his point of view it had been a moment of delicious reassurance – a woman from his past who had actively sought him out to bring their affair to fruition. From the point of view of any dispassionate observer, and certainly a hostile one, she was an enemy who had seized her opportunity to infiltrate the military.

But she had saved his life – again. And he wanted so desperately to see her – again. The thought that he might not be here if she needed him was maddening. Far more upsetting than the news stories which were probably at that moment winging their way back to England.

Sergeant-Major Cullinan was a chunky man, no more than average height but clearly as strong as an ox, with the rugged features to go with his physique.

"Glad to have you along, sir," he announced, regarding both Harry and Todd somewhat speculatively.

"We're in your hands, Sergeant-Major," Harry told him.

"Yes, sir. I gather it's a rush job."

"I'm afraid so."

"But at least you don't have anything to learn about weapons."

"No, we don't," Harry said. "Or how to use them."

"Very good, sir. What we are going to do is go on patrol for a week. We shall not enter known enemy-held territory, but we will do everything else a patrol would do. I am assuming that you are both one hundred per cent fit?"

"Ninety-nine," Harry replied.

"It'll have to be a hundred by the end of this trip, sir," the sergeant-major said sceptically.

A jeep was waiting for them, as was Cantrell to say goodbye. "Good luck, sir," he said, shaking hands.

"I am gaining a distinct impression that I am not expected to come back," Harry said, and reflected that he had been in this situation before. At least, he had never been so comfortable when going to war. Although he was carrying a considerable amount of equipment in his pack, which the sergeant-major referred to as a "bergen" – not to mention an unfamiliar but very large knife called a "parang", his service revolver and a tommy-gun – he was nevertheless wearing an open-necked and short-sleeved bush jacket and loose trousers over his soft boots, with a slouch hat instead of a tin helmet. It was a distinct improvement on battle-dress. Todd and the sergeant-major were similarly equipped.

They drove out of town for some distance, passing through several villages, while the ground gradually rose – not that there was any thinning of the thick forest they could see ahead.

"Here will do," the sergeant-major said, and the driver obligingly pulled over. The road, not much better than a track, disappeared emptily into the trees in front of them – as it appeared equally emptily from those behind.

"Is it really as deserted as it seems?" Harry asked.

"Probably not, sir. In any event, we are going to assume that it isn't. One week," he reminded the driver.

"One week," the sergeant agreed, and turned his jeep.

"Now, sir," Cullinan said, checking his compass. "We will proceed in a north-easterly direction until we come to the river. This will take most of the morning. Follow me."

Harry glanced at Todd and gave him a thumbs-up sign, then they followed the sergeant-major down the parapet beside the road and plunged into the trees. The sun was now quite high and it was already hot but dry – at least in the beginning. Rapidly the sweat began to flow and they discovered that the jungle was never that dry, as leaves dripped on their heads and muddy patches appeared under their feet. For the first hour the going was fairly easy, but gradually the trees thickened, the vines clustered, and the undergrowth became almost solid.

"Are we allowed to speak?" Harry asked.

"Normally, no, sir," Cullinan said. "But you may on this occasion."

"Can we hack away some of this stuff?"

"No, sir. The sound of someone cutting their way through the bush carries a long way."

"We're going to be cut to ribbons," Todd complained.

Both he and Harry were already bleeding from several small nicks caused by thorns and branches; fortunately their thick bush jackets protected their chests and shoulders.

"You'll get used to it," Cullinan assured him. "Now, please, sir, from here on we operate on hand signals only. Just keep your eyes on me."

It had become a world Harry had never thought existed. The heat increased until it became an almost physical presence, and was not in the least alleviated by the sudden heavy downpour of rain in the middle of the morning. This left the three men soaked and uncomfortable, but Cullinan pressed remorselessly forward.

Now the jungle was so thick it was like a green and flexible wall. Several times they lost sight of the sergeant-major altogether, but he was always close enough to turn round and give them a fierce glare at any undue noise. This was unavoidable, however, as the two newcomers trod on fallen branches and dislodged twigs, and tripped over unseen obstacles.

The jungle was alive. Birds sang overhead, which was pleasant enough, but they were also surrounded by nerve-tingling slithers and seethes. Once Cullinan had to check them before they walked into a huge ants' nest, and on another occasion he checked them again and they watched a large snake wriggling away from them.

"The thing to remember," Cullinan whispered, "is that all these creatures are more afraid of you than you are of them. If you don't trouble them, as a rule they won't trouble you."

"But it's only a rule," Harry suggested.

"Well, yes, sir. There's no accounting for mavericks."

It was noon when they reached the first river, which was about thirty yards wide and came down from the slopes above with a fair rush, its waters brown but surprisingly clear.

"It's about four feet deep," Cullinan said. "And at least the movement means there'll be no crocs. If it were any deeper we'd use a rope, but it shouldn't be necessary here. But the bottom will be slippery, so watch it. Now, the drill is, one man covers the others at all times."

Harry nodded, and unslung his tommy-gun, kneeling on the bank as the sergeant-major entered the water, weapons held above his head.

"Do you reckon he's right, sir, about the crocodiles?" Todd asked.

"I don't see any," Harry said.

"They sneak up on you," Todd said.

"In the Tarzan movies, the head and eyes are always show-ing," Harry pointed out. "In you go, Corporal."

Cullinan had reached the far bank and was beckoning. Todd drew a deep breath and slid into the water, making his way steadily across, arms held high. The water gushed at him, and once or twice he staggered, but he reached the far side safely.

Cullinan waved his arm again, and Harry went in. The water surging about his thighs was quite refreshing. He stepped out confidently, and without warning a stone turned under his foot. Taken entirely by surprise he went down and under, head and all. He managed to keep his hands and his weapons above his head, but his hat floated away.

He staggered upright again, and saw Todd in the water downstream of him, gallantly retrieving the hat. Cullinan was waiting to help him out.

"Sorry about that cock-up, Sergeant-Major," Harry said.

"Could have happened to anyone, sir," Cullinan said magna-nimously.

Todd returned with the sodden hat.

"I think we could all do with a cup of tea and some lunch," Cullinan said, and began removing various pieces of equipment from his bergen.

They ate – concentrated canned food – drank some tea, and then resumed their march, the empty tins having been washed in the river and then re-stored in their bergens. "Mustn't leave any trace of our presence," Cullinan explained.

By mid-afternoon Harry was feeling distinctly uncomfortable, with an almost painful itch around his buttocks which he could not relieve no matter how much he scratched.

Cullinan had noticed. "Is there a problem, sir?"

"Just an itch, Sergeant-Major."

"Do you mind if I have a look, sir?"

Harry raised his eyebrows.

"One can't be too careful in the bush, sir. If you'd drop your pants and bend over . . ."

Harry glanced at Todd, who looked extremely embarrassed. Then he released his various belts, placed his equipment on the ground, undid his pants, and bent over.

"Like I thought," Cullinan remarked. "Leeches."

"Shit," Harry said.

"Not right now, sir, if you don't mind. They're already festering where you've been scratching. Vicious little buggers. They can give you a nasty fever."

"Is there a cure?"

"Get rid of them. This may hurt a bit, but it's all for the good."

Harry looked over his shoulder, saw the sergeant-major light a cigarette. He braced himself, and a moment later felt the tip burning his flesh. And then again, and again and again. He was reminded of Green removing the shotgun pellets, six years ago.

"There's just one of these that's stuck in a bit far," Cullinan said.

More déjà vu.

"I'll just have to uncover him," the sergeant-major said. He struck another match to burn the end of a needle he produced from his first-aid kit; there was a little sliver of pain as he opened the flesh, and again as then the cigarette tip was applied to it. "There we go. Don't move, sir."

"For how long?"

"Just till I can apply some antiseptic cream. Then you'll be as right as rain."

"Until the next lot get at me."

"They're a menace, and that's for sure, sir," Cullinan agreed, applying the cream to Harry's bottom. It stung almost as much as the cigarette tip, but it was reassuring; a few moments later he was able to dress himself.

"That's an impressive array of scars you have there, sir," Cullinan remarked.

"To which I seem to be adding every day," Harry said.

The discomforts of the first day were intensified over the next three, and were not alleviated by the nightly laying up. It invariably rained, and although the sleeping bags in which they wrapped themselves were waterproof, the ground on which they lay rapidly turned into a bog. They were assailed by hordes of insects, of which mosquitoes were the most voracious; to resist these they were required to take daily doses of anti-malarial drugs – to Harry's great relief he did not have an attack. They went through various exercises, which often involved keeping absolutely still for more than an hour, regardless of which bugs might be attacking them at the moment, or even, on one occasion, a snake which burrowed around them inquisitively – and there were always leeches to contend with.

They also climbed, steadily if not steeply. "We're not going very high on this trip," Cullinan said. "But up there," he pointed through a break in the trees at some considerable peaks, "you'd be almost clear of the insects. Then it's pretty good going."

"I can hardly wait," Harry said. "What's that? Smoke!"

It rose from a valley to their left.

"That would be Reed's Rubber Plantation," the sergeant-major said.

"Did you say Reed's?"

"That's right, sir. He's a planter who won't move out. Making too much money, I reckon."

Harry deduced that Cullinan had not had time to hear about what happened in Singapore before they had left for Kuala Lumpur. But to be here, with Jutta *there* . . . The temptation was irresistible. Besides, if Reed's allegiance was in question, a surprise visit might be a good way to find out.

"I think we should pay him a visit," he said.

"I'm not sure that would be wise, sir," the sergeant-major said. "Mr Reed has made it pretty clear that he doesn't like the Army nosing about his property."

"Then he'll just have to put up with it."

Cullinan scratched his chin.

"How far away is it?" Harry asked.

"We could get there by nightfall. But . . . it'll add half a day to our return trip. The jeep will be waiting."

"No, it won't," Harry said. "There's a road into his property, isn't there?"

"Well, yes, sir."

"So, we'll get him, or one of his people, to drive us back to where we would be, or the equivalent, tomorrow."

"With respect, sir, this is supposed to be a training exercise."

"To teach me about the jungle. Am I going to learn a lot more on the return journey?"

"Well . . . no, sir. It's a matter of fitness versus fatigue."

"I don't think either the corporal or I have let you down there, Sergeant-Major. I intend to pay that plantation a visit. Are you coming?"

Cullinan sighed.

As the sergeant-major had estimated, it took them all afternoon to cover the few miles to the plantation, and it was dusk when they found themselves in the first orderly row of rubber trees; it was not the bleeding season, although the scars from earlier crops were clearly visible. Now the going was easy; not only were the trees separated but the undergrowth had been cleared.

They passed through several of these groves, and came in sight of the compound – a large area of small houses surrounded by a high fence; in the distance they could make out some larger buildings.

"There's a gate just round here," Cullinan said leading the way, but he had not reached the gate when there was a challenge.

"Who comes?"

"British soldiers," Cullinan replied. They stood before the gate, listening to a bell ringing and the barking of dogs.

"What do you want?" the voice asked. The speaker was certainly not a Malay.

Cullinan looked at Harry.

"I am paying a call," Harry said. "I am Colonel Harry Curtis, First Commandos, seconded to Brigadier Calvert's command."

"Wait a moment, Colonel Curtis," the voice said.

"Do you know Mr Reed, Colonel?" Cullinan asked.

"As a matter of fact, no. But I know of him."

A few minutes later the gates swung in and they found themselves in the middle of a considerable crowd of people, several of whom carried flaring torches. It all looked very romantic, but Harry surmised that it wasn't actually like that at all.

"Colonel Curtis?" The speaker was a European, large and blond. "Johann Schnell. I am Mr Reed's manager."

He did not offer to shake hands.

"Sergeant-Major Cullinan, Corporal Todd," Harry introduced.

"I have met the sergeant-major," Schnell said. "If you gentlemen will come with me."

They walked up a broad drive towards the main house, still surrounded by the crowd, while dogs barked and snarled. Harry could not help but wonder what he had got himself and his comrades into. A generator growled close by, and the house showed a lot of lights. A man stood on the verandah to greet them. He was short and slender, fair-haired and wore a little blond moustache. He was totally unlike the mental picture Harry had formed of him.

"Colonel Curtis?" His voice was also somewhat high. "The famous Tiger himself."

"How word travels," Harry said. "Or did your wife mention it?"

"It has been in all the papers for weeks. I must say, Colonel, you are the last person I expected to see. Or is this an official visit?"

"It could be," Harry said. "I must apologise for my appearance, and that of my men. We've been walking in the bush."

"Would it not have been simpler to come by car?"

"No," Harry said.

"Well, as you're here, I imagine you feel like a bath and a change of clothing. You do have a change of clothing?"

"I'm afraid not. But I wouldn't say no to a bath."

"Of course." Various servants were waiting, and Reed gave rapid instructions in Malay. The two NCOs were hurried off in different directions, Harry being escorted upstairs to a luxurious bathroom where a maidservant was filling a tub. But then, the whole house was luxurious: the floors were polished wood, and there were various islands of furniture dispersed about a very large, open-plan ground floor. Apart from Reed himself, there were several servants present, all staring at him. And there was a strong scent of . . . coffee, Harry realised. In fact, in the far corner of the room, two of the servants were clearing away cups and saucers.

At six o'clock in the evening, an English planter had just been drinking coffee – with several people, Harry surmised, judging by the number of cups. People who had suddenly disappeared. And surely in the normal course of events the drink at this hour should have been whiskey?

The first floor was surrounded by a deep gallery, off which opened the bedrooms and the bathroom to which Harry was shown. He was followed into the room by two more maidservants, who somewhat distastefully removed his belts and weapons, then his mud- and sweat-stained uniform, socks and boots. They did this with no trace of embarrassment, nor did he feel any. He was here for a purpose.

"Do any of you speak English?" he asked.

"I have English," said the obvious eldest of the three girls.

"Oh, good. Tell me, is your master not married?"

"Mr Reed is married," she agreed, and indicated the tub. "You will sit?"

Harry sank into the hot water; nothing had ever felt so good. "But Mrs Reed is not here now," he suggested.

"Mrs Reed is here," the girl said.

Then all he needed was patience. Very probably, she did not yet know that he was here. He relaxed, watched the three girls as they removed their sarongs – they wore nothing underneath – and allowed himself to be bathed by the gentle fingers, even allowed his eyes to close . . . but opened them again when he heard movement in the room. He almost expected, and certainly hoped, to see Jutta standing by the tub, but instead he saw a manservant removing his uniform – and his weapons.

"Hold on a moment," he said.

"These will be returned to you, sir, as soon as they have been laundered," the man explained.

"You're not going to launder my guns," Harry told him. "Just leave them there."

The man hesitated, then gave a brief bow and replaced the gun belts.

The girls had been waiting patiently; now they held towels to envelope him as he stepped out of the bath. Once he was dried, they wrapped him in a sarong – an amazingly comfortable garment, even if it was not something he would normally have worn to dinner. While they were attending to him, he heard some noise from outside the open window; as soon as he could he went to it, and watched several men proceeding down the wide drive towards the gates. Obviously these were the coffee-drinkers, departing. One of them now turned and saluted the house before continuing on his way. His face was difficult to make out in the darkness, but it was clean-shaven and Harry got the impression that he was quite young. More important, to whom had he been bidding farewell? It certainly had not been to *him*, therefore it had to have been to someone standing on the front verandah beneath him, and that could only be Reed.

The girls appeared to be finished. They bowed to him, hands pressed together, resumed their own sarongs, and left the room. Harry gazed at his gun belts. He did not really wish to be separated from his weapons, but he knew he would make a ridiculous figure wearing a sarong and a revolver holster. He left them lying on the chair and went on to the gallery.

A manservant waited at the head of the stairs. "The master is waiting, sir."

Harry followed him down the stairs and across the huge expanse of lounge to the far corner, where Reed was waiting for him. Standing beside him was Jutta.

The Women

Harry checked in a mixture of relief and embarrassment. "I must apologise for my appearance," he said. "There wasn't anything else."

Reed was wearing a dinner jacket and Jutta an evening gown. Harry guessed the disparity in dress was deliberate on Reed's part, to place him at a disadvantage.

"I think a sarong suits you." The planter flicked his fingers, and a servant – also clad in a sarong – hurried forward with a tray of champagne. "Welcome to Reed's, Colonel. It is seldom we have the pleasure of entertaining such a famous soldier."

"Thank you." Harry sipped and looked at Jutta, who had not yet spoken. Her features were composed, but there were pink spots in her cheeks. Harry wished he could gain some inkling of how she wanted him to handle this – how, in fact, she had already handled it.

"Do sit down." Reed sat himself on a settee; Jutta took a seat beside him. Harry sat opposite them. "Have you heard from Singapore?" Reed asked.

So it was all out in the open. That was a relief. Or was it? He was really in this man's power at the moment.

"I'm afraid I don't know," he answered. "I have spent the last few days in the bush."

"Ah, yes. Walking, you said."

"Acclimatising myself to the country in which I shall be operating," Harry said.

"Quite. And then you felt you would like to see Jutta again."

"Yes," Harry said, looking from one to the other and still trying to obtain a lead. "I wished to be sure she was all right."

"And as you can see, she is. Reassure Colonel Curtis, my dear."

"I am all right, Harry," Jutta said.

"However," Reed said, "there remains the future. Will my wife be charged, Colonel?"

"I'm afraid she will have to appear in court," Harry said. "As will I. But as it was self-defence, there will be no question of a charge – or at least, a charge that will not immediately be dismissed."

"By the courts, yes," Reed agreed. "But she will remain convicted, in the eyes of the public at large, of having killed a man while in the act of committing adultery."

Again Harry looked at Jutta, but again it was impossible to tell from her expression what she was thinking, or what might have taken place between her husband and herself over the past few days.

"It was not meant to happen like that," he said lamely.

"These things never are," Reed agreed.

"I think we need to know exactly where we are in this," Harry said.

"Are we anywhere? Are you in a position to be anywhere, Colonel? I understand you have a titled wife, and a family. Suppose I told you I intend to throw Jutta out on her ass, as I am entitled to do, and obtain a divorce. What would you do about it? What *could* you do about it?"

"I would certainly regard her as my responsibility," Harry said.

"There, you see, my dear," Reed said. "Is that not reassuring? However, I do not propose to do that, Colonel. I like having Jutta around. She is so decorative, don't you think?"

Harry gave Jutta another glance, and she gave a quick shake of her head. So he swallowed what he would have said, and instead remarked, "That has to be between Jutta and yourself, Mr Reed. I just wanted you to understand that I shall not shirk my responsibilities."

"And, of course, you love my wife."

"Yes," Harry said. "I love your wife."

"Well, then," Reed said. "Let's have dinner."

* * *

What an incredible conversation, Harry thought as he lay in bed, which felt almost as good as lying in the hot bath. But then, what an incredible situation. One in which he was entirely helpless – which was not a position he enjoyed. Without some sort of sign from Jutta, he had no idea how to proceed. But there had been no sign. No doubt she had been too conscious of having been watched by her husband throughout the evening. He had hoped she might have been able to arrange for them to have a few minutes alone together, but that had not been possible either. And as she was no doubt sharing a bed with Reed at this moment, there was no possibility of her coming to him during the night. And tomorrow he must just walk away. He began almost to hope for a police summons for them both to appear in court in Singapore.

At least his weapons did not appear to have been tampered with, even if they had been moved from the bathroom into the bedroom he had been given for the night. He also reassured himself that Cullinan and Todd were being well looked after. But sleeping remained a problem – he almost regretted declining Reed's offer of a maidservant for the night, but that had been quite impossible with Jutta virtually next door. By morning he was beginning to feel that his decision to visit the plantation had been a mistake.

"We were going to ask you to give us a lift part of the way back," Harry told Reed at breakfast. Jutta had not appeared.

"It will be a pleasure," Reed said.

"With respect, sir," Cullinan said. "I think we should walk it." To Harry's surprise, Cullinan was in the best of humours.

"But the rendezvous?"

"If we're late, we're late, sir."

Harry looked at him, and the sergeant-major waggled his eyebrows.

"Very good," Harry said. "It's up to you."

"He is a dedicated soldier," Reed remarked, contemptuously.

Reed waved them off – there was still no sign of Jutta – and they walked through the rubber trees towards the jungle.

"Would you mind telling me what this is all about?" Harry asked.

"Well, sir, we may have had a stroke of luck. Mr Reed was entertaining when we arrived last night."

"I had worked that out for myself."

"They were Commies, sir."

Harry frowned. "I'm not with you."

"A bunch of Chinese," Cullinan explained. "They left while we were being hurried off to our baths."

"I saw that," Harry said. "I thought they were labourers going home."

"No, sir. They were Chinese, not Malays, and they were leaving the compound. What is more, they passed quite close to where I was standing at my window, and I saw their faces. I recognised one of them. Their leader in fact. A chap called Chin Sen. We have a photograph of him back at the barracks. He's a known Commie leader."

"You mean Reed was entertaining Communists when we turned up?"

"He was certainly having a meeting with them. Then he had to get rid of them in a hurry."

"My God! I'm surprised he didn't get rid of us, instead."

"He couldn't risk that, sir. He had to assume that Kuala Lumpur knew about our visit to him, and would come looking for us if we didn't turn up."

"So that definitely puts him in their camp," Harry mused. And Jutta? No wonder she had not tried to communicate with him. But he simply refused to believe that she could be an enemy. "Trouble is," he said, "how do we prove it? If we go back, he'll simply deny those people were there."

"Yes, sir. But if we could get hold of those Commies . . ."

"How do we do that?"

"I can track them, sir."

"There were eight of them. And three of us. What sort of weapons did they have?"

"Oh, they'll be well armed, sir. But so are we. I would have said this is right up your street, sir – you being a VC and all."

"If you can catch up with those people, Sergeant-Major, you're on," Harry said. Suddenly he felt like action.

*   *   *

Cullinan was fairly sure the Communist group had gone north. He led Harry and Todd round the plantation and then traversed west, parallel to the northernmost grove of rubber trees. This took some considerable time, and by late afternoon Harry was beginning to feel they were wasting their efforts. Then the sergeant-major said, "Here we go."

He had uncovered human excreta, not more than twenty-four hours old.

"How do we know it's theirs?" Harry asked.

"This is no place for anyone to be, sir. Save going or coming."

Harry took his word for it, and having found the trail the sergeant-major soon picked up other signs, including an obvious campsite.

"They're certainly not attempting to conceal themselves," Harry commented.

"Why should they, sir? This is their country."

"You mean we never come up here?"

"Oh, indeed we do, sir. But only in strength, which gives them time to disperse. It'll never occur to them that a three-man patrol will venture into their back yard."

"And you don't reckon we're biting off more than we can chew."

"Not if we can catch up with them before they link up with a larger body, sir."

The Communists were not only not bothering to conceal their tracks, but they weren't hurrying either. By the next evening the soldiers, who *were* hurrying, smelt their campfire.

"Now, sir," Cullinan said. "The three of us can't capture eight men. Even if we could, there is no way we could take them back to Kuala Lumpur. I reckon we can manage just one prisoner. But one will be enough, both to give us info on their general set-up around here, and also to incriminate Mr Reed."

"And the others?"

"Well, sir, once we move in, they are going to try to kill us. And there can be no doubt that they, or their close friends and relatives, are guilty of quite a few murders."

"I take your point," Harry said, and turned to face Todd. "Corporal?"

"Whatever you say, sir."

"Very good. Your show, Sergeant-Major. You know the ground."

"Yes, *sir*! There is a river only a hundred yards further on."

Harry nodded; he could hear the swish of the water.

"That is where they'll be camped," the sergeant-major said. "If we go in from three different directions, and if they try to escape across the river, they'll be sitting ducks. The important thing is that they shouldn't know how many we are until it's over."

Harry nodded. "Make your dispositions."

"I'll take the right, sir, and the corporal the left, if you'll take the centre."

"Very good. The signal?"

"When I open fire, sir. Unless our approach is detected before then, in which case whoever is exposed will fire first and the others will join in."

"Hold on a moment," Harry said. "Don't we at least call on them to surrender?"

"Risky, sir. Those men are trained assassins."

"You're quite certain of that?"

"If they're with Chin Sen, yes, sir. If we don't shoot them, they will shoot us."

Harry sighed; he was back to square one. "Very good, Sergeant-Major. However, do remember that we need at least one of them alive."

They advanced more cautiously now, taking every precaution to conceal their progress; Harry and Todd were both uncomfortably aware that they were still making too much noise, although they were partially protected by the sound of the water. Certainly the Communist group remained unaware of their presence, and just on dusk they could hear voices and laughter. Cullinan pointed, and both Todd and Harry nodded. Cullinan then tapped his watch, and held up his right hand, opening and shutting the fingers twice. Again Harry nodded, and the sergeant-major and the corporal wriggled away into the bushes.

Harry crouched, studying his watch, waiting for the ten

minutes to elapse, increasingly aware of the sweat dribbling down his neck and chest. Never had he worked in such heat. As for what came after . . . He didn't want to think about that, about the possibility of Jutta being imprisoned . . . she had to be innocent. He was staking his life on that.

The ten minutes were up. He moved forward, on his hands and knees, until he reached the trees fringing the river bank. Now he could see the eight men seated round their fire, totally unsuspecting of what was about to hit them. He unslung his tommy-gun, checked it out, and unclipped his revolver holster just in case he needed the back-up.

A shot rang out, and then the whole evening was filled with the chatter of the automatic weapons. Harry sprayed the encampment with bullets, watched the men diving and falling to and fro. Two of them dived into the river, striking out for the far bank, surrounded by spurts of water as Cullinan followed them with his fire.

Nearly all the Communists on the bank had been hit, but only one appeared to have been killed outright. The others rolled back and forth as they gained their weapons and returned fire. Both Harry and Todd sent two more bursts, and they subsided. Harry stood up.

"Mind how you go, sir," Cullinan called.

Harry went forward, and Todd emerged from his left. The massacre was complete. Four men were dead, two wounded, one seriously. Of the two who had gone into the water, one was floating downstream, head down. The other had gained the bank and disappeared.

"I'm sure I winged him," Cullinan said in disgust. "That was Chin Sen himself. The bugger must have more lives than a cat. He'll be after help."

"How far away?" Harry asked.

"Haven't a clue, sir. Could be quite close."

"Then we'd better get out of here, p.d.q."

"He will kill you all," declared the slightly wounded man, who was in fact hardly more than a boy.

"You reckon?" Todd asked.

"He will avenge us. He is my brother."

"Well, that's good news," Harry said. "You're coming with us, young fellow."

"And this one?" Cullinan indicated the other wounded man, who was lying on the ground, bleeding and moaning dreadfully. "I don't think he can walk, and we sure as hell can't carry him."

"You say his friends will be along pretty soon. Bind him up, give him a full canteen and some painkillers, and we'll leave him here. You . . ." He nudged the young man with his gun barrel. "Let's go."

The boy scrambled to his feet. "My brother will kill you all," he said.

"I can see where you got your reputation," Calvert commented. "I send you out for a training exercise, and you shoot up a Communist cell and bring one of them back for interrogation."

"It was Cullinan's idea," Harry said. "He's a very good man."

"I know it. But you were the commanding officer, and it is you I am congratulating. Now we really have something to work on."

"You mean as regards Reed?"

Calvert shook his head. "That's rather a hot potato at the moment. Before we go arresting a prominent planter we have to be absolutely sure of our ground. The fact that he entertained a known Communist leader is not a certain indication of where his sympathies lie, especially as our young friend claims the meeting was held in the hopes – Reed's hopes – of buying off the enemy from attacking his plantation. That might be morally poor, but it is not a criminal offence. I'd have thought a delay would please you."

"It does," Harry agreed. "I still don't believe Jutta can be involved."

"I would say she probably is, whether she likes it or not. We'll have to see what comes out of that Singapore business. No, I'm more interested in what our young friend has to say. He's a talkative bastard."

"You can say that again," Harry agreed. "He talked virtually the whole three days it took us to get back."

"And he's hardly stopped since. He doesn't think he's giving anything away, but we're piecing together quite a picture, especially in these references to Ipoh. That's a town on virtually the far side of the Highlands, and our Intelligence has long held the opinion that it is a Communist base. Moving on it, however, will be a major operation, and the powers that be have been reluctant to sanction an attack because of the possibility of high civilian casualties. But if this lad will provide us, knowingly or not, with sufficient certainty that we'll find an assembly point, I may be able to twist a few arms. We certainly can't stand on the defensive forever."

"How soon will you be able to move?"

"Not until I can get the permission to do so. But that may be all to the good. It will give you the time to get to know your men, and for them to get to know you. Obviously I'm allowing word of your little coup to spread – and not only in the Army. The more the enemy get to know about what they're up against, the better. So, go to it. By the way, how are things on your domestic front?"

"I have no idea."

"It's been a fortnight since that Singapore business. I happen to know it was fairly well reported in England."

"I'm sure it was."

"And there's been nothing from your wife?"

"Not a word."

"Would you regard that as a good sign or a bad?"

"I can't make up my mind about it. We had a sort of open arrangement. In theory."

"Useful." Calvert was unmarried.

"Talking about Singapore . . ."

"The case comes up in six weeks. There will be a subpoena along in a month or so. However, if you happen to be in the field at that time, I shall merely inform the court that you are unable to attend because of military duties."

"And Mrs Reed?"

"As she has no military duties, officially, she will have to attend."

"To be charged with at least manslaughter."

"Well, Harry, she did kill a man."

"I have just killed at least five men."

"In the line of duty."

"I regard Jutta's saving my life as being very much in the line of duty."

"I have no doubt at all that a good attorney – and I am quite sure Reed can afford the best – will make that point stick. I am sure she'll be acquitted."

"My evidence could be vital. I was there. I saw what happened."

"And you made a statement, which, in your absence, will be read out in court in her defence – suitably edited, of course."

"Edited in what way?"

"Edited in keeping with the Official Secrets Act. That is why I do not wish you there, Harry. Too much may come out. As far as the police are concerned, a man broke into your room to rob you, you attempted to defend yourself, he drew a knife, and your companion very gallantly leapt to your assistance, possibly a shade too vigorously. Because that companion happened to be someone else's wife, it's a great big juicy scandal. But just a scandal. I do not wish, I cannot risk, you being put in the witness box and asked questions about our security arrangements on oath. Please understand that. You came out here to do a job. Let's get that done. Then you can do what you like about the beautiful Mrs Reed."

Harry recognised the common sense behind Calvert's decree, and he had the comforting reflection that should things turn out badly for Jutta, he could always insist on giving evidence at a later date; he did not think even Calvert would object in those circumstances.

But he had still promised her his support, and as things stood he could offer no physical evidence of that. He did not even feel he could write her a letter, as he had no doubt that her mail was read by her husband. Clearly she was being kept a prisoner on the plantation – she had never called him from their house in Kuala Lumpur, which indicated that she had not been allowed to come into town since her return from Singapore.

There was one ray of hope. He summoned Cantrell. "I shall not be attending the court case," he said. "That is the brigadier's decision. However, I wish you to be there, as an observer."

"I understand I am being called as a witness, sir," Cantrell said.

"Fine. I am going to give you a letter, which I would like you to deliver to Mrs Reed without anyone else knowing. That particularly applies to her husband, if he happens to go down to Singapore with her. Can you do that?"

"I think so, sir."

"Good man."

Harry wrote, begging her to get in touch with him and tell him the truth about her situation, and assuring her of his undying love. He could do no more than that.

But he could get down to the business of his command. The regiment consisted of about six hundred men, of whom about a third were regulars – mostly Gurkhas. The rest were Malay volunteers in various stages of training. All were excited at being commanded by so famous a soldier, and the more so because of the exploit Harry had carried out within a week of joining the force. He had an adjutant, Major John Hallis, six captains, and twelve lieutenants; all of these were British and regular, and were no doubt necessary at this stage, but as he told Calvert, "I would like to get some of the Malays commissioned just as soon as it can be done."

Calvert entirely agreed.

Harry also had Cullinan as his regimental sergeant-major, which was a great asset. Between them they trained their people to the ultimate degree over the next few weeks, not only in the jungle – with which most of them were fairly familiar in any event – but in battle tactics as devised by Harry himself, conditioned with regard to the enemy he anticipated meeting. Additionally, he carried out Calvert's "hearts and minds" campaign, sending his men into the villages to make friends with the local populations, lending a hand at everything possible from repairing houses to improving plumbing, assisting with domestic problems and giving medical advice where necessary. Lieutenant Codrington of D Company actually delivered a baby!

There were also regular meetings with Calvert, for the Communists were still active, perhaps the more so after the destruction of Chin Sen's cell. Chin Sen himself had an ultimatum delivered, demanding the return of his brother:

I and mine know all about you, great British War Hero, but your fame means nothing to us. They call you Tiger, but I kill tigers for sport. Return my brother, unharmed, or you will die a thousand deaths.

"Should this be taken seriously?" Harry asked. "Or is it merely rhetoric?"

"It is our business to make sure that it *is* rhetoric," the brigadier said. "You'll have extra protection when in town. When you're with your men I'd say you're all right."

As Calvert had prognosticated, the continued presence of bodies of soldiers where they were least expected made the insurgents' tasks the harder, at least as regards small-scale attacks. Soon there was clear evidence that the Communists were planning a major strike, and thanks to Chin Fu's careless talk, Intelligence had a fair idea of where the insurgent concentration would be – even if they had no ideas of when. Calvert remained certain that the time was right for a strike on Ipoh, but officialdom was still hanging fire.

He went ahead and planned the strike anyway.

"The timing has to be perfect," he told his officers. "We have to hit them before they hit us, but we don't want to hit them until they have concentrated sufficient men to make it worthwhile."

"What about Chin Sen?" Harry asked after the meeting. "As we haven't replied to his ultimatum, he should be working himself up to doing something."

"I imagine he is," Calvert agreed. "But I should think it's to be part of the offensive. If he wants to try something beforehand, that's up to him. There's no way he's going to get at his brother."

"I was thinking more of some act of revenge. As, for instance, a raid on Reed's Plantation."

"He won't do that if Reed is his friend."

"And if he actually isn't?"

"Look, he's been invited to abandon his plantation until the emergency is over, and he has refused. It's his bed, if he wants to lie in it."

"And his wife? I think perhaps someone should go out there and put the situation to him."

"What situation? There is no way he can be allowed to know our plans. As far as he is concerned, things are proceeding as normal. What you mean is, you'd like to go and get her out of there. I'm not giving you permission to become involved with that woman again, Harry. In any event, she'll probably be in Singapore when we make our move. Just get ready for it."

Once again Harry had no choice but to obey, knowing that his CO was right. He threw himself even more wholeheartedly into his work, and was taken entirely by surprise when he was summoned from Battalion Headquarters – a few miles out of town – by an urgent radio message from Kuala Lumpur. He returned immediately, was shown into Calvert's office, and found himself facing Cynthia.

For a moment Harry was lost for words.

Cynthia smiled at him. "I thought I'd come and pay you a visit," she said. "In all the circumstances."

"But . . . is Julian with you?"

"Julian is with Mumsy and Daddy. He'd never stand the heat. Is it always this hot?"

"Just about," Harry said, and looked at Calvert.

"I'm sure you two have a lot to talk about," Calvert said. "I'm going to step out for a few minutes. Lady Curtis. May I have a word, Harry?"

He gave Cynthia a brief bow, and left the room.

"Excuse me a moment," Harry said, and followed.

"Bit of a turn-up," Calvert commented.

"Yes."

"You understand that she's a weak spot. When Chin Sen finds out that you have a wife here . . ."

"Yes," Harry said again.

"Your best bet would be to put her on the first ship back to England."

"Easier said than done. She's a law unto herself."

"She's your wife," Calvert reminded him, and went down the stairs.

Harry returned to the office.

"What a nice man," Cynthia remarked. "Do sit down, Harry, and stop looking like a delinquent schoolboy."

Harry sat down. "When did you arrive?"

"Last night."

"And at which hotel did you spend the night?"

"I slept on board and came up here this morning. Is it important where I spent the night? And do you know that you haven't kissed me?"

"Do you want to be kissed?"

"Of course I do. You're my husband. Or have you entirely forgotten that?"

He kissed her, and she put her arms round him to hold him close.

"Where you spent the night is not important," he said when he got himself free. "What is important is how many people know you're in Malaya."

"Well, I imagine everyone, now. Are you afraid it will upset your popsie?"

"I am afraid it may excite quite a few people who would give their all to get at me, one way or another."

"Oh, really, Harry. Are you pretending I may be in some kind of danger?"

"I wish I were pretending. We are going to have to be very careful. At least at my flat you'll be safe until we can get you a passage home."

"I have seen your flat," Cynthia said. "Brigadier Calvert very kindly allowed me to take my stuff there. However, I decided against staying. It really is a little Spartan. I have taken a suite in a hotel. It has a room for Annie."

"Annie?"

"My maid. You didn't think I'd come all this way on my own?"

"Shit," he muttered. "Well, I'm afraid you will have to put up with the flat. I'll have my man Todd go along there now and move you out – with Annie, of course. I'm sure we can find room for her."

"Harry," Cynthia said. "You have simply got to get rid of this idea that you can tell me what I must do and what I must not do. I intend to stay in that hotel. You are perfectly welcome to stay there with me, if you wish. If you do not so wish, well, I am sure we can arrange to meet from time to time. As for a passage home, we shall have to talk about that. I certainly did not come all this way to go straight back. I have things to do."

"I was sleeping in a hotel when someone tried to murder me."

"With your friend. I am looking forward to hearing the truth about that."

"The truth is that I cannot adequately protect you while you are in a hotel. Even if I am there with you. And I cannot be with you all the time."

"I am sure I will manage," Cynthia said. "Now, I would like to meet this Jutta person."

"Why? You didn't allow me to meet your Caribbean boyfriend."

"No one knows anything about him. Except you. But you have managed to have your name linked with this woman in every newspaper in England."

"Inadvertently. Why do you wish to see her?"

"I think it is my right to do so."

"Well, you may find it difficult. She is being kept incommunicado by her husband. At least until the court case."

"When she will be tried for murder."

"She will be tried for manslaughter, and acquitted."

They gazed at each other, and there was a tap on the door.

"All sorted out?" Calvert inquired.

"Not really," Harry said. "But we have used up enough of your time."

Cynthia stood up. "You've been very kind, Brigadier Calvert. May I expect you to dinner, Harry?"

Harry hesitated only briefly. Then he nodded. "Yes. Do you have transport?"

"I have a taxi waiting. Good afternoon."

She swept out of the office.

"Sticky?" Calvert inquired.

"It promises to be. But the main problem is that she appears to have no intention of going home, at least for a while, and that she insists in staying at the hotel – which makes her an obvious target for Chin Sen's people, once he knows she's here."

"Which will be by tonight at the latest," Calvert agreed. "We can take care of that, Harry. I'll put an armed guard on the hotel. As for her wanting to stay here, well, it's her funeral. I'm sorry, I shouldn't have said that. But if she's determined to stay . . . Who knows, we might pick someone up – even if it goes against the grain to use your wife as bait."

"She'll enjoy it," Harry said. "Supposing she ever finds out. I'm committed to staying in town tonight, Mike."

Calvert nodded. "You can take a couple of days off, if you wish."

"I will rejoin my people tomorrow," Harry said. "If you'll assure me that Cynthia will be safe until next time I get into town."

"She'll be protected," Calvert said.

The evening went off better than Harry dared hope. The hotel staff were in a state of high excitement at being able to entertain two such guests – heightened by the presence of several plain-clothes policemen – while the other clientele, as word spread, gawked at the two rich and famous people in their midst. Cynthia was at her scintillating best, and with her hair piled on top of her head, her most beautiful as well as her most charming. She wore an off-the-shoulder dinner gown, and her skin glistened excitingly with a thin layer of sweat.

They were in bed before the subject of Jutta came up – and then it was Harry who raised it. Cynthia had just been as tempestuously sexual as ever; the contrast to Jutta's quiet fervour was enormous. And the event was in any event overlaid by the memory that the last time he and his wife had had sex was before she had gone on her Caribbean fling.

"Do you wish a divorce?" he asked.

"What a question to ask of a woman with whom you have just had sex and who is your wife," she commented. "Of course I do not wish a divorce."

"But you have come all this way . . ."

"I came all this way to make plain to the newspapers that we are *not* getting divorced."

"Ah. But you still wish to see Jutta."

"I am curious to see this woman you travelled twelve thousand miles to have sex with, when you had me at home."

"Darling, I did not travel twelve thousand miles to see Jutta. I came here to do a job, and she happened to be here too. I had no idea that she was."

"How long had you been lovers?"

"We had never been lovers, before that night in Singapore."

"But you had known her a long time."

"She happened to have saved my life during the War."

"As the White Rabbit might have said, curiouser and curiouser. I simply must meet this woman."

"Well, I will see if it can be arranged. For the time being, however, you must stay in the hotel."

"Say again?"

"You must stay where you can be protected."

"That is absurd. I wish to see something of the country. I almost certainly will never come here again."

"Right now it is not safe."

She made a sweeping gesture. "And all these people aren't safe?"

"You happen to be a special case."

"I don't believe you. You're making it all up."

"Believe what you like. You stay in the hotel."

She glared at him. "Are you going to be here?"

"Not for the next couple of days. I have work to do. But I'll be back at the weekend, and we'll have some fun."

"So for the next few days I sit here and twiddle my thumbs."

"I'm afraid so. Do co-operate, darling. It won't be for long. We happen to be in the middle of an emergency. Hopefully we'll have it sorted out within the next month."

"The next *month*? You simply have to be joking."

"You'll be surprised how quickly the time flies."

To Harry's great relief, she did not refer to the subject again, and next morning she was once more all sunshine and light. "I'll be back on Saturday morning," he promised.

"I'll be here," she promised in turn.

At last he had the time to think, as his jeep drove him out to regimental headquarters. He had actually not anticipated this crisis until after he had returned to England – but then, he had always been an optimist: in his profession it was essential. Now . . . it was a choice between a woman he did not love, but who happened to be his wife and the mother of his son, who he *did* love . . . and a woman he did love, but who just happened to be someone else's wife, in deep trouble on his account, and whose real feelings for him he could not be sure of.

What a mess!

Getting back to drilling and preparing his men was a relief. It was the following day, when he returned to his Headquarters hut for lunch, that he found Calvert waiting for him.

"Trouble?" he asked.

"Yes. A word alone."

"Would you mind, Major?" Harry asked Hallis, who promptly left, as did Todd, who was waiting to serve the meal. "Sounds grim."

"It is," Calvert said. "Or it could be. They have your wife."

"What did you say?"

Calvert laid a piece of paper on the desk. Harry bent over it, swallowed as he saw that it was stained with blood. The words were printed:

YOU HAVE MY BROTHER, GREAT TIGER. NOW I HAVE YOUR WOMAN. YOU BRING CHIN FU REED'S PLANTATION NOW AND WE EXCHANGE. YOU COME ALONE WITH MY BROTHER. CHIN SEN.

"How the hell did this happen?" Harry asked. "You said she would be protected."

"As long as she stayed in the hotel. But it appears that she went out to Reed's plantation."

Harry sat down, slowly. "I told her to stay in the hotel."

"I'm sure you did. But she seems to be a lady of independent mind."

"Yes," Harry said grimly. "Tell me what you know."

"It appears that yesterday she simply called a taxi and told the driver to take her out to the plantation."

"And your security squad did nothing about it?"

"Their orders were to stop anyone getting at her, not to prevent her moving about."

"And you think that she went out to Reed's?"

"That's where her maid says she was going. The taxi certainly took the road north."

"I'd better have a word with the driver."

Calvert looked grimmer than ever. "The fact is, Harry, he never came back."

Harry nodded. "That's Cynthia, all right. She's hired him for the week, or whatever."

"Harry, neither she nor the taxi ever got to Reed's."

Harry frowned at him. "How do you know?"

"As I said, the security guard did not feel that he had the authority to stop Lady Curtis leaving the hotel. It was only when she did not return by nightfall, and he learned from other taxi drivers that she had left town, that he became worried and checked with the maid; then he reported to Headquarters. They immediately contacted Reed's by radio, and was told that she was not there. They called back a couple of hours later – ample time for the taxi to have completed the journey – but she had still not appeared. This was then reported to me. I immediately sent out a patrol, and they found the taxi. The driver was still behind the wheel, this note pinned to his chest with a knife. The knife had penetrated his heart. I am most terribly sorry, but this was always a possibility if she refused to take precautions."

Harry sat down. He didn't know what to think. He wasn't sure he wanted to think, at that moment. "I have to go after her, Mike. You know that."

"I know that's what you want to do, Harry. But this couldn't have happened at a worse time. I've been given the go-ahead to move on Ipoh."

"With my people?"

"Ah, no. I'm taking the Malayan Scouts. They're already moving out. Your people will remain here in reserve. And you will command in my absence. The point is, this exercise has to be carried out in total secrecy. If they get word of it, the Commies will just melt away."

"Do you think you can get up there without them knowing of it?"

"Hopefully, yes. I am using small units of fourteen men, who will infiltrate the jungle and close in on the town. It's going to take some co-ordinating, but it can be done. What we cannot afford is for something to stir them up on the south side of the Highlands."

"I don't agree," Harry said. "Surely the ideal situation would be for something *to* stir them up in the south, to distract Chin Sen and his people while you are getting into position. In any event, we now know that Chin Sen is in the south. Our business surely is to keep him here while you get your people into position."

Calvert stroked his chin. "I cannot allow an exchange, Harry. If we once go down that road, exchanging prisoners for hostages, we're on a hiding to nothing, and every prominent person in the Federation is at risk."

"I understand that," Harry said. "Let me handle it my way."

"Harry," Calvert said earnestly. "If you go out there alone, you are a dead duck. And so is your wife. If . . ." He bit his lip.

"If she's not already dead," Harry said. "I know that's a risk. But I'll bring in Chin Sen, Mike. For you to hang."

"How? He certainly isn't going to come single-handed."

"Neither will I, entirely."

"He'll be watching your every move. If you have a back-up, he won't play."

Harry grinned. "This is my kind of business, Mike. And here's something else. He's named Reed's as the meeting place. That could be neutral ground, as it is intended to sound like. If it isn't . . . I'll bring you back proof positive that Reed is involved."

"And his lady?"

"If the proof is there, I'll have it."

Calvert gazed at him for several seconds. Then he said, "I'll wish you Godspeed."

*   *   *

Harry sent Cantrell into town with Calvert to obtain a search warrant for Reed's plantation. He did not really expect to find Cynthia there; he just wanted to upset as many people as possible, as rapidly as possible. Then he summoned his men and told them what had happened. "I need a volunteer who at a distance can pass for Chinese," he said.

Several of the Gurkhas stepped forward; Harry chose the youngest looking – his name was Bukit.

"Corporal Todd will drive," Harry said. "Sergeant-Major?"

"Count me in, sir," Cullinan said.

"Thank you. You understand the risk?"

"Yes, sir."

"Very good. We move out immediately we've eaten . . ."

"With respect, sir," Hallis said. "You must have a back-up."

"I intend to," Harry said. "But Chin Sen's people will certainly be watching the road. Therefore we cannot move until he is fully committed. Which means, hopefully, after I have regained Lady Curtis and placed Chin Sen under arrest. You will have one company standing by, ready to move with all possible speed when I call for you. I will use Reed's radio."

"Standing by, here, sir? Fifty miles over a bad road . . . We're talking about two hours."

"Hopefully less, Major. But when you come, I wish it to be with all possible publicity."

"Sir?"

"You will fire your guns into the air. You will also bring the battalion band, playing their loudest."

"I don't understand, sir. Surely this operation calls for the utmost stealth."

"On my part, yes. But if I need you, I wish the whole world to know you are on your way. Especially any insurgents who may be making themselves a nuisance. We will hold and wait for you. We leave in fifteen minutes."

Harry used those fifteen minutes to have a brief lunch.

Sergeant-Major Cullinan joined him. "All set, sir," he said.

"Thank you, Sergeant-Major."

"Do you think . . . Well, sir, they're right bastards. And having it in for you . . ."

226

"I prefer not to think, right this minute, Sergeant-Major."

"Yes, sir."

Todd, busy fussing about Harry's gear, said nothing but looked volumes.

There was another visitor a few minutes later; Cantrell arrived with the search warrant.

"Permission to accompany you, sir?"

"It's going to be mucky, by any standards."

"I understand that, sir. But I would like to come."

"Then you shall."

Harry had forced himself to eat, although he was not in the least hungry: he knew that the biggest mistake he could make would be to panic. He had never done so before, no matter how grim his situation. But then, it had always been *his* situation, not that of his wife. He had to believe that Chin Sen – if it had been Chin Sen – was seeking only the exchange of his brother. In which case Cynthia would be unharmed, if perhaps somewhat ruffled. But she had brought it on herself. What did not bear thinking about was if Chin Sen was *not* seeking an exchange – or if it had not been him at all.

"All ready, sir," Todd said.

Harry went outside. The entire battalion had assembled to see him off. "Let's go." He sat in the back of the jeep with Cantrell and Bukit, who wore a scarf wrapped round his head to conceal his features; his wrists were handcuffed and he was clearly meant to be a prisoner. Cullinan sat in the front beside Todd. They were armed with revolvers, tommy-guns and a string of hand grenades, just as if this was a Commando operation. Harry was determined that it should be. Major Hallis brought the regiment to attention, and the jeep drove out of the yard and on to the road leading north into the jungle.

They reached the plantation in late afternoon. They had not travelled very fast; Harry wanted any watchers to see them and get a message off to Chin Sen.

Their coming was certainly known. The gates to the plantation compound were open, and several people watched their approach, amongst them Schnell the manager.

The jeep pulled to a halt.

"Good morning, Colonel," Schnell said. "On patrol?"

"I am looking for my wife," Harry said.

"Your wife, Colonel? I didn't know she was in the country."

"Now you do," Harry pointed out. "Has an English woman been out here during the past twenty-four hours?"

"Not to my knowledge."

"Well, I wish to have a word with Mr Reed. Very good, Todd,' Harry said.

One of the labourers had already left on a bicycle, peddling up the drive to the plantation house. Todd now drove behind him, slowly.

As on the occasion of Harry's first visit, Reed was on the verandah to greet them, and again wearing a dinner jacket. But this time Jutta stood beside him, very becoming in a sarong, with her hair loose.

"Why, Colonel Curtis," Reed said as Todd stopped the jeep at the foot of the steps. "What a splendid surprise. But you are looking for your wife."

"Yes," Harry said, stepping down. As before, he looked at Jutta, seeking some sign – and as before there was none. It was impossible to believe that they had so unforgettably shared a bed in Singapore.

"And you think she may be here. That is what they said on the wireless last night. But I told them she wasn't."

"So you did. But she was coming here."

Reed shook his head. "She was very unwise. It is not safe for a white woman to drive out here, alone."

"I'm sure. By the way, this is Captain Cantrell. The Sergeant-Major and Corporal Todd you know. Do you mind if we search your house?"

"I do mind," Reed said. "I will not permit it. You have no right to do this."

Harry took the search warrant from his breast pocket. "I'm afraid I do, Mr Reed."

Reed glared at him.

"Your wife is not here, Harry," Jutta said in a low voice.

"But you know where she is, what has happened to her. Or your husband does."

"This is outrageous," Reed declared.

"So is the kidnapping of my wife, Mr Reed. Shall we go inside? I will remain with you, downstairs, while my people carry out the search."

"I will make a formal complaint to the governor," Reed announced.

"That is your privilege," Harry said. "Carry on, Captain Cantrell."

Cantrell beckoned Cullinan.

"You had better go with them," Reed said to Jutta. "Just to make sure they do not steal or damage anything."

Jutta hesitated, looking at Harry as if afraid the two men might fight when she left. Then she followed the two soldiers.

"I know absolutely nothing about your wife," Reed said.

"Then you have nothing to worry about. I also want secure accommodation for this young man." Harry indicated Bukit.

"Who is he?"

"Someone your friend Chin Sen wishes to get hold of, urgently."

Reed snorted. But he still did not betray any knowledge of what the Communist commander had in mind. He gave instructions to one of his servants.

"You stay with him, Corporal," Harry said.

"Sir." Todd held Bukit's arm and urged him to the stairs, where the servant was waiting.

"I won't offer you a drink," Reed said.

"I wouldn't accept it," Harry agreed. "What you can do is show me your radio room."

Reed's head jerked.

"I may need to keep in touch," Harry explained.

"It is through there." Reed indicated a door in the far wall. "Show me."

Reed glared at him, then led him to the door and opened it. As Harry had expected, it was very modern equipment. "Very good," he said. "Tell me, does Chin Sen have one of these?"

"How the hell should I know?"

"I think you probably do. However, it is no matter. What I am going to do is give you some instructions, which you will carry out immediately."

"I am not one of your soldiers."

"You are a suspected terrorist."

Reed's head jerked.

"Who I know is in constant touch with Chin Sen's people. Now, I agree that it is extremely unlikely that you would take the risk of holding my wife here. But she is certainly being held by Chin Sen, and I imagine somewhere fairly close to here. You know where to find him. I wish you to send one of your people to him, now. Tell him that I have come here as he wished, with his brother, and that I want my wife back, now."

"That was Chin Fu?"

"Yes," Harry said. "Old friend of the family, is he?"

"I know him only by name. You say that Chin Sen set this up?"

"And you're saying that you did not know of it?"

Reed's eyes flickered. "Until last night I had no idea your wife was in the country."

"I'll believe you, for the time being."

"Where does this business leave my wife and I?" the planter asked.

"If you co-operate, fully, you may escape charges."

"May?"

"That's the best I can offer, Mr Reed."

Reed considered for a few moments, then rang the brass bell beside his chair. Instantly one of his servants appeared, and Reed spoke rapidly in Malay. Harry had no idea what he was saying, and he didn't much care; it was going according to plan.

"Where will you wait for your wife to be delivered?" Reed asked.

"I will wait right here, Mr Reed."

Reed's eyes narrowed. "You will wait on this plantation?"

"This is where Chin Sen expects to find me."

Reed looked as if he would have said something, then changed his mind and instead spoke again in rapid Malay. The servant bowed and left the room.

"How long will the message take to reach Chin Sen?" Harry asked.

Reed smiled. "I am not going to answer you, Colonel. But I can assure you that a reply will be here by morning."

"Well," Harry said. "Perhaps you would like to invite my men and I to dinner?"

The search completed – predictably neither Cynthia nor anything incriminating was found – Harry went on to the verandah to survey the plantation, which seemed settled for the night, with various lights flaring and sounds of voices and the barking of dogs carrying through the stillness. He turned at a sound, to find Jutta standing behind him.

"This is madness," she said. "What can the four of you do against Chin Sen and his people?"

"You reckon he's on his way, do you?"

"He will be. And if you're thinking of setting a trap . . . they will be overseeing every movement of your men."

"We'll have to see how good he is," Harry agreed. "I really would like to know your place in this, Jutta."

"I . . ." She bit her lip. "I will help you, if I can. But I have nothing without Patrick."

"I have said I would take care of you."

"How can you? Your wife . . ."

"Will have to understand."

Jutta hugged herself. "You wish me to be a kept woman for the rest of my life."

"I wish to take care of you for the rest of your life."

"And your life? You know that Chin Sen means to kill you."

"I've an idea he means to try. But a lot of people have had that idea."

The sound of a gong drifted through the evening. "Dinner is ready," Jutta said.

He caught her hand to prevent her from going inside. "Will you come to me tonight?"

She gave a little shudder. "I cannot. You should not stay here. It is too dangerous."

231

"Meaning that Reed may be having ideas about me as well?" She licked her lips.

Dinner was a surprisingly relaxed affair. Reed maintained a flow of conversation and the waiters kept the wine flowing also – although both Cantrell and Harry did no more than sip theirs.

"When exactly do you expect a reply from Chin Sen?" Harry asked.

"By dawn. You can have a good night's sleep." Reed looked at his wife. "Are there rooms arranged for our guests?"

"Yes," Jutta said.

"We would prefer to share," Harry said.

Reed raised his eyebrows.

"It's a habit," Harry said. "I will share with Captain Cantrell, and the sergeant-major will share with Corporal Todd – and the prisoner, of course."

"Watch and watch," Harry said when he and Cantrell were in their bedroom. "Two hours on, two off."

The time was ten o'clock.

"Mind if I have first go?" Cantrell asked. "I'm not going to sleep anyway."

"Have you ever seen action?" Harry asked.

"Not really, sir. I came out in '45, but on the staff."

"Well, take your lead from me. Just remember, when we open fire, it's shoot to kill. Aim at the body."

"Did you say, when, sir?"

"I'm afraid that is how it is going to be," Harry said.

"But . . . your wife . . .?"

"I don't think she'll be involved," Harry told him.

He lay down fully dressed save for his boots, and was asleep in seconds – and awake it seemed in seconds more, as Cantrell touched his shoulder.

"Midnight, sir."

"Anything?"

"Not a sound, sir."

Harry sat up and checked his weapons, while Cantrell lay down in turn. Harry moved to the window, looked down at the

232

yard and the drive and the houses beyond. As Cantrell had said, there was no sound and no movement. He opened the door, looked out at the gallery. There was no sound there, either. He wondered if Jutta was sleeping, and if she was not, what she was thinking. He supposed he might be considered to have brought catastrophe upon her. But if her husband was involved with the terrorists – as now seemed certain – she would have suffered catastrophe in any event. Whether or not she now escaped it was up to her.

He closed the door, sat in a chair, and waited. His brief sleep had left him totally refreshed, eager for action. There were so many things to be thought about, and he did not wish to think about any of them: having set up this situation, he could now only react to Chin Sen.

At two o'clock he awoke Cantrell, who seemed to be surprised at having slept at all. Then he lay down, and once again went right off. To be awakened at four.

"Sir," Cantrell said. "Listen."

In the distance there was a roaring sound.

"Tiger," Harry said. "If it's real."

He went to the window. There was a dawn breeze now, sweeping down from the mountains and quite chilly. It was the wind that was carrying the sound, and at the same time obliterating other sounds, those closer at hand. It was still very dark, but he knew it would lighten in the next hour.

"Downstairs," he said. "Bring your shoes."

Harry slung his weapons and carried his shoes outside. The NCOs were next door, and were both awake, as was Bukit. "You stay up here for the time being," he told the Gurkha.

He went down the stairs. At the foot of the steps a manservant appeared, and Harry put his finger to his lips. The Malay looked thoroughly bewildered. Harry had to assume that he would go straight up and alert his master and mistress, but that was inevitable.

He went on to the front verandah, inhaling the damp air – it had drizzled during the night – and then suddenly becoming aware of sound. A great deal of sound, seeping towards him. He stared into the gloom, which was now definitely beginning to lighten, and made out a large body of men – Harry estimated about forty – approaching up the drive, the gates having been opened.

He strained his eyes, but couldn't determine if they had Cynthia with them.

There was movement behind him, and Reed arrived with Jutta; both were fully dressed.

The men were within thirty yards of the steps.

"That's far enough," Harry said.

They checked, and one of them stepped forward. In the gloom Harry could not clearly make out his face, but he didn't doubt it was Chin Sen.

"You are the British Tiger," Chin Sen said.

"So they say," Harry agreed.

"And you have come to surrender my brother."

"I have come to regain my wife."

"She is a beautiful woman," Chin Sen remarked.

"I think so. Where is she?"

"She is here, Colonel Tiger. Where is my brother?"

"Come inside," Harry suggested.

Reed drew a sharp breath.

"You have him here?" Chin Sen asked. "That is what I was told."

"Let me see my wife."

Chin Sen considered for a moment, then waved his arm. Two of his men came forward, marching between them a veiled and shrouded figure. Her hands – if it was a woman – were tied behind her back, and she stumbled, being kept on her feet by the men holding her arms. What might lie beneath the veil Harry did not care to imagine.

"Bring her here," he said.

"Show me my brother."

"He is in the house. Come into the house and see him, and then show me my wife."

"No!" Reed shouted. "It is a trap."

"Cover me," Harry snapped, and ran down the steps, drawing his revolver as he did so. "Sergeant-Major!"

Jutta screamed.

Chin Sen reached for his own weapon, holstered at his waist, but Harry, moving at top speed, was already upon him. Chin Sen threw up his hands to protect himself, and Harry swept them aside and brought his pistol butt down on the Communist commander's head with a sickening crunch. Chin Sen fell forwards into Cullinan's arms as Harry sidestepped him.

Then he went up to the two men holding Cynthia, shooting the first man in the leg. He went down with a squeal of pain. The other man released Cynthia's arm to draw his own weapon. Harry shot him in the chest. Blood flew, and he went back without a sound.

Harry ducked his head to throw Cynthia over his shoulder; in all the excitement she had not uttered a word, but he could not consider the implications of that now – he was at least sure it was her, from the flutter of golden hair behind the veil.

Chin Sen's people had recovered from the shock of Harry's pre-emptive strike, and now surged forward, but were halted by a burst from Cantrell's tommy-gun. Cullinan followed Harry's example and threw Chin Sen over his shoulder in a fireman's lift, then they both backed to the steps, revolvers thrust forward. Cantrell had fired over the heads of the Chinese rather than into them. Now they advanced again, parangs drawn but not using their firearms for fear of hitting their leader.

"Bastard!" Reed shouted, and drew a revolver of his own, then gave a gasp as Jutta hurled her shoulder against his. The revolver flew from his hand and he fell to his knees.

"Fire into them!" Harry snapped, gaining the verandah. Cantrell and Todd sprayed the charging mob with bullets, and several men fell. The rest halted, and then retreated.

Harry laid Cynthia on a settee and turned to Jutta. "You really have a habit of saving my life," he told her. "But it's one I can live with." Her eyes were filled with tears; now she had really burned her bridges.

Next he turned to Cantrell. "Captain Cantrell, get Reed in here. Corporal Todd, call Company. Private Bukit," he shouted up the stairs, "come down."

Cantrell urged Reed into the room with the muzzle of his

tommy-gun. Cullinan backed into the doorway and laid Chin Sen on the floor, not at all gently.

"You are a bitch," Reed growled to Jutta. "I will skin you alive."

"When you come out of gaol," Harry remarked, closing and bolting the door.

Jutta ignored her husband as she rolled Cynthia on to her side to pull away the cloying material and reveal that she was both gagged and bound. She freed the gag first.

"Water," Cynthia gasped. "My God, water."

Harry looked up and surveyed the half-dozen sarong-clad servants, male and female, who had accumulated behind him. "You," he pointed, "fetch some water. The rest of you clear off. Go back to your houses and stay there until this is over." He knelt beside Cynthia as Jutta freed her hands. Cynthia's face was distorted with discomfort and humiliation, but she did not look as if she had been cut there. She still had breasts, although lacking shoes her toes were bruised and bleeding. She was wearing only her slip and underclothes, and these were torn.

She glared at him. "Don't touch me," she said.

The servant arrived with a silver tray on which there was a carafe of water and a glass. Harry poured and held it out. Cynthia sat up, snatched the glass, and drank, greedily and noisily.

"Would you like something to eat?" Jutta asked.

Cynthia clearly hadn't realised who she was. "I wish a hot bath," she said. "And," she shuddered, "to be left alone."

Jutta looked at Harry, who nodded. "Then, if you'll come with me," Jutta invited. "Can you stand?"

"Of course I can stand. I—" She stood up, and promptly fell over. Harry caught her, and she threw his hands away. "Don't touch me! My feet," she complained to Jutta.

Jutta put an arm round her waist. "Lean on me," she said, and helped Cynthia to the stairs.

The men watched her go.

"Seems your wife isn't too happy, Colonel," Reed remarked.

Harry ignored him. "Captain Cantrell, check the back door. Did you get through, Corporal?"

"They're on their way, sir."

"Then give Captain Cantrell a hand at the back. Get rid of these people."

Cantrell shepherded the servants out of the huge lounge. Harry heard shouts from outside, and moved back to stand beside Cullinan, but the Communists were not about to charge the tommy-guns. However, a shot now rang out, the bullet smashing into the woodwork beside the door.

"Inside," Harry said, and they closed and bolted the door while some more shots were fired.

Chin Sen sat up and rubbed his head, and stared at Bukit, who had joined them. "Now you will die," he said. "All of you. Slowly."

"I have not betrayed you," Reed protested.

"They know you are with us, now," Chin Sen said. "You are dangerous."

Reed swallowed, and stood up; Harry turned his tommy-gun on him. "Just sit," he said. "Any movement from the back, Captain Cantrell?" he called.

"A lot of talk. If the labourers join in . . ."

"They won't," Harry said, hoping he was right, and looked up at the gallery as Jutta appeared. "How is she?"

"Lying down. I have given her a sedative. She is hysterical."

"She can't have had a bath already."

"She hasn't. She'll feel better after a rest."

"She'll be lucky," Reed commented.

"Was she . . ." Harry hesitated.

"I don't know," Jutta said. "I don't think so."

"Will you stay with her?"

"No," Jutta said, and showed him that she was carrying a single-barrelled pump-action shotgun and a box of cartridges. "If I'm going to go, I'm going to take some of those bastards with me."

Before Harry could remonstrate, a new voice shouted from the yard. "What is happening in there?"

"Which side is he on?" Harry asked as Jutta came down the stairs.

"He works for my husband," she said, feeding seven cartridges into the magazine.

"Then he may have some authority," Harry said. "You!" he shouted. "Schnell! Call these people off before anyone gets killed."

"Two are already dead," Schnell called back. "They will not go without Chin Sen."

"You'd better tell them there will be a company of my Scouts here in a little while, looking for blood," Harry said. "Tell them to clear off and they may get away with their lives."

"You're surrounded, and don't have a hope in hell," Schnell pointed out. "Your people can't get here for at least two hours. Send out Chin Sen and I'll hold these people back."

"You are under arrest," Harry said. "For aiding and abetting the insurgents. If you kill anybody in here, you will be hanged."

"I could bring him down now," Cullinan muttered.

"I want the first move to come from them," Harry said.

"He's going off," Cullinan remarked regretfully.

Harry considered. Everything Schnell had said was true: he doubted they could keep out a concerted attack, especially if the insurgents were supported by the labourers. But he still held a trump card.

He stood above Chin Sen.

"Get up."

Chin Sen looked up, and blanched at the expression on Harry's face.

"I wish you to come outside with me," Harry said. "And command your men to withdraw."

"Why should I do this? I will not."

"I'll tell you why you should," Harry said. "It is because if you do not do as I wish, I am going to blow your head off, right there on the front verandah."

There was a moment's silence. Even Cullinan seemed to gulp.

Chin Sen drew a deep breath. "You will not do this," he said. "It is not what British officers do."

"Let me tell you something," Harry said. "I am not the sort of British officer you have ever encountered before. I am a Commando. I am the Tiger. I spent the entire War going behind enemy lines to kill people my government wanted dead. I am quite sure this government wants you dead, and I will save them a lot of trouble by doing it now. Up."

Chin Sen stood up. "You cannot allow this," he told Reed.

Reed swallowed; his life had just also been threatened, by this very man.

Jutta looked as if she would have spoken, but then did not. Bukit merely checked his weapon.

"Cover me," Harry told Cullinan.

"With respect, sir," the sergeant-major said. "You're taking a hell of a risk, going out there. Those were rifles they were using."

"Just cover me," Harry said, and pushed the door open. He had hold of the neck of Chin Sen's shirt, pushing the Communist leader in front of him, and carried his revolver in his other hand. It was now quite light and the compound seemed to be deserted, but Harry did not doubt the insurgents were still there. "Do your stuff," he said.

"They will not obey me," Chin Sen panted.

"I'm sure they will. They are your people."

Chin Sen drew a deep breath. "Listen to me!" he shouted. "Disperse. There are soldiers coming. Go back to the hills. I will join you later."

There was no sound from the compound.

"You'd better try again," Harry suggested. "I'm not a very patient man."

"Go away!" Chin Sen screamed, obviously terrified. "I command you!"

A single shot rang out. Chin Sen made a gurgling sound and sagged against Harry, who actually felt the impact himself; the bullet had smashed through Chin Sen's body and into his.

"Colonel, sir!" Cullinan burst through the door to grab Harry's shoulders and drag him back through the door as he fell; Harry retained his grasp on Chin Sen's collar and they both fell inside. Cullinan slammed the doors, while the firing again became general, replied to by Bukit from one of the windows.

"Harry!" Jutta knelt beside him, rolling Chin Sen away from him; the Communist leader was dead. Now she tore at Harry's bush jacket. "Oh, thank God. It hasn't penetrated. Don't move."

He lay on the floor, propped against a settee, while blood

stained his jacket. "I never thought they'd shoot their own man," he said.

"They intend to kill us all," Reed said, his voice shaking.

"They're your people," Harry pointed out.

Cantrell came in from the back. "Are you badly hurt?"

"I don't believe so."

"Shall I take command?"

"No," Harry said, and watched Jutta returning with a large first-aid box. "What would I do without you?"

"Take more care of yourself, I would hope."

"Something's happening, sir," Cullinan said.

"Just keep still," Jutta said. She had lifted Harry's bush jacket over his head and now removed the bullet – it had just entered the flesh – before wrapping bandages round his chest.

"Tell me, Sergeant-Major."

"They have a lot of torches."

"They're going to burn us out," Reed said dolefully.

"What do you reckon, Sergeant-Major?"

"It's a fact, sir, that they have torched villages in the past, where they don't reckon the people are on their side."

"Do you have a cellar?" Harry asked Jutta.

"Nothing that will keep out fire. These floors, and therefore the cellar ceiling, are wood."

"Then we'll just have to keep them away from the house. Let no one approach the back, Cantrell."

Cantrell hurried off to rejoin Todd.

"You won't keep them out," Reed said. "They'll use arrows. We're done. Why in the name of God couldn't you leave well enough alone?"

Jutta tied the last knot. "It'll be painful, but you can stand." She picked up the shotgun.

"Jutta . . ." Harry caught her hand. "I seem to have brought you a hell of a lot of bad luck."

"It's been exciting," she told him.

He got to his feet, leaning on her. The pain in his chest was severe, but it was definitely external. He moved to the window, peered out at the morning. It was broad daylight now, and there were glimpses of people moving about in between the houses, but there were no flaring torches to be seen there. These were at a distance, and there seemed no point in wasting ammunition.

"What do you reckon, sir?" Cullinan asked.

Harry looked at his watch: a quarter past seven. It had only been fifteen minutes since Todd's call to Company. His mind flickered over all the previous tight situations he had been in. Some had been, superficially, tighter than this, but he had always been in control. Well, he supposed he was in control here, but only in his knowledge that help was on its way. The trouble was, Schnell knew that too. Just as he would also know that *his* only hope of ultimate survival was utterly to liquidate the defenders so that no one would remain to give evidence against him.

"We hold, Sergeant-Major," he said. "Every second is to our advantage."

"Yes, sir," Cullinan said, clearly not entirely convinced.

Jutta joined them. "Will they attack?"

"Yes," Harry said. "They have to. Scared?"

"Not as long as I'm standing next to you."

"Jutta," he said. "When this is over . . ."

"We'll talk," she said. "When this is over, Harry. *When.*"

"I think they're coming, sir," Cullinan said.

Harry moved back to the window and saw people closer than before. Several carried torches.

"Hold your fire," he said. "Jutta . . ."

"I am staying right here," she said.

"Here we go," Cullinan said.

"Open fire," Harry said. "Captain Cantrell!" he shouted. "Hold that door."

"Yes, sir," Cantrell replied, and a moment later he and Todd were also firing. Cullinan and Bukit had sent several shots into the advancing mob, but Jutta was saving her shotgun until they came closer; her husband had fallen to the floor and was crouching with his hands over his head.

Harry joined in the shooting. The insurgents certainly did not lack courage; several had fallen but still they came, waving their torches. Now they were at the foot of the steps and the torches were being hurled, while from behind them the defenders could see fire arrows arching out of the houses to come plummeting on to the roof.

One of the torches had been hurled from sufficiently close to smash through the big windows and land in the drawing room – moments before Jutta blasted the thrower with her gun, pumping another round into the chamber as she did so. But behind her the torch had landed on an upholstered settee and this was blazing.

"They're destroying my house," Reed wailed.

"Beat it out," Harry told Jutta, and then joined her as the assault died down and the insurgents retreated to shelter.

Jutta dashed into the kitchen and returned with several tablecloths with which she attempted to smother the flames, but she couldn't get close enough to be effective. Now the insurgents had resumed shooting; bullets sang into the house, mostly smashing into the ceiling and the gallery but nonetheless threatening.

"Aaaagh!" Cynthia stood on the gallery, stark naked. "Fire!"

"The roof!" Jutta snapped.

Harry ran up the stairs, Jutta behind him.

"Fire!" Cynthia screamed again. "It's burning."

Harry could hear the crackling of flames now, but as he ran along the gallery towards his wife she turned away from him.

"Don't touch me," she moaned.

"For God's sake," he said. "Jutta, can you find her something to wear?" He ran past her, opening first one bedroom door and then another. The roof in the second room was well alight, and starting to smoke. He certainly did not have the means to put it out. He backed into the corridor, looked down on the blaze in the centre of the living room. That too was giving off a good deal of smoke, and he could hear someone coughing. The whole house was going to be untenable in a very short while, and this was so obvious to the insurgents that they had even ceased firing, content to await the necessary evacuation.

Jutta was wrapping Cynthia in a sarong.

"Who *are* you?" Cynthia demanded.

"My name is Jutta Hulin."

"Then you're—"

"Yes," Jutta said. "I am the other woman. But I do not think now is the time to discuss that." She looked at Harry. "What are we going to do?"

Harry paused to consider. The men outside this house were not highly trained professional soldiers, whereas he and his four men were. The problem was with the women . . .

"Colonel, sir!" Cullinan was standing at the foot of the stairs, looking up. "This is getting a bit heavy."

"I know it. We are going to have to leave."

"Just like that, sir?"

Harry grinned. "Just like that, Sergeant-Major. Stand by What's immediately behind the house?" he asked Jutta.

"A banana grove."

"That'll have to do. Now listen to me," he told Cynthia. "We are going to break out of here and run into the bush. No one is going to be able to attend to you personally; you will have to look out for yourself."

She stared at him. "I hate you," she said. "I loathe and despise you."

Harry nodded. "A little bit of hate is sometimes valuable for survival. You were trained as a soldier. You would be helping us – and yourself – if you reverted to that, and used a gun."

She licked her lips, and he drew his revolver and handed it to her. "Just remember that your aim is to shoot them, not us. Let's go."

Jutta squeezed his arm. "Can we do it, Harry?"

He kissed her. "We sure as hell are going to try."

They went down the stairs. "Back up," Harry told Cullinan and Bukit. "They're not going to come through there while it's burning."

Reed seemed to wake up. "What are you doing?"

"Evacuating."

"If you go outside you'll be killed."

"That also goes for staying. It's your decision."

He waved his people into the kitchen, where the air was cleaner, and Cullinan closed the door.

"Any movement?"

"Not a lot," Cantrell said. "Just some fire arrows – some got in."

"That's right," Harry said. "So we have to get out."

Cantrell gulped, and looked at the two women. At least Cynthia seemed prepared to do her bit.

"When the time is right," Harry said. "We want to delay this as long as possible, to give Major Hallis time to get up the road. Just remember – when we do go, we stick together. That may make more of a target for the insurgents, but it also concentrates our firepower. Anyone hit has to keep moving; there can be no stopping. Understood?"

Even Cynthia nodded. She was understanding that this was what he had been trained to do, and if she could remember anything of the files she claimed to have read, she also knew it was what he did best.

"Now," he said. "Check your weapons."

They all did so. Jutta looked in the larder and found a carrier bag, into which she emptied her box of cartridges and the first-aid kit; the bag she suspended from her wrist. She gave him a quick smile, and then looked away again. He didn't know if she was afraid or not; it was not an emotion she had ever revealed, even when she had been Lawton's prisoner. As for the future . . . At this moment, only the present mattered.

Now the house was clearly well alight. They could hear the roaring of the flames from beyond the door, and wisps of smoke were starting to infiltrate the kitchen; the heat was intense.

"Do you think we should do something about Reed, sir?" Cullinan whispered.

"It's up to him to do something about himself," Harry said.

And a few minutes later they heard the planter shouting, "Don't shoot. I am coming out. I am your friend."

A moment later a shot rang out. No one in the kitchen said anything. Now there was a considerable amount of smoke in the room, and the crackling of the flames was very loud. Harry looked at his watch. It was half past seven. And it was time.

"Remember," he said. "We have massive firepower. Use it. And stay together. On the count of three, Captain Cantrell."

Cantrell, standing by the back door, nodded.

"One," Harry said. "Two. Go."

He had taken up a position immediately behind the captain,

and as the door was thrown open he was first down the steps, tommy-gun chattering at the nearest houses. For a few moments there was no reply, the insurgents having been taken entirely by surprise. Then they began shouting and firing wildly, but they were also showing themselves, and several went down before the hail of bullets. In only a few seconds Harry was amidst the bananas, checking there to see if his people were all right. Amazingly, they all seemed to be, although Cynthia was screaming – whether with fear or excitement he couldn't tell.

"Right," he said. "An orderly withdrawal into the bush, facing front."

Now bullets were thudding into the hands of fruit, but the insurgents were still firing, blindly and wildly.

"Cease firing," Harry said in a low voice. "No point in letting them know where we are. Withdraw."

They backed through the grove, and were nearly out the far side when Cantrell gave a groan and went down. Harry, bringing up the rear, knelt beside him. "Where?"

"I don't know," Cantrell gasped.

There was a lot of blood and he was obviously badly hurt, but Harry had no intention on this occasion of abandoning anyone. "Jutta," he said, "see what you can do."

She knelt in turn, taking out her first-aid box.

"Form a perimeter," Harry commanded. "Here we stay."

The soldiers lay down, and after a moment Cynthia did likewise. She was in any event already covered in mud and her hair was a tangled mess; she never had had that bath she had wanted.

"Daddy will throw a fit when he hears about this," she remarked.

"I should think he will. Just remember it was your idea."

He peered through the huge leaves. He could hear movement, and a good deal of chatter – the insurgents were advancing very slowly and carefully.

"Make every bullet tell," he said.

Cantrell groaned as Jutta bandaged him.

"What is it?" Harry asked.

"It's in the gut. There are several ribs broken. And it's still in there. He needs help, Harry. Quickly."

Harry could only squeeze her bloodstained hand.

"Can we hold them?" Cynthia asked.

"For a little while. How many bullets do you have left?"

She checked the gun. "Two."

"Sergeant-Major?"

"Half a box, sir."

"I have a full one, sir," Todd said.

"Less than half, sir," Bukit said.

So, Harry thought, we can repel one all-out assault. And then . . . He looked at Jutta, but she was bending over Cantrell, making him as comfortable as she could. At least they had got together, once.

"Why don't they come and get us?" Cynthia asked.

"They will, when they're ready," Harry said. They—" He checked, listening. Drifting through the trees there came the beat of drums and the squeal of fifes playing *Colonel Bogey's March*.

"Hallelujah," he said. Now he could hear the roar of the truck engines.

"Some coup," Mike Calvert remarked. "I'm afraid we haven't been able to locate Chin Sen's body."

"You probably won't," Harry said. "He was incinerated."

"But we've got Schnell. He's facing a list of charges as long as your arm."

"And Reed?"

"Oh, we found something identifiable there. Your Jutta is a widow. And you're the hero of the hour – despite what your wife says."

"Such as?"

Calvert indicated the newspapers on his desk. "She's had a ball. Kidnapped by terrorists. Sexually assaulted . . . Was she sexually assaulted?"

"I don't think so."

"Escaped, revolver in hand. Rescued by British soldiers. You are not mentioned by name at all. And of course, every story is accompanied by a photograph and headlines like 'Earl's Daughter's Harrowing Experience'."

"Well," Harry said. "If it makes her happy. She's on her way home now. There will be a divorce. In some odd manner she seems to consider that I was responsible for the whole thing."

"I'm sorry about that," Calvert said. "The divorce, I mean. What about your son?"

"I will have access, whenever I'm in England."

"Tough. On the other hand, I suppose some people might say that you *were* responsible for the whole thing," Calvert ventured.

Harry raised his eyebrows.

"I'm thinking of that Singapore business, and then your arrest of Chin Sen's brother, which sparked Chin Sen's reaction. Don't get me wrong, Harry. Getting rid of that bastard is a big plus. It's just a pity about the publicity, which somewhat overshadows our success at Ipoh."

"I never did congratulate you on that."

"It wasn't quite as big a success as we had hoped. They knew we were coming, and managed to get most of their people out. I'm afraid we have a long business on our hands, and a messy one. Are you game?"

"You mean you want me to stay?"

"I certainly don't want you to go. There is a problem, however."

"I was sure of it."

"The powers that be, both here in Kuala Lumpur and in Singapore, are a little concerned that what is happening may take on the nomenclature of a civil war."

"Isn't it?"

"That may be the reality of it, but reality is seldom something politicians care to consider too deeply. They want us to continue our efforts to extirpate the Communists, but not to give the impression that it is a business of Malay killing Malay. They therefore want our commands to be renamed and in fact restructured. I have been in contact with the War Office about this, and they are willing to have our regiments incorporated in the SAS. How does that grab you? You have fought with the SAS before, haven't you?"

"During the War I fought fairly close to them."

"Will you accept a commission with them? Same rank. And a great number of advantages, such as the very latest equipment and the ability to insist on complete secrecy as to what we are doing."

"Field rank?"

"You will continue in command of your regiment."

"Then I'm flattered. I assume they accept married officers?"

"In your case, I am sure they will. But . . . you tell me that you are no longer going to be married, in the near future."

Harry grinned, got up, and walked to the window. "I said I would be divorced, Mike. That allows me to remarry, which is what I intend to do."

Calvert got up and stood beside him, to look down at Jutta, who was seated on a bench in the yard while she waited for him.

"Allow me to be the first to congratulate you," he said.